SPANCIL HILL

LEARA RHODES

To Jessica, Christiana, and Viviana
May you all have stories to share

The Ballad of Spancil Hill
Michael Considine (1870 - 1873)

Last night as I lay dreaming of pleasant days gone by
My mind being bent on rambling to Ireland I did fly
I stepped on board a vision and I followed with
    the wind
And I shortly came to anchor at the cross of Spancil Hill

It being the 23rd June the day before the fair
When Ireland's sons and daughters in crowds
    assembled there
The young and the old, the brave and the bold their
    journey to fulfill
There were jovial conversations at the fair of Spancil
    Hill

I went to see my neighbors to hear what they might say
The old ones were all dead and gone and the young
    one's turning grey
I met with the tailor Quigley, he's a bould as ever still
Sure he used to make my britches when I lived in
    Spancil Hill

I paid a flying visit to my first and only love

She's as white as any lily and as gentle as a dove
She threw her arms around me saying "Johnny, I love
you still"
"Oh she's Ned the farmer's daughter and the flower of
Spancil Hill

I dreamt I held and kissed her as in the days of yore
She said, "Johnny, you're only joking like many's the
time before"
The cock he crew in the morning he crew both loud and
shrill
And I awoke in California, many miles from Spancil
Hill.

PART I

West coast of Ireland, Mannin Bay
1885 - 1887

1

To sit and wait is hard for Cahey. He must move, must react, must win this race. Through his father's life, he has seen that hard work does not win, perseverance does not win, and building a family does not win. What works is to take chances and to depend on just one person: himself. His rigid posture makes his horse snort. His Connemara pony bought at a farm fair is stocky and sturdy. The other horse in the race is a black mare stomping her feet in anticipation of starting the race. Suddenly the black mare rears to show off her strength. Cahey's horse backs up, ready to flee. The two horses are side by side on a flat beach area on the Irish coast. Cahey holds his horse tightly with the reins to stop her from fleeing. He must hold her steady and win this race. Though he has never raced the horse before, his father had and won; Cahey plans to win. With no money in his pocket, a winning race will help him get by until he can get a job in Galway, another half-day's ride. He glances at the horse next to him. The horse prances about with energy matched only by the smile on her rider's face. Cahey's horse continues to back away, but Cahey has his eyes on the start of the race when the hat drops.

The horse next to him begins to move. Cahey sees the hat drop but his horse has backed up too far. He clicks his heels and his horse begins to move. He clicks again and the horse picks up speed. Cahey can smell the seaside salt air mixed with the oil he uses to groom the horse's ankles. The saddle is one he had taken care of and then hid in the brush to allow him to take the horse and ride away from the farm. He fits easily in the saddle's creases.

The horse's muscles bend and pull Cahey forward. He sees that the black horse is a good head in front. He leans down closer to his horse's mane and begins encouraging her. He has always talked to the horses on the farm and this horse, his horse, has been his companion. The horse knows and responds to Cahey and his every move. He hopes this will hold true today. Cahey tells his horse what to do. "Go like the wind," he says. The horse picks up speed. Cahey feels like he is flying down the beach, flying with the afternoon sun burning off the morning rainwater on the rocky shore. His horse is surefooted on the wet rocks, not sliding, not shying away, running and racing to win.

Cahey hears shouts from the sidelines from the men watching the race on Sunday afternoon. None of the shouts encourage him to win; they call for the rider next to him, Donovan, to win. Cahey leans closer to his horse's neck and speaks louder than he normally would but with their speed and the men's voices, he needs his horse to hear him. He tells his horse, "Fly, girl, fly." The horse lengthens her stride. Cahey gains a few more inches on the black horse. The rider, Donovan, shouts something but Cahey cannot understand it. He is interested only in what his horse is doing, and that is for his horse to pull ahead of the black horse.

Then the race is over. The men at the finish line signal that both horses have crossed. Slowing his horse down and patting the glistening fur on the horse's neck, Cahey offers encouraging words. "Great run, good girl."

He turns and looks back at where the men on the beach have gathered around the village leader, Ryan. All are talking at once and gesturing. Cahey glances at Donovan, who has turned his horse about and is watching the men. Both riders walk their horses toward the group.

"Well, who won?" asks Donovan.

Cahey sits silently on his horse behind and to the side of Donovan and his black horse.

"Too close to call," says Ryan.

"Too close to call? My horse always wins," says Donovan.

Cahey is not sure what this means. He is sure that his horse ran a good race, but if he does not win, he will have to continue on to Galway with no money and no job. The men continue to argue and point to both horses.

Finally, Ryan waves his hands to quiet the men. He looks at Cahey and Donovan. "There is nothing to do but to do it again. What say you?"

The men shake their heads but agree. Ryan looks at Cahey and Donovan, "Are you men willing to do it again?"

Cahey nods and begins walking his horse back to the start line. He can hear Donovan shouting at the men on the beach to stand where they can see the horses cross the finish line. They have to see that his horse is the true winner. He reminds them that his horse always wins. With that, he follows Cahey down the beach.

"Same rules," shouts Ryan, and when the men and horses are in place, he drops his hat. Both horses lunge forward. Cahey can feel that they are running side by side. Then Cahey feels something jab at his horse's side. He glances down but does not see what it could have been. He needs to stay focused on the race. He quickly looks at Donovan, who is looking back at him with a smile on his face. Cahey's horse pauses just enough to have Donovan's black horse pull slightly ahead.

The men on the beach are shouting. The race is over, and Cahey hears Ryan announce, "Donovan wins the race by a nose." Cahey gives free rein to his horse and allows her to saunter to the end of the beach. Then he turns around and heads back to where the men are gathered.

Donovan has dismounted and is gesturing to those gathered on the beach. "Well, men, I guess that one will go down in the books as the day I won again!"

Cahey slides off his horse as Donovan, who is stocky and walks with a swagger, approaches him. "Good race, lad, but I warned you that my horse always wins."

Still flustered as to what made his horse pause, Cahey does not immediately put out his hand to accept Donovan's handshake. Instead, he walks his horse over to Ryan.

"Something happened during the race to make my horse pause," says Cahey to Ryan, who has stepped away from the group of men to talk with Cahey.

"What? Did you see what it was?"

"No, we were going too fast."

"Then I guess you have to accept that it was nature and be done with it."

Donovan approaches Cahey again. "You are not from here, are you, lad?"

Cahey can hear the men cheering Donovan's win. "I'm from near Mannin Bay," he says.

"Will you be staying around here?"

"No, sir, I'm off to Galway."

"Right, you are, lad." Donavan is looking over the Connemara horse. "So, do you want to sell your horse?"

"No, sir, she's all I have, and I plan on racing her and working in Galway."

Donovan does not reach out to shake Cahey's hand but instead says, "Then great is the luck that is on you." He immediately turns to join the men on the beach.

As Donovan walks away, Cahey quietly says, "It is not just luck that I need."

2
———

After losing the race, Cahey is restless to be on his way. He has no money in his pocket but he has never had money in his pocket; he'll make do. There are no formal goodbyes. Muirghein, Ryan, and Séan say their good wishes at breakfast. Cahey loads his horse and just as he is about to ride down the lane, Muirghein hands him a small feed sack with something inside.

"Bread, jam, and berries, for when you get hungry along the way. Don't you be forgetting us now."

"No, ma'am. I won't forget." And he will not forget them for taking him in and giving him shelter in front of their fire on the cold rainy nights. He had met Séan on the roadside picking berries and had been taken to the thatched cottage in the small fishing village where he was offered fish stew and soda bread. In the few days he has stayed in the village after leaving the farm up north, he has fished with Ryan, the king of the village who represents the heritage the village has kept for centuries, and who in an effort to help Cahey, organized the horse race to give Cahey money to continue his journey. Though he did not win the money, his new friends made him feel he could now continue his journey into Galway.

As he passes the last house in the lane, Cahey sees a young woman, Sophie, whom Séan had called out to and greeted when the two young men entered the village the day before. Now Sophie is looking out from behind the corner of a house. Cahey has seen her watching him during the few days he has been in the village. Though he admires her long raven hair, she seems young, like the age of one of his two sisters, and he needs to go on his way. Maybe he will see her another time. He tips his cap to her. She leans back into the shadows. Cahey rides to the top of the hill and does not look back as he goes down the lane heading to Galway.

The landscape changes. Whereas the seashore is covered with rocks and lichens, the track headed south takes on more shrubs and trees. He watches the birds soar above and listens but cannot hear the sea. All he hears is the clicking of his horse's feet on the hard-beaten sod and the caw of a bird in the trees. He has dreamed about leaving the farm and finding a new future in the city. He often would lay awake in the evening glow of summer and think about what it would be like. Now as he rides, he remembers the quiet times with his papa, times when they didn't talk but just sat still waiting for a bird to rise out of the heath. His papa taught him how to listen, how to stay still, and wait for the tiny sound of the bird pushing through the heath flowers, and then to stay poised until the bird is extended to get a good clean shot. Listening was used with the horses, too. His papa would stand still near a stressed horse and listen to the horse's labored whinnies and snorts in order to scare the human away. His papa would simply stand and listen. Soon the horse stopped and began to listen to papa, who would talk softly and reassure the horse that all would be fine. As the horse listened, papa walked closer and closer and finally was able to put a bridle around the horse's head and lead the horse back to the lean-to. Cahey has learned to listen from his papa.

He dismounts and walks silently to the ridge and looks over the rock wall lining the field. He sees large seagulls dash about on the rocks and swoop down on the shore. As he stands and listens, he does not know what he is listening for. He slowly mounts his horse and rides on. The day is still young and he has miles to ride before reaching Galway.

The city he sees is a town with few trees. There is a bridge. The road is busy with carts and horses and people going into and leaving town. He dismounts and leads his horse to make his way easier. His hearing is absorbed by the travelers on the road. Most of the people he sees are men in work clothes and farmers with carts hauling products. He joins in and moves over to the side of the road to allow carts and wagons to lumber past him. As he is moving slowly down the road, he hears a cart rumbling fast behind him. He moves further over to the side to allow the horse-driven cart more space. Just as the driver passes him, one horse stumbles and nearly falls. The second horse stalls almost sending the driver and the cart with oak barrels head over heels on top of the horses. Everything comes to a halt on the roadway with others moving to go around the cart. Cahey stops and watches as the cart driver hops down to see about the horse. Cahey moves closer. The stumbling horse is in agony and Cahey cannot leave a hurt horse. As the cart driver unbuckles the harnesses holding the horse to the cart, Cahey hears him talk to the horse but in a disgruntled way. "I don't need this today, you hear? I don't need you giving out on me and me still so far from the stable."

Cahey leans over and looks at the horse's legs. "Looks like the shivers."

The cart driver jerks back and looks at Cahey, "What?"

"Shivers," repeats Cahey. "The horse has a spasm in her hind legs. Does she have difficulty backing up?" Cahey leans over and begins to gently massage the horse's hurt leg, and though the horse is having none of it, Cahey talks gently to the horse. He begins to massage the other leg and the horse is quieting.

"Well, yes, she does," says the cart driver, who nudges Cahey over a little in order to look closely at the horse's leg. Cahey moves to the front legs of the horse and begins rubbing.

"Shivers," confirms Cahey.

The cart driver unhooks the horse from the cart and stands holding the leather harness. "Can anything be done?"

"Nothing here," says Cahey as he stands up and pats the horse on the neck. "But you are correct to unharness her. She cannot pull the cart with the spasms in her leg."

"Ah, too bad; she is a good horse," says the driver. Cahey cringes; he knows a good diet would help the horse. He speaks up. "I have a good horse; we can hook her up and get you to where you need to go. We can tie the other horse to the back of the cart, go a bit slower so she can stumble along with us and get her back to the stables where there is something you can do to help her improve."

Cahey is aware that the driver is sizing him up, much as Séan did on the road when picking berries. The driver looks down the road both ways, and then he shakes his head. "I don't know, but you seem to know something about horses and I need to get back to work."

"I have worked with horses," says Cahey assuring both of them that he is right. He is hoping he is right.

"Let's do it," says the driver, handing the harness to Cahey. It only takes a few minutes for Cahey to remove the gear and saddle from his horse and tuck it underneath the cart bench. The men hook up Cahey's horse to the cart and tie the lame horse to the back. As the men leap up into the cart and head down the road at a much slower pace, the driver says, "I'm Michael O'Flaherty."

"Cahey Ó hArrachtain."

"It's a good day to have you on the road, Cahey. Where are you headed?"

"I've come to Galway to find a job."

Michael laughs so loudly that the horses' ears prick back to see if there is danger. "Good luck with that! We need to go up the road here to the stables. There, we'll be able to change out the horse and I can then get to the quay for a pickup."

They do not talk as the road is crowded and they must wait their turn as they wind their way into the city. Cahey glances back at the stumbling horse to make sure she is not in too much pain.

"What goes into the barrels?"

"Don't you know, now, it is liquor that goes into the barrels. I deliver them to the pubs about town and out this road to the next village. I work for Nun's Island Distillery."

"A distillery?"

"That's right. The River Corrib is where Mr. Burton Persse put his distillery so he could have water to make the ale."

"And you deliver the ale?"

"Yes, I load the cart, deliver in town and out to some of the villages, and then pick up goods from the ships in the harbor out at the quays."

"How long have you been working there?"

"About a year. I came up from the south of Galway to find work."

Cahey listens as Michael explains his work at the distillery. Cahey does not need to ask questions; Michael is on a tell-all lecture. He explains that a dozen horses are used to deliver the ale and to pick up shipments of barley and malt from the quay. Michael continues his one-way dialogue as they rattle down the road with the empty barrels, dodging other carts and the people walking along the road. Cahey glances over at Michael along the way. He is impressed with Michael's sinewy arms and broad chest. He obviously works those muscles all day long to get them so bold-looking. His neck is thick and taut. Cahey also watches how Michael guides the two horses and moves the cart from one area of the road to another to avoid deep ruts worn by so many travelers. The ride is not long before they see an arch. "That's the Spanish Arch and that road leads into Galway town proper. I do that route in the morning."

They pass the arch and begin crossing the river by guiding the horses over a narrow wooden bridge. Cahey looks over the edge and sees the churning river eddies swirling below. "Since you are looking for a job, there are many mills along this river and many grain stores along Merchants Road. These might be places to begin looking for work." Cahey sees the direction Michael points to and makes a mental note to remember.

When Michael hollers at the cart in front of him to move along, Cahey looks out toward the river and sees many men sitting idly on the riverbank. Some of the men have rope fishing lines and others lean on the stones by the river with their hats pulled down over their foreheads to hide their eyes. They look away when Cahey looks at them. He's seen many of the same faces in Connemara. Haunted eyes and gaunt faces are the signs of people who have seen others die of starvation as the potatoes got the blight and the kale harvests declined due to the weather. Cahey remembers the men's talk at gatherings in Connemara. They talked about people being evicted from their houses, owing more than three years' rent, and having only a fortnight of food left in the larder. Many of them went to towns and cities, hoping for work, and hoping for food to feed their families. Cahey has seen these people's faces in the countryside; now he is seeing them in the town. With no money in his pocket, he could easily be one of them if he doesn't get a job.

The speed of the horses picks up as they cross the bridge, and Cahey shifts on the bench to get a better grip as their speed increases. He glances back at the horse tied behind the cart but turns and looks at Michael when he asks, "You say something will help the horse?"

"Yes, when the horse gets the shivers, we feed them only oats and a little pig oil."

"What? I have never heard of pig oil."

"It's a mixture of sulfur and oil."

"Ah, you do seem to know a lot about horses," Michael says again. Cahey is uncomfortable under Michael's gaze; he is not sure what Michael means by the look he is giving Cahey.

Cahey clears his throat from the road dust. "Their ankles need to be groomed and cleaned to avoid the scratches, since they have all the long hair around the hooves."

"Yes, we do that. Wait till you see the stables." Pride fills Michael's voice as he begins to make a right turn into a gate with guards on both sides. As they enter the compound for the distillery through a courtyard, Cahey sees stacks and stacks of wooden barrels. A cooper stands in the middle counting barrels and barking orders to his assistants, who are moving many types of barrels: puncheons, hogsheads and quarter-casts. Some are stacked five barrels high. Quickly Cahey looks about and sees that the buildings surrounding the compound are all stone with slate roofs. Each building stands alone. At the far end of the compound are the stables where Michael is heading. Cahey has never seen anything so grand. The stables are built of enameled brick with an ornamental open roof. Michael stops the cart at the harness room. Cahey sees a weighing machine and other appliances; he has no idea how they would be used.

"Seámus," Michael calls out. "Seámus! I've had a bit of a problem with one of the horses. We need to change about."

A blonde-haired man stands up from behind a bench and

looks out at the horse. "Take him to the sick box. And who's that riding with you? You know you can't take on any riders. You know the rules, lad."

"This isn't a rider. This is Cahey, and his horse got us back to the stables and just in the nick of time, too, I hear there is a big load coming in at the quay and I better be getting down there to get it."

Seámus steps out into the courtyard and reaches out to help Cahey down from the cart and shakes his hand. He is as tall as Cahey but has too much weight on his body, even for a man as tall as he is; the weight causes him to stagger rather than walk. "Well then, I better say thank you. Can you help Michael change out your horse? We are shorthanded at the moment. I have no idea where Stiabhna is. He was here and now he's gone. Can never keep up with that boy. If it was left up to me, he'd be long gone." Seámus barely stops talking. "Where are you heading?"

Thinking that he might have a chance to get some work here, Cahey answers him with, "I'm looking for work."

"He knows a lot about horses," says Michael over his shoulder as he works to unhook the harness on the Connemara horse. "He says the lame horse has the shivers and can get better with a diet of oats and some pig oil. He also knows how to clean the Shire's feathers."

Seámus looks at Cahey with renewed interest. "You do now? That's all very good, but we are not hiring and you would need to go into the office to apply anyway."

"I can do that," says Cahey. He sees a small pasture off to the side with a gate from the compound where a few horses are grazing. "Can I put my horse in the pasture while I help here?" Cahey asks with barely a pause and with the hope that the boss guy will agree. "She's tired from pulling the cart."

Seámus hesitates but then says, "All right, but just for a while." He returns to the harness room.

"Yes, sir!" says Cahey. He quickly leads his horse over to the pasture. He speaks to the horse and pats her on the side to close the gate and return to the cart area.

Barrels are removed from the cart and Michael has the lame horse untied. He points in the direction of the stables. "Just take the horse over there to the sick box. They'll take a look at her and I need to head off to the quay. I'm running late as it is."

Across from the stables is a horse hospital or 'sick boxes' built of enameled bricks. The sides of each stall are lined with closed fiber matting and paved with blue bricks. A coach house along with several other buildings complete the horse area of the compound. As a groomsman takes the horse from Cahey, he hears Michael whistle at the horses, turn the cart around, and quickly exits through the courtyard.

Cahey looks about the courtyard and sees a door where men are lined up. He looks into the harness room for Seámus. "Where do I apply for a job?" he asks.

Seámus nods to the line of men. "There. Go join the queue."

Cahey turns but then straightens his back and walks over to get in line. The line moves quickly. The men who leave grumble about there being no jobs using the skills learned by farmers. Cahey hears them and bounces his heels on the ground with nervous energy. He has never asked for a job. He has food for today and tomorrow, but then he remembers that all of his gear, including the food, is stowed under the cart bench that Michael has taken to the quay. How could he be so careless? It is everything he owns minus his horse. At least he has his horse. He looks out to the pasture to confirm that the horse is still there. The man in front of him enters the door to the office. Cahey waits outside. He tucks his hair under his cap and brushes off dirt from his trousers. The man before him leaves; it is Cahey's turn.

The clerk sits behind a table with a sheet of paper and a pen.

"Next," he says. "Name please."

Cahey takes off his cap. "Cahey Ó hArrachtain."

The clerk looks up at him and puts the pen down without writing anything down. "Cahey, then, what do you know about working in a distillery?"

Cahey pauses. "I know about taking care of horses and driving a cart." He hasn't actually driven a cart but he saw what Michael did and is confident that he could too. "And I can lift barrels. I just helped Michael empty a cart out in the courtyard."

The clerk picks up his pen and makes some notes on his paper. "Where did you work with horses?"

"Mannin Bay."

"Did you work on a farm?"

Cahey does not want to be seen as a farm laborer. He hesitates. "The horses I worked with often did chores on farms in the area," he says. "My job was to groom, feed, and take care of them."

"I see," says the clerk. "The harness room just hired a guy."

"Yes, Seámus says he can't find him to work. I'm here. I can work," says Cahey.

The clerk looks at Cahey for a long minute, and then he stands. "Wait here." He goes out into the courtyard. Cahey paces back and forth in front of the table. In a few minutes the clerk returns and sits down. "Seámus says he will give you a trial run. Go report to him."

"Thank you, sir, thank you."

Cahey bounds out of the office and races over to the harness room. Seámus is waiting for him. "I see you talked your way into a job; now, let's see if you can actually do the job."

Cahey is confident but knows he needs to pay attention and learn what he needs to do. Seámus goes over the different harnesses and gear used on the horses. He shows him the carts and points out places he will need to know around the courtyard. Cahey counts five warehouses with hoses and pipes lying all over the ground.

"What's with the hoses and pipes?"

"Fire. Fire is always a big concern. We are located at the fork of the river to get water up here fast. We even have our own fire brigade." As they finish the courtyard tour, Michael comes racing into the courtyard with a fully loaded cart from his trip to the quays. He stops over near another warehouse.

"Go help Michael," says Seámus.

Cahey jogs over to the cart to help Michael unload the barley.

"You stayed around," says Michael.

"Yes, my gear is under the bench."

Michael looks and sees the gear. "I forgot you put it there. I was in a hurry."

Michael hops down and begins unleashing the barley from the cart. Cahey starts to help but Michael stops him. "We have to have it tested before we unload," says Michael, who takes a portion of the barley and hands it to a man in a white apron. As they stand and wait, Michael explains that there is a barley, oat, and corn sampling clerk. A portion of each delivery is handed to one of them for comparison with the samples that hang in bags upon a frame on the wall. If a sample is not up to the mark, the sampling clerk can refuse delivery and report this to the buyer's office. So, they wait to see if they have to return the barley. The sampling clerk gives his approval and Cahey helps Michael unload the barley. When they finish unloading, they lead the horses over to the harness room. As they unharness the horses, Seámus instructs Michael to show Cahey how to wipe down the horses.

Cahey offers Michael a grin. "I got a job working with you."

Michael smiles back. "Then I'll tell you what I know. We brush down each horse."

Cahey interrupts. "I know how to brush a horse, tell me what you pick up at the quays."

"Right," says Michael. "At the quays we meet the ships carrying the barley needed to make the liquor. Each evening, the ships are berthed to unload the cargo, and I—we—bring it back here. We reverse that once the whiskey is made by taking barrels to load on ships called hookers to take back up the coast. In the morning, we load the carts with barrels to deliver to alehouses in the area ready to meet the demand for that day. With hard times, much whiskey flows, right?" says Michael.

Cahey's papa seldom drank ale except when they went to the fairs. Cahey was offered a drink once in a while when they were out with the men at a race or on a special lending job where they went to pick up or deliver a horse.

The two men finish their job, and Michael offers to show Cahey where they stay. Cahey gathers his bed roll, saddle, and rucksack that he had left next to the harness room and meets up with Michael who leads the way up an outside stairway to a loft area over the harness room. Cahey had not slept on straw palliasses before. They are placed on wooden platforms about twelve inches off the floor. The beds on the farm had frames and ropes that held the mattresses, which were stuffed with straw. There are pegs for holding clothes on the wall above each platform. Doors are at both ends of the long room, with windows all along the side, offering plenty of air flow and breezes. Michael points out a shed in the back where Cahey can heat water for tea and where their midday meals are served. Because they work with animals, they don't eat in the employee dining hall with everyone else but could grab breakfast and have dinner in the dining room. Michael explains that the smaller rooms off to the side of the long room are for longterm workers, with one of them being the water closet.

"Come on, I will show you around outside," says Michael. They go back down the stairs and out among the many buildings in the distillery compound. As Cahey walks with Michael, he counts many rooms within the buildings. There are excise and clerks' offices, waiting rooms, the dining hall, sampling room, private offices for the partners, telegraphic and telephonic rooms, and lavatories. Cahey learns from Michael that each warehouse and each room of the compound is cleaned daily to lessen the likelihood of fire. Michael also explains the blue brick in the stable walls was made in Staffordshire, England, and is designed to be used in heavy construction. Michael's father had worked in the foundry making bricks, so he knows that when the local red clay is heated at a high-temperature fire with little oxygen, the brick takes on a deep blue color with a hard surface resistant to crushing strength and does not absorb a lot of water. Cahey could understand that with all the horses coming and going, the tough stable walls are a necessity.

As Cahey looks at the blue walls he can almost hear his papa say back in the cottage on the bay, "Boys, don't be throwin' yourselves about and against these walls. They're fragile and all we have between us and the cold." Solid walls might be a good thing to get accustomed to, Cahey thinks.

3

———

Days go by, and Cahey gets into a routine: deliveries, pickups, and grooming the horses. Sunday comes and he has no deliveries just cleaning the harness gear, checking over the carts to make sure they are ready to go, and brushing down his horse. Then Seámus tells him that he has half a day off to do whatever he wants. He could go into town, but he hasn't ridden his horse in a week and misses the feeling he gets when the horse takes him along. He decides to go by way of the road to the quays where there is a beach; he can ride his horse there.

The salt hill beach is rocky but still good for a canter. He guides his horse carefully past the stone outcrops and when he hits the beach, he can feel that the horse is primed to go. Cahey lets her take off, moving into the water when people are too nearby. Luckily the beach is not crowded, just a few groups of people enjoying the afternoon sun. When Cahey reaches the end of the beach, he slows the horse down and makes a smooth turn. He barely gives a twitch to the reins. "Good girl," he says to the horse. Slower, he lets the horse take him back down the beach. As he reaches a large outcrop of stone, Cahey dismounts and leads the horse gently down the beach where he had seen a group of people finishing up a picnic. Some of the young men were hurling on the beach, and Cahey wants to watch. One has a *camán* and hits a *sliotar*. They practice hitting the ball back and forth, not trying for any real goals like with a team during a game. As Cahey watches, one guy catches the *sliotar* and takes four steps to toss it in the air and hit it with the *camán*. Cahey has not played a game with other young men in quite a while. He and his brother would join neighbor friends at gatherings along the hillside and they might kick a ball or throw one, but with all the work they needed to do on the farm, they seldom had time to practice hurling. Though he is still walking his horse while absorbed by the activity on the beach, he is surprised when the horse pauses. He realizes that a young woman, tall with long blonde hair flowing down to her shoulders in wavy strands, has walked into his path. He looks at her and admires her off-white beach dress that has long sleeves covering her arms but leaves her slender fingers free to smooth the horse's mane.

"You have a nice horse," she says after Cahey abruptly stops so as not to run over her.

"Thank you." Cahey continues to stare at her.

"Your horse looks different. Are you from here?"

He glances at his horse. "No, I am from Mannin Bay."

And before Cahey can assess her, though he likes how she looks, she asks, "Do you offer rides to women on your horse?"

He answers quickly and honestly. "Only if the woman has ridden before."

Cahey jumps up on the horse and reaches his hand down to lift her. The most beautiful woman he has ever seen swings easily up behind him and catches her arms around his waist.

"What's your name?" she asks.

"Cahey, and yours?"

"Micil."

Without a moment's pause, Cahey clicks his heels and the horse canters down the beach. He can feel her touching his waist. He smells something, a pleasant smell. The beach is not long so Cahey turns the horse and they race down the beach several times. He can feel her fingers, those long slender fingers he saw touching the horse's mane, grip his waist when the turns the horse and heads in another direction. As they near the group again, one of the other women comes running out.

"Micil, Micil, we have to go. Come now. We have everything packed; we are ready to go."

Micil leans forward, and into Cahey's ear, she says, "Shall we ride again on Sunday week?"

Cahey holds her arm as she slides off the horse. "Of course."

She dashes away with her friends. Cahey watches her turn at the top of the bluff and wave. The last thing he sees is her blond hair blowing in the breeze. He almost forgets to wave back since he is still staring at where she had been. He then turns his horse. "Go girl. Go like the wind." They gallop down the beach. Cahey feels the strength of his horse under him and feels his heart pounding in his chest.

After a burst of speed, Cahey changes course and wanders slowly back to the stables, thinking only of Micil. He sees her face, her chin, her brown eyes. What he doesn't see is anything he passes. There is Miller's bonded store; Cahey doesn't see it. John Gray's factory for making corks and Palmer's flour mill, where they bake the "Star of the West" bread, might as well have been in London for all Cahey is taking in. He passes by twenty-five businesses that all need a water line to the river and are located on the right bank of the River Corrib. Cahey ignores them all. He sees only the woman on the back of his horse holding onto him. The scent, he finally decides, is lavender.

Though daylight is long in the summer months, Cahey knows he must put in a full, long day in the morning so he returns to the stables. As he brushes down his horse, for the first time since leaving home, he sings as he brushes.

"One morning early I went out
On the shore of Lough Leinn
The leafy trees of summertime,
And the warm rays of the sun,
As I wandered through the townlands,
And the luscious grassy plains,
Who should I meet but a beautiful maid,
At the dawning of the day."

4

The week has nine days in it, Cahey is sure, but when Sunday afternoon finally arrives, Cahey brushes down his horse and mounts eagerly. He heads for the beach. As he nears and looks down the rocky slope, he sees groups of people, but he does not see Micil. His hopes drop and he realizes that he has no way of knowing if she will be here. Add to that, he has no idea of how to even find her. All he has is the memory of her lavender scent following him down the beach. He moves down to the water though he isn't as up for a ride as he thought. Just as he is coming to a group of boulders, Micil stands up.

Cahey smiles. "How did you know I was coming?"

Micil smiles back. "I've been listening for you."

Cahey reaches down and Micil swings up onto the horse behind him and wraps her arms about his waist. He takes the horse down the beach. At the end of the beach is a path through the wetlands. Cahey glances back at Micil. She squeezes his waist and he is off again through the path and through the bushes. The horse finds an easy gait, and soon they are in the countryside, riding briskly as though there is no time for them to be anywhere. Cahey lets the horse choose where to go. Ahead he sees a small grove of beech trees with grass nearby. Cahey halts the horse, dismounts, and reaches to lift Micil down.

"We can let the horse rest a bit here with the grass," he says as he feels her body in his arms.

Micil nods and, with feet on the ground, chooses to sit on the grass under a beech tree. She spreads out her skirt and then begins to pick at the wildflowers growing around her. "What do you do in Galway?"

"I work at Nun's Distillery with the horses and carts. And what do you do?" Cahey's heart is pounding in his chest so he does not sit down next to her. Instead, he paces around the grassy area picking his own wild flowers and a grass blade here or there.

"I am training to be a telegraph operator," says Micil. "I come from a small village, Labane Village, where there are no jobs. Since I have an uncle working at the post office, he got me the training. How did you get to Galway?"

Cahey looks confused; he wants to say his horse but feels that there is something more to the question. He is not used to talking with young women who are not his sisters, but Micil is easy to be with. She is a natural on the horse. He paces and paces and though he tells her about his mum, papa, brother, and two sisters, he does not tell her what happened to make him leave the farm. He does tell her about his decision to come to Galway; describes his side trip to the village where he met Muirghein, Ryan, and Séan; and then the luck he had in finding work so quickly. These are all positive stories and they come out so easily as Cahey talks with Micil.

"And where do you go from this job? Is there more advancement at the distillery?"

Cahey is momentarily distracted by the wind blowing Micil's hair, making it look like golden silk flowing in the breeze. He shakes his head before answering. "I don't know. I haven't asked. I am just pleased to have a roof over my head and food in my stomach. I never thought to ask about anything more."

They talk easily about how the town is changing with more and more destitute people coming into town with no jobs for them because even with the mandatory primary education, many of the hungry people are illiterate and have dropped out of school to work the farms to feed all the children and take care of the families. Micil talks about her own family and how, though they were farmers, her mother in particular saw to it that Micil and her two sisters had their education and knew how to read, write, and figure their numbers. Many an evening after chores, the girls were required to go over all their studies with their mother and to listen to each other's studies as well. "Things have a way of sticking in your brain when you do a lot of listening," says Micil.

Cahey is indeed listening. He attended school for a while when the school was in session, which was not that often with the remoteness of where they lived and with the difficulty of finding knowledgeable teachers. He has basic reading and writing skills. He was the oldest and had to help with the horses and with the farm. To hear Micil talk about her education makes him wait to tell her how little he knows. He wants her to like him and not judge him so soon.

"Where are your sisters?" asks Cahey.

"They are both older and have married and moved away to start their families. One is in Dublin and the other is in Cork." The quiet between them is comfortable, and Cahey moves over to sit next to her. They talk about Galway since they are both new to the town. Cahey leans back to lie all the way down and stares up at the clouds. So does Micil and soon they are creating stories about what they see in the clouds.

"I need to get back," says Micil. Cahey does not want the

afternoon to end but stands and offers her a hand to get up, holding her hand a bit longer than needed while he whistles for his horse. He mounts and then reaches for Micil like before. Together, they wend their way back down the paths to the beach.

"Where do you live? I'll take you there." Cahey hopes to prolong the visit; he doesn't want it to end.

"No, it would be better that I walk to my lodging."

He dismounts before she can and reaches up to assist her. He holds her at her waist as he lifts her down and can smell the lavender wafting out around her. He could tell the scent when they were on the horse but now that he is holding her in his arms, he breathes in deeply, not wanting the scent to dissipate nor for her to leave. She smiles at him, a smile that fills his chest with his own heart. Micil then pats down her bright blue skirt and straightens her blouse trimmed in blue lace. Cahey wants to remember every detail.

"Micil, when can I see you again?"

She is walking away. "Like today, I'll be listening for you on the beach." And she goes over the ridge.

Cahey moves to sit on the boulder where Micil had been sitting to greet him. He wants to spend a little more time thinking about her in this spot.

5

———

Early on Monday morning, Cahey sees Seámus.

"Good morning, Cahey, how are things going for you?"

"Just fine, sir, just fine."

Seámus is taking inventory of the harnesses. "Good, that's good to hear. By the way, the remedy for the horse you offered has been tried and the groomsman says the horse is doing much better."

Cahey moves along with Seámus as the harnesses are being counted. "Ah, that's good to hear," he says.

Seámus asks, "Would you like to work more with the horses than with the driving? You do seem to know a bit about them."

Now we're going somewhere, thinks Cahey. "Yes, sir, I like to work with horses and would like to improve my chances at work. What would I need to do for that?"

"Well, the men we have working with the horses have many, many years of experience; however, you could apprentice to the saddler and learn a good solid trade."

The work was not exactly with the horses, but it was close. "Yes, sir, and how long would the apprenticeship last?"

Seámus pauses and sorts through some reins below the harnesses. "About three years, when there is an opening."

Cahey is eager to advance. He heard Micil ask about his future—three years might as well be forever. He pauses to think before he speaks. "Please, sir, I would like that. In the meantime, I will work with the horses and the harness room and learn all I can." At least now he has more of an idea what kind of a future he could share with Micil.

"I know you will, lad, I know you will." Seámus shuffles down the row to continue his task.

With no errand to attend to, Cahey is at a loss as to what he should do so he decides to go to the sick box to see about the lame horse. The horse is the only one there. He takes a brush and combs through the feathers on the ankles. He sees a canister of oil on a nearby shelf, applies a little, and gently rubs it into the horse's hair. Just as he is finishing with the back ankles of the horse, the groomsman comes into the sick box.

"What are you doing here? You have no business here. Get going. Get out of here before I call Seámus and tell him that you are not where you should be."

"But Seámus..."

"Go on, get out of here."

Cahey backs out of the sick boxes and starts to head back to the harness room.

The groomsman, looking at Cahey leave, calls to him. "Wait a minute. Aren't you the guy who told us what to do about the horse?"

Cahey stands at the door and waits. He doesn't know if the groomsman liked his advice or not so he remains silent.

Impatiently the groomsman asks again, "Well, aren't you?"

"Yes, sir, I am," Cahey says, deciding to stand his ground.

"Good advice," says the groomsman. "The horse is improving and we won't have to put her down. Good job."

Cahey nods several times but leaves quickly to go and find Seámus.

"Seámus, did you mean for me to work with the horses today?"

"No, lad, I have to get it straight with the groomsman first."

"Ah, I hope that works out. I was oiling the feathers of the lame horse and he threw me out without hearing why I was there."

"Not to worry; I'll straighten it out. In the meantime, hang close to the harness room and get everything ready for the fair coming up. We have some old harnesses that need repair and oiling to use as backups."

"A fair? When?" Cahey's hopes surge as he remembers going to fairs with his papa. He remembers one fair in particular. Several years earlier, Cahey was told that he would be going to a fair with his papa to buy a new horse. He got up earlier than anyone and quietly went outside to take care of the chores. He dashed through feeding the horses in the lean-to next to the shed. He let the sheep out of the closure and into the pasture. He rushed to pile the peat up in the bin to be taken into the house and then he ran to the stream and filled a bucket with water. When he entered the cottage, he ladled some water in a kettle and placed it in the embers in the fireplace for a cup of tea. By that time, his papa, Richard, was up and moving about the main room of the cottage. He ruffled Cahey's hair and motioned for him to come with him outside so as not to wake the rest of the family. At the lean-to, Richard brought out two horses and Cahey got the saddles and began preparing the horses. When the horses were ready, so was Cahey, who jumped on his horse.

"Don't you want a cup of tea before we leave?"

Cahey shook his head no.

"All right then, let's go to the fair!"

The men went down the lane with Richard singing a song

he always sang when he'd leave for the fields early in the morning.

Then Cahey hears Seámus describing the fair in Ballinasloe, which brings him out of his memories.

"The fair is in October, and we take barrels out to quench the thirst of those buying and selling horses. We pick up a horse if we need one as well. So, get those harnesses ready."

Cahey's spirits improve with the day. He polishes and repairs every harness on the pegs and stops frequently to help change out the horses from the carts and to lead them over to the groomsmen. He also thinks about the fair.

Cahey has been trying to make mental notes of the importance of where he is working so he can impress Micil with what he does and how he thinks his future might turn out, especially since she asked. He knows that though there are many ale shops around town and in the villages nearby, Nun's Distillery is the only legal distillery in the area. Cahey knew plenty of people up where he was from who made poteen, Irish moonshine, with private stills, but the government always found a way to shut them down. Nun's Distillery takes making alcohol to a different level. Micil should be pleased that he is working for such a distinguished company.

In a day's work—because he now wants to learn—Cahey has been schooled on the city's history as he asks men working at the distillery and at the quays. They tell him that Galway is growing again after many people have left. They point out that the canal, the Eglinton Canal, has been constructed to connect the Claddagh Basin Lake with the sea so produce can be transported to the markets much more easily. Cahey asks many questions. The men tell him about the railway line coming into Galway at Eyre Square, and that though the Galway shipping line is no more, the Allen Line out of Canada sails from Galway to America, into Boston rather than New York. At the quay, Cahey notices that there is no big dock for the ships to unload;

the bay is not deep enough. He asks more questions. To board the ships, he learns, passengers have to take a tender out to the ship anchored in the bay near Mutton Island.

"Cahey!"

Cahey breaks out of his reverie and hustles over to Seámus who has just called for him.

"We have a double delivery to an alehouse on Academy Street in town. Harness up another one of the carts with horses and let's get them moving."

Cahey runs to get the harness and then runs to get the horses. When ready to go, he drives the cart over to the cooper where both he and Michael load the full barrels. Once loaded, Michael leads them out of the compound and down the road.

Cahey watches the route so that he can do it again if he has to make a delivery later. He sees the storefronts and then sees the turn onto Academy Street. Michael pulls in front of the alehouse, a timber framed pub with two stories, and dashes inside. Cahey drops down to the roadway and begins to unlash the barrels on Michael's cart. He heaves a barrel up on his shoulders as Michael comes out and gets a barrel. Two more trips and the barrels in Michael's cart are unloaded. Michael hops into his cart and calls out to Cahey. "I've got to get down to the quay for pickups; can you manage this without me?"

Cahey waves and off Michael goes. Cahey begins to unlash his barrels and retraces his path into the alehouse, through the back door, and into the courtyard. As he passes through the door, he sees a young woman behind the bar, older than he by a couple of years, watching him as he passes. He nods his cap in her direction but keeps on working. When he comes through with his last barrel, she is not in the alehouse. He heads out to the back courtyard and puts the barrel with the others.

"Thought you'd never finish," came a voice from behind the open door. The woman steps out into the courtyard. "I haven't seen you make deliveries before. Are you new?"

All Cahey sees is how she is dressed. She has a low-cut bodice tied in ribbons down her front with a half apron covering a bright flowered skirt. Her hair is tied back with a ribbon at her neck. Her cheeks are red with rouge and so are her lips.

Cahey takes his hat off and nods. "Yes, I have been driving the carts, but then I haven't." His statement makes no sense but he is somewhat rattled; he has never seen a woman dressed so.

She comes nearer to Cahey. "I'm Sheila."

Cahey remains silent. She steps closer to him until she is near enough to whisper in his ear. "What's your name?"

"Cahey. My name is Cahey." He eyes the back door and how he might exit.

"Well, hello Cahey. Do you have time to sit with a glass of ale and talk awhile?" Sheila reaches out to touch Cahey's arm, but he slides by her.

"No, ma'am, I have to get back to my cart. Thank you though." Cahey dashes through the alehouse but hears Sheila laugh and then call out to him, "Okay, but we're having a special *ceilidh* on Saturday night. Why don't you come back?"

Cahey waves his hand over his shoulder and moves through the alehouse to the door.

"There will be lots of music, food, and drink. You should come, you know." Sheila has followed him into the alehouse.

Cahey nods to Sheila and dashes to his cart. As he heads away from the alehouse, he looks back and sees her at the door. He thinks to himself, going to hear some music and dance might be just what he needs on Saturday night. And he is curious as to how the alehouse can play music with the British ban on anything Irish.

6

Carts are slow to get back, meaning Michael has not returned. Cahey is anxious to go to hear the music. Michael has agreed to go, but he is still out collecting a pickup from the quays. Cahey paces and wipes imaginary dust off the harnesses. Seámus watches him pace around the room.

"If I didn't know better, I would think you have a meeting with a lovely maid tonight."

Cahey stops pacing and sits on his stool. "No, Michael is going with me to hear the music at the alehouse tonight, where we made the double delivery. The owner says there would be music tonight."

"You mean Sheila told you."

Cahey turns redder than his hair.

"Everyone knows about Sheila. You just watch your step with that one. She lures you with drink and then you're engaged. Men are few and far between in these parts with the famine, the leaving, and the joining up with the army, and she'll be snagging anyone in pants." Seámus laughs and returns to his work. In a more serious voice, he says, "Just be careful with the music as well."

Cahey sees Michael drive fast into the compound. He joins him to help unload the barley from the cart. Together the two men unharness the horses and lead them to the stable where a groomsman takes them to brush down. Cahey hangs up the harness. Just as he starts to dash up the side stairs to change his shirt, he hears Seámus say to Michael. "Don't you and Cahey get in any trouble at that alehouse tonight. I need all of my men to remember who they work for, you hear me?"

"Yes, sir," says Michael and soon he's right behind Cahey on the stairs. The men stumble into the loft area, change their shirts, and wet down their hair a bit. Cahey's red curls are a bit difficult to wet down so he pulls a cap on top. Michael's hair is straight and trimmed. The men bounce around the room and slap at each other like brothers along the way, full of fun and out to have a good time on a Saturday night.

Finally, they are ready and fast walk down to the Spanish Arch and turn up Main Street. It is getting later and they know the music has started. Right so, they can hear the jig as they turn onto the street. Two men as sentries look them over and let them pass by on the street. Men are standing outside smoking pipes and talking. Cahey and Michael have to wedge themselves through the crowd and into the packed room. Four men are sitting in a corner. One has a fiddle, another a bodhrán, another a tin whistle, and the fourth a melodeon going full speed with a tune Cahey has not heard. Four couples are in the middle of the floor dancing a quadrille. Cahey didn't recognize that dance either. The two men shuffle around until they find chairs. Everyone is enjoying the music and is dancing, keeping time with their feet, or clapping their hands. Suddenly, Sheila pops her head between them.

"Hello, guys. I brought you a drink." She deposits the two drinks on the table in front of them and disappears.

"I don't have money for a drink," says Cahey, but Sheila is gone. Besides, he is paying more attention to the music, something he enjoys and taps his feet to the rhythms he hears.

As the band plays, people join in and sing merrily. They sing "

Eileen Aroon."
"Fain would I ride with thee, Eileen Aroon,
Fain would I ride with thee, Eileen Aroon,
Fain would I ride with thee
To Tirawley's tide with thee
Eileen Aroon"

Then the band plays "Bank of the Roses" and without stopping move into "Parting Glass" and "Saint Anne's Reel" and then "The Hills of Connemara." Cahey feels the music he has heard all his life. Whenever people of his area get together for a wedding, a wake, a harvest—if there had been a harvest—music happens. Sometimes they would gather at the crossroads and have *sean-nos*, if they did not have instruments. He knows that music fills people's souls when food and money are scarce. And though the British have banned much of Irish culture, Cahey has experienced how folks find a way to have their music, like here in the pub with sentries watching and people being careful as Seámus has warned them.

Cahey sees Michael pick up one of the mugs. "She didn't ask for money." Michael looks about for Sheila and sees her up at the bar.

"Yes, but if the bill comes, we'd be owin' for things we can't afford." Cahey is determined not to be swayed.

"True, but there are other ways to pay for a drink," says Michael with a wink and a nod to Sheila.

Cahey looks quickly at Michael to see if he is joking. "I'm not wanting to do that."

"Yeah, but I'm just sayin'."

Sheila looks at them and smiles from across the room. "Suit yourself; it's your own business," Michael says.

The music changes to a jig. Several guys jump up and begin to dance. Their hands are at their waists as their feet leap and kick and tap. Sheila comes back around to them.

"Doesn't look like you are drinking much tonight."

"We have no money for drink," says Cahey.

"But the drinks are on the house," says Sheila, who winks and whisks away to get more drinks for other customers.

"There, you see," says Michael, "the drinks are on the house," and he takes a gulp of one of the drinks on the table.

Cahey concentrates on the dancers and listens to the music. At the *sean-nós*, old style dancing back at the farm, there would be no wooden floors like in the alehouse, so someone would take off a front door, polish it well and put it down at the cross roads where everyone gathered on a warm summer's night. The door was their stage. People would take turns putting on a pair of wooden-soled shoes with nails driven into the soles to produce more sound and they would dance the night away. Their nearest neighbors could play instruments; the wife was good with the melodeon and her husband could play the fiddle. Everyone would dance and sing songs way into the night. Then at the end of the summer on the first day of August when Lugh-nasa takes place, they would go up into the hills, search for bilberries, build a bonfire, and celebrate the beginning of the harvest, when there had been harvests. Sometimes they just needed to celebrate the time of the year in memory of a harvest. Poteen became the drink of choice for many of the celebrants.

Cahey's reverie is broken when Sheila begins to pull him forward out of his chair. "Come on, then, let's dance if you aren't going to drink."

They join the quadrille just forming and the music begins. Cahey remembers all the steps as though it was just yesterday when he danced them at the crossroads. This particular quadrille has solo dances. Cahey remembers steps his papa had taught him and he steps high with skill and force. As he backs into position with the other dancers, the room cheers and people clap and shout out to him. Sheila smiles broadly. "Where did you learn to dance like that?"

"Back in the hills," he says and twirls her around to end the set, "from my papa, who was always the first person to dance when the music started."

As he moves back to join Michael, people clap him on the back and shake his hand. Everyone seems to have enjoyed his dancing and he did too. It has been a long time since he had some fun.

"Well, I never," says Michael. "I had no idea you could move like that. Man, oh man, we are going to have some fun at *ceilidhs* this summer!"

Cahey smiles at his new friend and notices a second drink is in front of Michael. There's still a lot of music to be heard and the men sit awhile just listening and enjoying the tunes. Michael takes an excuse to go out back and soon Sheila is sitting in the chair next to Cahey.

"I notice you didn't drink your drink."

"I told you I had no money for drink." Cahey does not look at her.

"But it was on the house," she says and lays her hand on Cahey's arm.

He moves his arm to another position. "I pay my own way and will not be taking things for free."

Abruptly, Sheila stands, "I give you a gift and am generous to you and all you can say is you'll pay your own way?"

Cahey did not mean to upset her; it was nice of her to give them free drinks, but he was told by his papa to listen to what others say. He remembers what Seámus said about Sheila. He remembers overhearing what Seámus said to Michael. No, he would not take a free drink.

Cahey remains firm. "I'm sorry, Sheila. I don't mean any harm or bad wishes. I just cannot take the free drink."

Just then, Michael returns. "I'll take one," he says.

Sheila steps away quickly and leaves the two men looking at each other.

Cahey stands. "I think it is time we went on back." He takes his friend's arm and leads him through the crowd and into the night. They walk down Main Street with Michael muttering. Cahey guides him up the stairs and Michael falls onto his mattress and is asleep before Cahey can even take his own shirt off.

7

The week is full of repairing harnesses, loading carts, driving when needed, and helping out with the horses. The lame horse has healed and is out in the pasture. Cahey is busy all day long and late into the night. He rarely sees anything more of the compound than the stable area unless he drives loads in and out.

The week seems like a month before he is free to go to the beach on Sunday afternoon. He is looking forward to seeing Micil. She said she would be there, but as he looks around, he does not see her. He rides down the path they had taken; he sits in the spot where she had sat. She is constantly in his thoughts. In his mind he can see her standing at the boulder waiting for him. He can smell her lavender scent. He has no idea where to find her; all he knows is the telegraph training program and that she lived in Labane Village, wherever that is. Finally, he gets up and whistles. His horse comes and he rides slowly back into Galway the way he had come so many weeks earlier. He thinks about what he knows most about, and that would be horses, definitely not women.

As the days pass and he drives through town to deliver

barrels, Cahey will see a woman walking along with Micil's same gait and same hair and he almost cries out to her only to realize that it is not Micil.

"Cahey!" Seámus pokes his head out of the harness shop. "Cahey!"

Cahey has just unloaded a cart of barley and is pulling the horses over to the stable.

"There you are. We are busier than ever, and I know I promised you to work more with the horses, but I need more carts and more drivers. So, I must ask that you use your horse and take a small cart to deliver a barrel for a special occasion. I will pay you extra to do so."

"Yes, I will do it. Let me get my horse ready."

Cahey goes to the pasture and whistles. His horse stops grazing, perks her ears, and trots over to the gate. Within minutes Cahey has her harnessed and ready to go.

"Where am I headed?" He feels as though he is just going through the motions of work. He knows he needs to have energy to keep this job, but all he can do it think about Micil and wonder why she has not shown up any Sunday he has gone to the beach.

"To Middle Street, a long grey building at the end of the block. You'll see it, I'm sure, and someone will be watching for you to let you know where to put the barrel. There's to be a special celebration; the telegraph trainees are completing their lessons and management is hosting a special party for them this afternoon."

Cahey does not move. He stands still and just stares at Seámus.

"Cahey, get on with it. Is anything wrong?"

Cahey does not want to tell Seámus why he lacks spirit. Quickly he says, "No, sir. Yes, sir, I mean. I'm on my way." He drives over to pick up the barrel. Off he goes to Middle Street. He finds the turn and sees the long grey building at the end of the block. A cook with an apron is standing near the entrance of an alleyway.

"Here, this is where it goes," the cook says and then races down the alley to an open doorway.

Cahey heaves the barrel up and slings it on his shoulder. He goes down the alley and through the doorway following the cook's directions. He places the barrel on a tabletop and retraces his steps to his cart. He looks through the windows and sees women milling about in a hallway preparing to go into a room. He sees a woman he recognizes. She is the woman who called to Micil on the beach the first day they met.

"Hello," he calls through the open window. "Hello, do you remember me?"

The woman pauses and is about to turn away when she looks again. She comes to the window.

"You're the horseman on the beach with the red hair," she says. "Yes, I do remember you."

"I am the horseman; I have been looking for Micil. Do you know where she is?

"Oh, right, you don't know. Her mother is very sick and she had to go back to Labane Village. She has been gone the full term and will not finish with us. Sorry."

Cahey is both relieved and saddened. Relieved that he isn't the reason she did not return to the beach but saddened that she is now at home and out of his reach. He drives slowly back to the stables. He takes time to think through what he should do next.

On his return to the stables, he goes over to the harness room to find his boss. "Seámus, I have a proposal for you."

Seámus answers with a lack of enthusiasm. "Yes, what is it this time?"

Cahey disregards Seámus' tone and plunges into his idea. "If I came up with two horses and we build an extra cart from leftover cooper's trimmings, could you afford to pay me a fee to use the horses and cart for the small extra trips? We could do them when we had down time and no big loads. You wouldn't have to hire a new driver because Michael and I are already on the payroll and we can drive them."

Seámus scratches his head. "How are you going to come up with two horses?"

Cahey grins. "I have an idea is all. Are you game if I make it work?"

"Yes, if you can turn it around, I'm game."

"I'll need a day off, a day during the last week in June."

"Somebody told you about the Spancil Hill horse fair, right? I can tell by the look on your face that you have heard about the fair."

"Yes, some of the guys were telling me that it is one of the biggest horse fairs and has been going on for centuries down between Ennis and Tulla in County Clare. I figure I could ride down the night before and see what I can come up with."

Clutching his notebook where he writes everything down, Seámus says, "You seem to have a plan. The fair is on a Sunday this year. Yes, take off on Saturday evening, then."

Cahey's grin covers his face. "I do have a plan, thank you. You'll see, it will be fine." Cahey has grown fond of Seámus and believes that Seámus trusts him to do the right thing.

"All right, then, give it a try."

Cahey is excited but nervous. He is really taking a chance. He has saved money from using his horse for special deliveries and the wages for his job. He has even put a few provisions aside here and there just in case his plan works out. He estimates that he needs two additional horses to begin building his transport business and creating a future where he can include Micil; that is, if he can find her.

8

The Saturday night before the fair, Cahey has his bedroll ready and provisions in his rucksack. He is ready to go. With the sun shining long hours in June, he can get down the road before dark. He whistles for his horse, loads her up, and swings himself up onto her back. As he starts through the compound, Seámus comes out of the harness room. "Good luck, you hear?"

Cahey tips his hat and picks up the horse's gait as they go down the road. He has managed the last few months to learn some of the distillery business; now, he has to learn how to buy a horse.

He did go with his papa to the horse fairs around the farm. At these fairs, men would be selling horses and sometimes cows and sheep. He has watched how his papa would look at the horse from afar. When he found one that he thought was strong with legs good for work in the fields, then he'd go closer to take a look. He'd look in the horse's mouth at the teeth to tell how old the horse was and look at the horse's coat to see if the horse was healthy.

Cahey's papa told him, "The nicer you are to a horse, the more they will work for you." Then he laughed and said, "There are three things that are good in a horse: high hips, low shoulders, and a hollow back." Cahey was not sure what his papa meant but remembered what his papa said. He'll have to remember a lot more about horses before he gets to the horse fair. He hopes the long ride ahead will give him time to remember.

As darkness begins to thicken in the night, he sees a campfire off to the side of the road and a group of people talking and eating around the fire. As he approaches, he calls out, "Good evening." Several of the men turn and look. "I'm off to the horse fair tomorrow. Are any of you going?"

One of the young men stands up and comes towards Cahey. "Yes, we all are. Come join us and rest here with us through the night."

Cahey thanks him and dismounts, pulling his gear with him and letting his horse wander off with the others to graze on the grass.

People introduce each other around the fire, and it is hard for Cahey to remember which child belongs to which family member. Everyone seems to know each other. Then Cahey figures out that the three men are brothers and the women are their wives. The relationships make more sense after that. People drink their tea and after a short while, everyone finds their bedrolls and lays them out around the fire for the short night, light comes early in June in Ireland.

The first light has Cahey up, but someone has already stoked the fire and has put a kettle on for tea. He accepts the water in his cup and lets the tea leaves steep as he gets his bearings. He figures there will not be much of a ride this morning; he is close to the fair site. The three brothers are with the horses, and Cahey walks over to where they are.

"Good morning," Cahey says and all the men nod. "I have a proposition for you."

The men all turn and face Cahey. "We're listening."

"This horse I have is a racehorse and wins flat races."

His new friends look carefully at the Connemara horse. "This horse?"

"Yes, and I am wanting to organize a race to get some money to buy a horse." Cahey pauses to let the idea sink in. "Will you help me organize the race?"

One of the brothers straightens his back. "What's in it for us?"

"Part of the till?" says Cahey.

There is a pause as the brothers look at each other and consider Cahey's offer.

"Okay, how will it work?" one asks.

"You locate someone at the fair who wants to race and then we will set it up and race."

The brothers think that might work. They agree to meet at the site where the ale tents are set up.

Cahey wants to get to the fair and see what is there. He thanks the brothers, loads his horse, and is off to the fair. "I'll meet you at the ale tents."

The brothers reply with a wave.

People have come from all over the county. Cahey has never seen so many people in one place. Groups of men are gathered around other men who are holding two or three horses on a rope. Boys with their papas are traipsing from one group to another, each with an eye on the horses. Cahey looks out over the pasture where the horses are and sees hundreds of these groups. Over to the side are tents where women are boiling potatoes in large pots and have kettles of water for tea warming on the open stone circled fire pits. Another tent has baked bread sitting in their roasting pots nestled in the coals. Then he sees an area where there are several ale tents. He heads in that direction skirting along the back sides of the crowds. He passes the benches and the roped-off area where the auctions will be held. He dismounts and walks his horse slowly over to the site of the ale tents. A group of men are gathered. Cahey doesn't see the brothers. Maybe there are other ale tents; this is really a big fair. Cahey decides to wait. He takes this time to look over some of the men. They are rugged farm men with soft cheeks and jowls and red blotchy faces from too much weather and too much ale. Their clothes are work pants, woolen vests and shirts, few jackets. One man has brown woolen pants with similar but dark green wool patches on the knees and across his bottom, neatly sewn and stitched to last. Cahey's mother was careful like that. She stitched clothes together to make them stronger and to make them last.

Soon, he sees the three brothers walking through the crowds. Two of the brothers see Cahey and wave. As they approach, they say to Cahey, "We have a race!" The third brother comes from behind them and introduces James Donovan, who wants to race.

As Donovan sees Cahey, both men look at each other and laugh.

"James Donovan, how is it that you are here?" Cahey clasps his hand and shakes it vigorously.

"I could be asking you the same question, Cahey."

The two men catch up on what they have been doing while the three brothers look on with amusement. Finally, it is settled. They would race a flat race with the bets given to the eldest of the three brothers to keep track. At the end of the race, the eldest brother would get a percentage of the till and the winner would get the rest. Now, they need to get the bets going.

The brothers walk about among the men at the ale tents letting them know that a race would begin shortly so they need to get their bets in. Fairs often produced races and games, and though early in the morning, these men seem ready for a race. "There are two horses," the brothers announce and Cahey and Donovan parade their horses among the crowd so people can see.

One man shouts out, "Can't be no race between that big black horse and the short brown one. No race a'tall." One of the brothers goes to pace out the distance for the race and marks it with a red sash. The second brother checks the distance and marks the finish line with a length of rope. Finally, the bets are in, and the men with their horses go down to the starting sash.

"May the best horse win," says Donovan to Cahey, who tips his cap and sits nervously on his horse. He remembers how Donovan won the race on the beach with King Ryan. Again, it is just Cahey and his horse, and though he had wanted to win the first race, this time he is determined to win. Cahey listens as the eldest brother explains that when he lowers his hat, the race will begin. He and his brother will mark which horse passes first and the other brother will stay at the start line to make sure the horses are fair in their start.

"Did everyone understand?" asks the eldest brother.

Both riders nod yes.

"If all the bets are in, then let's start the race; men, get in position."

"Just a minute!"

Cahey sees a man wearing an expensive looking black jacket and black hat walk up to the finish line. "Who's in charge here?"

The men along the sidelines say nothing until the eldest brother speaks up. "I am in charge, sir."

The tall man walks over to the brother. "Then let's mark my

bet down too." He puts his money in the hat and speaks quietly to the brother acting as the bookie. Everyone cheers.

The eldest brother looks at Cahey and Donovan. "Get in position."

The men ride their horses to the starting point. As Cahey turns to get in position, he sees Donovan sit on his big black horse with a smile on his face. Cahey remembers the last time Donovan had a similar smile on his face. Cahey sees the eldest brother raise his hat high above his head.

"Let's start the race!" he says and slings the hat down.

Cahey, though nervous that something may spoil his chances to win, has his eyes focused on watching the hat. Donovan takes off with his horse and Cahey gets into a steady gait and leans far into his horse's mane. He keeps a wide margin from Donovan's horse. The black horse is half a length ahead. Cahey leans forward and pulls up to where the black horse is only a head up front. Cahey meshes into the fur of his horse. He sees the finish line ahead. His horse pushes forward. Cahey can feel the heat of the black horse running neck to neck with his horse. In what seems like no time at all, he has crossed the finish line. Who won?

"By a nose, the horse won by a nose." Cahey hears someone say.

He turns to congratulate his opponent. "Good race, Donovan."

"Easy for you to say when you won the race," says Donovan.

Cahey is flustered. "What?"

"Your horse won by a nose, came up at the very last," says Donovan, who dismounts and turns his back on Cahey to talk with men he knows who saw the race.

Cahey calls out to him. "Donovan!"

Donovan turns to face Cahey.

"May the luck be upon you."

Donovan tips his hat and walks away with his friends.

The eldest brother comes up to Cahey. "Wow, you won a pot! Plenty to buy a horse. Good race."

Men are lining up at the ale tent to celebrate the win even if they lost the bet. The tall man who had placed his bet last approaches Cahey.

"You have a good horse," he says and pats the horse's neck.

"Thank you, sir." Cahey is still in awe that he won against Donovan.

"Seems you know how to ride; do you know how to take care of horses as well?"

"Yes, sir. I work for Nun's Distillery in Galway, sir. I work with the horses there."

"Is this one of their horses?"

"No, sir, this one is mine; I brought her with me when I came down from Mannin Bay."

"I see. Well, if you ever want to leave Galway, come look me up, I live here in Spancil Hill."

"Yes, sir. Thank you, sir." Cahey is even more flustered than ever. He isn't sure exactly who the man is, but he knows that everyone else from around here did know and that means he is important.

The tall man turns back to Cahey. "What's your horse's name?"

"Name? I never gave her a name, sir."

"A good horse has got to have a name. Colleen is a good name."

"Then Colleen it is. Thank you, sir."

The tall man tips his hat and is gone into the crowds. Now, Cahey has to buy a horse. He looks at the money in his pocket. He counts it; then stops and counts it again. He looks up and sees the eldest brother. "Did you take your percentage?"

"Yes, I did. Thank you. You made us happy today."

"There is a lot of money here; it all came from the bets?"

"Yes, and a generous one made by his lord a-gin' you, which really added to your final amount."

"He bet a-gin' me?"

"Yes, and it really made the pot bigger for you 'cause most of the folks knew Donovan's horse and just based on size they figured he would win. So, his lord made the odds a lot higher."

Cahey smiles for the first time in a long time, tips his hat to the brothers, and goes off to find the perfect horse.

At the corner of the pasture, he sees a man holding the ropes for two horses, both mares. Cahey remembers what his papa taught him, look for their strength, strong legs, low shoulders, high hips, hollow back, and good coat. If the man is honest looking don't look in the horse's mouth, take his word for the age of the horse. Cahey looks over the horses and rubs his hand over their coats, "What are you asking for the horses?"

"Fifty pounds each."

"I don't have fifty pounds each. I can give you twenty-five pounds each."

"Much too low. The morning's early; I can sell them for fifty pounds by the end of the day."

Cahey shrugs and begins to walk away. A third man, who has been standing nearby and overhears the conversation, steps forward. "Wait a minute young man. If you have an urge to buy these two horses, then let's see if we can come to some compromise. If you are asking fifty pounds each and you are wanting to pay twenty-five pounds each, half of that would be thirty-five pounds give or take, since he wants to take two horses, right sir?"

The man holding the horses looks straight at Cahey and not at the man negotiating. Later, Cahey would think through how smoothly the price was increased by the third man, but for the time being, he does have the money, thanks to the race and his savings.

Cahey nods; the buyer nods.

"Okay, sold. Pay the man."

Cahey counts out the seventy pounds and still has a few pounds left over to get him back to Galway. He hands the man the money. The seller takes two eight-meter-long ropes and ties one to each horse. Then he pulls out of his pocket a couple of shillings and hands these over to Cahey.

"For good luck," he says.

Cahey tips his cap, takes the two horses and heads over to the food tent. Suddenly, he is hungry. With his nervous energy about to explode, he throws his cap into the air with a great big, "yahoo." He now owns three horses.

9

B usiness done, Cahey mounts Colleen, ties the other two horses to a third rope and proceeds to return to Galway. As he is leaving the pasture, he sees the three brothers. "Thanks for your help," he says.

"And thank you for the extra money," says the eldest brother. "If you are ever near our village, stop in and rest by the fire."

"Which village are you from?"

"Labane Village, just this side of the road on the way to Galway."

Cahey sits still for a moment. "Labane?"

"That's right. Go up the road a piece until you reach Gort, then just past Ardrahan is Labane. Ask for the MacMillans, everyone knows us."

Cahey tips his hat yet again and heads up the road.

The midday sun has come out and the three horses manage to find a good gait. There are few people on the road since everyone is still at the horse fair. He has heard that the buying and selling will go on all day and there will be music in the evening, but he has other plans. He stops to rest the horses near a lough with a stream. He takes time to brush down the two new horses to get to know them better. They seem even-tempered, which is good, and willing to make the journey. After they have had water and rest in the shade of some beech trees, Cahey goes on down the road. He passes through Gort and then through Ardrahan. Now he believes he must be in Labane Village. He begins looking for someone to ask about Micil. He sees a farmer come through a field and step over wooden steps placed to cross the stone fence and continue onto the roadway.

"Sir, if you have a moment, I'm looking for someone who may be living around here."

The farmer shields his eyes from the sun. "Who are you looking for."

"A woman named Micil, who had been in Galway learning telegraphing."

The farmer wipes his face and looks at the young man with three horses. "There's no one by that name living around here. Must be someplace else."

"This is Labane Village?"

"It is, but no one by that name lives here. I have an errand to attend to and I must go. Good day." He crosses the road and goes on his way across another pasture quickly.

Cahey senses that the man is too quick with him but doesn't know what to do. He can't follow him across the pasture with the three horses. So, he does what his papa taught him. He dismounts, goes to the side of the road, sits in the shade, and listens; he is going on instinct that the farmer will return this way. He doesn't have to wait long before he sees the farmer and a young woman coming down the road; they are carrying baskets of produce from a garden. The farmer stops sharply when he sees Cahey waiting beside the roadway. The young woman is Micil.

"Cahey."

Cahey stands, takes his hat off, and steps forward to greet Micil.

"I heard you had to return to your village to take care of your sick mother. I was down buying horses at Spancil Hill and met three brothers from the village, so I found out where it was and could get here easily."

Micil turns to the farmer. "Papa, this is Cahey Ó hArrachtain. I met him in Galway."

"Hello. I'm sorry I lied to you, young man. My daughter came home to nurse her sick mother, God bless her soul, who has died, and we are still in mourning. I was afraid that if I told you she was here, it would not be good for her."

"I understand sir. I understand your concern. I just want to visit a moment and catch up with how she is."

"Very well, I'll go on to the house. Come for a cup of tea."

Cahey watches as Micil's father leaves. "Yes, sir." Then he has eyes only for Micil. He looks at her and sees the spirited young woman in Galway but with sadness in her face. He steps nearer to her and smells the scent of lavender.

"I looked for you for weeks and had no word." Cahey reaches out and smooths back her golden hair.

"I'm sorry. It happened so quickly, and I thought I would be back to finish the term, then I had no way of getting word to you. I'm so sorry." Micil never takes her eyes off Cahey's face.

"Well, here you are now. *Ce bhfuil tú*? How are things going?" She pulls him over to the side of the road and they sit in the grass. They talk of many things, of her mother, the loss, of her papa and his grief, of Cahey's job and his future, and before they get to the house, they realize that they don't want the distance between them. Cahey reaches out and takes her hand.

"I have to stay here until the new term and then begin again with the telegraph training," says Micil, "but they say I can get in because I qualified and it was due to a family emergency that I had to leave."

"When does the new term begin?"

"Not until after Christmas."

"Ah, the summer and all of fall to go." Cahey pauses. "So be it."

"So, be it?" Micil is not pleased with his response.

"*Shin, shin*, that's that. We'll have to wait, is all." Cahey holds her close, leans over and kisses her. "We'll have to wait."

He savors the lavender scent. It is getting late; they must go in for tea with her papa. "You'll write, won't you?" Micil nestles her head into Cahey's neck.

Cahey holds her even closer and kisses her again. "Yes, I'll write." And though he has never written a letter, with Micil tucked close to him, he knows he can write to her.

10

Arriving back at the stables late in the day with his three horses, Cahey notices that the other workers gape and stare at him. But Cahey is most pleased with the tone of respect in Seámus' voice as he teases him.

"Look at you," he says. "Gone to the horse fair and brought back not one but two new horses. How did you do it? It is all honest and above board, right?"

"Yes, sir, it is all honest and they all belong to me. I have even some money left over in my pocket to make the cart for deliveries. You see, I have raced my horse before and she did well, so I met some fellows and we organized a horse race. Colleen won by a nose against a horse twice her size. I have to say the lord of the manor down there did a favor and put money in a-gin' my horse and really raised the odds, so I won more than one would expect. I was hoping for money for one horse."

Seámus claps him on the back. "Well done, lad, well done. Let's get these horses in and brushed down. We'll see to building the cart tomorrow and get them rolling the day after. What do you say to that, lad, what about that?" And Seámus actually walked away quickly even though he still swaggered with his weight.

Cahey keeps smiling; he feels really good that maybe finally the world is going his way. He puts Colleen out to pasture after brushing her down and making sure she has plenty of water. The other two horses are being brushed by the groomsmen. Seámus is bustling about, ordering stalls cleaned and picking over harnesses to see which ones would work best for the new horses.

Orders get busy, and Cahey jumps in to help load carts, unload carts, tend to the horses, size the harnesses, anything and everything to get the courtyard moving and be finished for the day. Out of the corner of his eye, he sees Michael watching him.

"Michael, *dia dhuit, Conás átá tú.* Hello, how are you?"

"Fine, just fine." Michael does not look at Cahey and continues fussing with one of the harnesses.

Cahey sees that he has some mending to do. "Wish you had been there."

Michael turns away from Cahey. "Didn't know you were going anywhere."

Cahey circles in front of Michael. "It happened quickly and was such a risk, I was just happy Seámus went along with it."

"Yes, but you won," says Michael.

"I did, but it wasn't so great to win when I didn't have friends like you there rooting for me." Cahey grabs Michael's broad shoulders with a friendly hug.

Michael shrugs Cahey off and says, "Yes, well, next time. I'll be there for sure, next time."

The men in unison begin to unload and load as though they have worked together their whole lives. It is good to have a friend.

At the end of the day, Cahey goes to check on Colleen. He stands at the gate and whistles. Colleen lifts her head and comes sauntering over to him. He rubs her ears and straightens her mane. Suddenly behind him is Seámus.

"You did good on your trip."

"Thank you."

Seámus doesn't move and leans against the fence near Cahey. "But something seems amiss. Did anything happen to you while you were away?"

Both men are looking at Colleen.

Cahey hesitates, he doesn't want to burden Seámus with his personal problems, but then again, Seámus has asked.

"Everything is fine. Well, almost fine. Remember me going out on the beach on Sundays?" Cahey turns to face Seámus. "I met a woman, Micil. She's now in Labane, her village, after going home to take care of a sick mother. Her mother died and it is just her papa and her. Well, we have gotten close and with her so far away and me not able to see her until maybe Christmas, well, she asked that I write her."

Seámus laughs. "That's a problem? That a pretty woman asks you to write her?" Seámus reaches out and strokes Colleen.

Cahey tucks his head. "Well, yes, it is. I did basic education at home but I had to work the farm and take care of the horses. She's educated and may laugh at how little I know." Cahey looks away from Seámus.

Seámus stops patting Colleen and looks at Cahey. "If she cares, she will not judge."

"I know, but I would like to be better educated."

Seámus stops leaning on the fence and stands as straight as his legs allow him. "Problem solved."

"Really, how?"

"My boys, they need a better chance at life than what I have. They have to get more education. I have a poor scholar living at my house. He does lessons with them for food and lodging. You can sit in during the evening lessons and learn with the boys."

This sounds good to Cahey, but there is a problem. "But what can I contribute?"

"A horse."

"What?"

"He likes to go to the gatherings down at the Coole Plantation with Lady Augusta Gregory, but he has no means to get down for these Sunday gatherings. Lend him a horse as payment for your lessons."

Cahey thinks a minute. Since he has not been riding to meet Micil on Sundays, he could offer Colleen to the scholar. Cahey looks back at Colleen and rubs her neck even more. "Thanks, Seámus. When do we start?"

"Nothing like the present; he's at the house tonight."

Faster than usual, Cahey finishes his chores and heads down the road with Seámus. Cahey is nervous that maybe he is too old to learn the things the boys are learning. Maybe there comes an age when learning slows down and all that book work doesn't sink in anymore. They arrive at the modest two-room cottage with a loft where the kids and scholar sleep.

Mrs. Kelly, Seámus' wife, has just put the platter of stampy on the table. Stampy reminds Cahey of his mum's table. She would peel raw potatoes, rasp them, and dry them in a cloth. Then she would mix a few boiled potatoes with these raw ones to hold them together and bake them on a griddle. Cahey's mum always knew ways to make food expand when there were children and extra people at the table. Cahey has picked up his portions at the employee dining room and opens the tin for Mrs. Kelly to see. She marvels at the vegetables already cooked: carrots, potatoes, broccoli, and kale. She puts all of them in a large pot, adds some water from the tea kettle and a little spice from her herb garden, and begins making a soup to go with the stampy. "Start with this and the soup will be ready soon."

Everyone sits and Seámus bows his head. Cahey didn't realize his boss was a religious man. Cahey bows his head, too.

"Lord, we thank you for the food and friends. May our table always be blessed with more than with less. Amen."

The children wait as their mother puts stampy on plates for them and then passes the platter to Seámus, the scholar, and Cahey before she takes any for herself. There is a pitcher of water from the well, and talk is quick and varied with children trying to tell their papa everything they had done that day. The soup is ready, and Mrs. Kelly carefully serves out portions in everyone's plates. When finished, the children go to the fire with the scholar.

Seámus stays in his chair at the table but stops the scholar. "John, tonight Cahey will join you."

"An extra pupil, sir?" John is direct with his question and does not seem to like it. Cahey notices that he tries to straighten his bent shoulders, but too many hours poring over books have curved them forward.

Looking directly at John, Seámus answers, "Yes, but in exchange, Cahey has a horse he is willing to loan you so you can attend the gatherings at Lady Gregory's. Do you think that is a fair exchange?"

This time, John is able to straighten his shoulders a bit more with his immediate acceptance, "Yes, sir," says John. "Sit here close by me, Cahey, so I can begin to see what you know and what you need to know."

Cahey's days begin to fill with a variety of work with the horses, with the carts, and driving when he is needed. He and Michael work well together and tease each other like brothers. In small moments, he finds time to build another cart and pulls Michael into the construction.

"Why are we building a cart out of our own efforts?" asks Michael, obviously not excited about the extra work.

"Because I have two new horses and made a deal with Seámus and, as you are my friend, of course, you would want to help."

Michael takes a moment to look at Cahey. "Okay, then." And the men continue their work to build the cart.

The long evenings are spent working with John, the scholar. Finally, Cahey is confident enough to write his first letter, but he has to ask where to buy paper. John takes him to a bookbinder shop; but not any bookbinder shop. He takes him to the L. Hynes shop in Galway that boasts a bookbinding service and circulating library on High Street. When Cahey walks in, he cannot believe the variety of stationary: post, letter, note, foolscap, and copy paper. He is just looking for paper to write Micil. Then he sees mourning and plain visiting cards, writing desks, escritoires, and quill pens in boxes. Along with these stationary goods, Hynes also sells books. Cahey has never seen so many books. Hynes has books on cookery, domestic economy, gardening, farming and rural affairs, ladies' knitting, netting, and crochet instructions. There are books on the essays of T. Davis; the *Rise and Fall of the Irish Nation*, O'Connell's memoir of Ireland; the Life and Speeches of T. F. Meagher; and ballad poetry of Ireland. And when Cahey picks up the history book, *Knocknagow* by Charles Kickham, a nationalist who was imprisoned for his opinions, John shows his excitement about the book. "Yeats describes the book as 'The most honest of Irish novels.'"

Cahey holds the book reverently. "Why do they consider it such a good book?"

John explains, "Writers who have dealt with rural issues have been of the landlord class like Lady Gregory, J.M. Synge, Emily Lawless, and Maria Edgeworth, who wrote from the outside looking in. Kickham writes from the inside, but don't buy a copy of Kickham's book. You can borrow mine."

Cahey makes his stationary purchase and looks forward to reading Kickham's book. He feels as though a whole new world is opening up for him, a world that is opening up for many in Ireland. He now understands the link between literacy and social-economic status. Seámus says that he wants more for his children, so he is willing to invest in a better education for them. Cahey discovers that many of his peers are investing in more education, like Micil with her telegraph training, to give them better options in the future. Some of his coworkers have others read letters from family in America or Australia. More Irish are learning better skills of writing and reading in preparation of emigrating to America or Australia to increase their chances of getting higher paying jobs or to be able to secure land to own.

When they return to the Kelly house, Cahey writes his letter and wants John to take a read. John scans the copy and then takes a pen and begins to add things.

"What are you doing? Was my writing so bad?" Cahey asks.

"This is a woman you wish to woo?" John continues to scribble and change words on the paper.

"Yes, I guess so. Yes," says Cahey.

"Well then, you need to put the 'woo' in. Here read this."

Cahey reads and has to admit that the letter sounds a lot better and a lot more romantic. He's pleased and plans on posting it first thing in the morning.

The summer wanes and autumn begins. He writes letters along the way and gets letters from Micil. He writes about his reading of Kickham's novel and the building of a cart with Michael. She writes about the farm, her papa, the crops, the cows, and then at the end of one of her letters she says, "I wish we were riding this Sunday afternoon down the beach."

11

A s October approaches and the big fair at Ballinasloe grows near, Cahey goes to Seámus.

"Seámus, I have an idea."

Without a pause or even a glance at Cahey, Seámus says, "I know, you want to go to Ballinasloe and buy more horses."

"Yes, but there is more."

Seámus stops what he is doing and looks at Cahey. "More?"

"Yes, I know you cannot afford to have us go for several days with all the orders and deliveries that have to be made, but I remember you said that the distillery would take barrels of ale to the fair to sell. Here's how we can do that. We can take two of the big wagons, load them with full barrels, have Michael and me drive them and take along two helpers to serve the ale at the fair. The sale of the ale would pay for the trip, plus you would not be missing any of your regular carts because we'd have the wagons and we would only be gone one day and two nights."

"How do you figure that? Sounds very confusing to me." Seámus scratches his head and tries to make sense of what Cahey is planning.

"Well, with two of us driving the wagons, we could drive all night by rotating the wagons and letting the driver sleep during his rotation in the rear. We'd all be rested and ready to serve the ale, and I could purchase the horses. Then we could head back doing the same thing. You know how big this fair is, and the locals are the ones serving up poteen, not the good ale. We'd be welcomed."

Seámus continues to scratch his head. "I will have to ask my boss about this. Sounds a bit chancy and he might not go for it. I know he wanted to take a delivery, but he was thinking of having one of the houses nearby sell the ale."

Cahey pursues. "If he does that, he will still have to deliver the ale with two drivers, two carts, and four horses gone for three days. He would only get what he'd make for selling the barrels, but this way he'd have the total sales of the ale and more ale if we take two wagons and only two men for two days. We need four people, but I know we can get two helpers who will go for the trip and the experience, and all we'd need to do was to pay them for just the work they do selling the ale."

"I'll ask." And Seámus, with a look of amazement, goes off toward the warehouses.

Cahey sees Michael coming out of the stables.

"Michael, did you hear? We're going to Ballinasloe in October."

"Seámus approved?"

"Not yet, but how can they turn something like this down?" Cahey smiles and claps his friend on the back. They go off to finish their work. Cahey calls after him, "Michael, by-the-by, will Sheila be able to go with us to help us sell the ale?" Michael grins and hurries off.

Two days later Seámus comes to Cahey. "I got word from the boss; you can go and take the wagons, but remember who you work for and be respectful and reputable."

"No problem. We have your interest at heart."

Seámus laughs heartily. "No, my friend, you have your heart at interest. Have you heard from the Labane lady?"

Cahey blushes. "Yes, we write regularly, and my lessons have improved my letters greatly. Thank you for letting me be a part of that."

"And the scholar, is he returning the horse properly and on time?"

"Yes, everything seems to be working nicely. Thank you."

"Good, then I will see you tonight."

As he turns to leave, Cahey says, "Then tonight it is and I have a special treat. It's a surprise so don't tell the wife or the children."

Seámus smiles and moves on to finish his work.

Cahey has been saving some of his funds and saw that the baker in the employee kitchen often has small loaf cakes left over from the day. He asked the baker if he could buy some of the cakes at a reduced rate rather than throwing them out. The baker could show extra money on his accounts and that would make him look good to his boss while the cakes could be taken to share with the family who had so welcomed him into their home. Cahey finishes his work, cleans up quickly, and goes to collect the cakes. There are four varieties, plenty for the entire family to choose and have some left over. Cahey is pleased. He pays the baker and carefully bundles the cakes so he can carry them to the house.

Everyone is sitting when he arrives. He joins in, hiding his parcels behind the bench. When dinner is over, he reaches down and pulls up the cakes and unwraps them. The children are speechless and Mrs. Kelly smiles, stands, and says, "I think we need special plates."

And Seámus says, "And a little special ale as well." It is a grand party with even the scholar laughing and sharing funny poetical sayings with the children, though Cahey has no idea what he is talking about, and truth be known, he thinks the children probably do not know either. For Cahey, though, he was creating a family in Galway.

12

Ballinasloe Fair is one of the largest and best known in the region, so the men at the distillery tell Cahey. People from Europe come to this fair to buy and trade horses. Cahey has carefully planned. He is to drive the first leg, with Michael resting, and then they switch around every two or three hours to keep them fresh and ready to work when they get to the fair. Sheila accepts and they get Seámus's eldest boy to assist as a helper to Sheila and with the horses.

After the day's work is finished, Michael and Cahey load the wagons with the barrels and put their provisions under the driver's benches. Sheila is to fetch the boy and meet them at the stables. Cahey has enough money saved to purchase two more horses and that would be without a race. He will see how that works this time.

Sheila and the boy, Pádraig, arrive and everyone settles in on their wagons. Seámus claps his son on the back. "Pádraig, you listen to Sheila, Cahey, and Michael. They'll take care of things. Don't be getting into any trouble."

"We'll take care of him," says Michael and ruffles Pádraig's hair, causing him to pull his cap down lower over his blunt haircut. "Is the hair cut new?" asks Michael, and without answering, Pádraig turns up his collar and slumps on the bench.

Cahey climbs up into the wagon and gives Pádraig a nudge with his elbow, offering him a smile, "Ready for our adventure?"

Pádraig returns the smile and sits up straighter on the bench next to Cahey.

Down the road they go. Ballinasloe is only thirty-four miles from Galway, and it would have been easy to get there on the railway line, but with the ale and purchasing the horses, it is cheaper to take the wagons. In October, the long light of the summer is gone. Evening comes early and it is dark by the time they leave Galway proper. Michael and Sheila say they are too excited to sleep yet. Cahey doesn't say anything; he just drives. Pádraig is also quiet. The wagon, however, is noisy and rattles down the winding road with barrels of ale sloshing in the back.

The night passes with the shifting of the drivers. Sheila has found a niche among the barrels to curl up with her quilts; Pádraig has found the same. Rather than just switch drivers, Cahey insists that they also change the position of the wagons to rest the horses so the lead horses can then follow for a while.

Dawn arrives as they near Ballinasloe. Cahey gets in line with many wagons hauling cows, sheep, and horses all funneling into the fields around Ballinasloe. He counts many hay wagons to feed all the cows, sheep, and horses. The going is slow. The fair is held inside the Clancarty estate of Garbally with the race park being the main trading arena for the animals. The men at the distillery told Cahey that Ballinasloe is the link in the food chain providing farmers of Leinster with young cattle and sheep.

Everyone in the wagons is wide awake. Cahey moves slowly through the massive crowds trying to get as close to the arena as possible to increase sales of the ale. He sees several other wagons lined up with their backs open to display food and drink. He goes a little distance from them and positions the wagons. Once they unharness the horses, Pádraig is sent to cobble them among any grass he can find; the field is already one wet, muddy mess. Michael and Cahey position the ale barrels to be sold and stack the barrels so that they could easily dispense the ale. Sheila takes off her headscarf, fluffs up her hair, and they are ready for business.

Cahey sees Michael looking at Sheila the way Cahey looks at Micil, and in all honesty, Cahey sees Sheila in a different light from their first meeting. He likes her but not the way Michael does. "Why don't I search out some tea for us?" he says. "And we'll have some bread from our provisions." He leaves to wind his way through the crowd of people, leaving Michael and Sheila minding the ale.

As Cahey moves through the crowd, two horsemen come through with a stick stuck in their Wellington boots to disperse the crowds and force their horses through. "Mind your backs," they say in English.

A man near Cahey responds in Irish, "Mind yours."

The horsemen stop. "What did you say?"

He repeats what he says in English and then Irish. "I said, 'Mind yours.'"

The men sit up tall on their horses. "Do you have any idea how stupid you sound speaking a language of peasants and impoverished people? You label yourself, sir."

"I do," says the man, lanky with long brown hair. "I do speak Irish, and I am from a poor family, and I work hard for my living."

Cahey sees the two horse riders stiffen in their saddles.

"Are you suggesting that we do not work hard for ours?"

"On the contrary, I believe there is work and then there is leisure. How one defines work and leisure depends on one's class."

"I think you mistake us for fools, sir. Is that your intent?"

"Only if you make it so by your words," says the man in Irish.

"What do you say?"

Cahey is silent but watches as the horsemen look about and see that many of the men in the crowd are now standing silently shoulder to shoulder backing the man, backing the Irish language, and engulfing Cahey into the dialogue. To move away from the crowd would be difficult and Cahey wants to witness how these men handle a difficult moment. Though the crowd around Cahey is quiet, the tension is high. Cahey feels it rippling through the crowd. Men stand with straight arms and tight jaws. Cahey can see in their faces that they do not intend to back down and are willing to take on a fight. Then in the back of the crowd a voice is heard. A man begins softly singing.

"When boyhood's fire was in my blood
I read of ancient freemen."

People step back and move. Cahey sees an old man with long wispy white hair is the one who is singing. The old man continues, slowly moving toward Cahey and the man who is confronting the horsemen.

For Greece and Rome who bravely stood,
Three hundred men and three men;
And then I prayed I yet might see
Our fetters rent in twain,
And Ireland, long a province, be.
A Nation once again!

Cahey turns to face the two men on horseback as the old man walks forward and stands with Cahey and the man confronting the horsemen. Cahey knows the song; it is considered the Irish anthem. He joins in.

A Nation once again,
A Nation once again,
And Ireland, long a province, be
A Nation once again!"
Other men and women join the singing.
"It whisper'd too, that freedom's ark
And service high and holy,
Would be profaned by feelings dark
And passions vain or lowly;
For, Freedom comes from God's right hand,
And needs a Godly train;
And righteous men must make our land
A Nation once again!"
Now many are standing shoulder to shoulder and
    singing.
"So, as I grew from boy to man,
I bent me to that bidding
My spirit of each selfish plan
And cruel passion ridding;
For, thus I hoped someday to aid,
Oh, can such hope be vain?
When my dear country shall be made
A Nation once again!
A Nation once again,
A Nation once again,
And Ireland, long a province, be
A Nation once again!

As the people finish the song, the men on horseback growl at the crowd and move hurriedly away. Cahey senses that there are too many Irish for them to fight that day.

The crowd disperses, but the fair seems to take on another feeling, at least to Cahey, a feeling of Irish pride. Suddenly,

Cahey is joined by two men. Both take an arm and walk with him to a place more remote from others' ears.

"Are you a brother?" asks the stockier man.

"What are you asking?" Cahey is caught between the two men.

"He's asking if you are a member of the Irish Republican Brotherhood," explains the other man, who resembles the stockier man. They might be brothers.

"No, I have no idea what you are talking about," says Cahey, attempting to break free from their arm grasps. "Who are you?"

"We are the brothers of the IRA. You supported the Irish."

"Yes, but those men were being rude and pushing through the crowd."

"Ah, so you don't care about the issues, only about yourself, do you?"

"What issues? I'm here to sell ale and buy a horse, that's all."

"Okay, if that is what you say. You'll say more if it was your rent and your job." The men begin to walk away.

Cahey thinks quickly. His papa would tell him to listen first. "Just a bit, tell me more about what it is that you are doing."

The two men lead him over to the side of the field. They squat to keep from sitting in the mud and begin to tell him what they are about. They tell him about Lord Clanricarde, the largest landlord in the area with more than 56,000 acres of land, who raised his tenants' rent in retaliation for their backing Captain Nolan in the last by-election. Nolan is an Irish nationalist landowner and Member of Parliament in the House of Commons as a member of the Irish Parliamentary Party representing Galway County. Something had to be done about rents and landowners, they explain to Cahey.

Then they tell him that the average wage for an agricultural laborer is nine shillings a week. If the laborers have no harvest, they have no wages; therefore, they cannot pay the rents. Cahey knew about not being able to pay rent. What he did not know is about the Irish Republican Brotherhood. This is the first time an association has been named, though he remembers the talk in Mannin Bay about how there needed to be one. Cahey wants to know how he can find out more about the issue.

"You must read Thomas Davis and Charles Gavin Duffy's work on the Young Ireland Movement," says the stockier man.

"And how do I find these?"

"The booksellers in Galway carry these, I know. Plus, they are read in the reading rooms of the Repeal Association."

Cahey has few words. He does not know any of what these men share with him. He will need to read about Gladstone's reforms and the Landlord and Tenant Act. The men tell him about Michael Davitt, who founded the Irish National Land League. They described Captain Charles Boycott who managed an estate in Mayo. Though he brought in people to work the harvest, the local people made his life so unpleasant that he was forced to leave. Now Gladstone has proposed a second land act. The sticky wicket, they say, is that the members of the Land League have agreed to let Parnell use Parliament to pave the way for land reform with a demand for home rule as well.

They pause to let all this soak in for Cahey, who feels he has just been introduced to ideas he is now curious to know more about. His family had suffered many of these things. Though he has heard of Parnell, he does not know a lot about him. He stands up between the two men. "Sirs, thank you for sharing all this with me. I will need to get on with my business for today, but I assure you, I will find out more when I return to Galway." With that, he tips his cap and prepares to move away.

"Just a moment," says the smaller brother. Cahey is sure they must be brothers now from their similarities. "How do we know you won't just go and mouth off to folks that we have had this chat?"

"You don't know," says Cahey. "You don't know me and you assumed I was one of your brothers because of my reaction to the horsemen. You will now have to take my word that what you have shared with me will not be revealed as coming from you."

Cahey turns and walks away, leaving the two men standing in the mud. He finds his way back to the wagons where sales of ale are going briskly even that early in morning.

"Where's our tea?" asks Michael between filling tin cups with ale.

"Ah, I got sidetracked." Cahey says no more.

"That we noticed. We're just happy no one took you off to the gael for standing up for the Irish."

"They would do that here?" Cahey is not convinced.

Michael looks over at Sheila, who nods and goes on to help another customer. Cahey has a lot to think about.

The day is spent taking care of selling the ale. Pádraig is a great help to Sheila and Michael. He catches Cahey's eye. "Will you tell my papa how hard I worked?"

Cahey ruffles his hair like a brother would do to a younger brother. "Yes, I definitely will do that. But before I do, I need to buy a horse."

Cahey saunters through the crowds of people and locates a horse that looks good. The man selling the horse has two men interested in the same horse. Cahey stands back and watches the men negotiate. What catches his attention is that each man tells the other the bad points about the horse in question. Each has something negative to say so that by the time they talk it out, the horse is a hag in their descriptions. The horse is definitely not a hag. The horse is a wonderful sable brown horse with white markings on her forehead and white markings on three of her four ankles. She has a bit of spirit and tugs on the rope as the owner tries to listen to the men in front of him. The owner of the horse sees Cahey listening to the talk and nods his head at Cahey. "And what do you think, young man, about this horse?"

Cahey responds quickly. "I think it is a fine horse and is worth three times what these men are suggesting."

The two men stop talking and look at Cahey. The owner smiles. "I totally agree." He turns to the two men. "I cannot sell this horse to either of you. Thank you." The men are outraged, but the owner of the horse motions for Cahey to join him and leads the horse away from the two men who remain arguing even though the horse is not there. Cahey gets in stride with him as they walk the horse down through the field.

"You ruined my sale to those men, back there, you know." The man is lean and taut with bulging arm muscles.

"I'm aware that they wanted a beautiful horse for nothing." Cahey has been stroking the horse's mane as they walk.

"So, you know something about horses."

"I'm learning every day."

"What do you know about this horse?"

"I know she is spirited and likes to run. And I think that you would not be selling her if you didn't need the money."

The man stops in his tracks and laughs out loud. Cahey sees him looking at him in a new way, not as a buyer but as a compatriot. "Were you not just talking with Lord Clanricarde's henchmen?"

Cahey pauses as they walk. "Those two rude men on horseback are men who work for Lord Clanricarde?"

"The same."

As they resume their walk, Cahey glances about him to see if those men were still around. "I'm doomed."

"Maybe, maybe not."

"How do you say?"

"Maybe there are others who will shield your back, as you witnessed with the singing of the anthem."

"Ah, but I have to belong to some brotherhood, I understand."

"And you are not a joiner?"

"No, I would rather walk my own path."

"Sometimes those paths force us to walk with others whether we want to or not; we have no choice."

Now it was Cahey's turn to give a hard look at the owner of the horse. "Who are you?"

"Some say I am a wanted man; others just give my name: Mickileen."

"And why would you be wanted?"

"Because I dare call a spade a spade and a crook a crook. I have stood up against Lord Clanricarde and now he wants my head. I am selling all I can to pay passage to Australia. I must leave."

Mickileen says all of this so quickly that Cahey cannot imagine having to make these choices. He thinks quickly. "Do you not have family or friends who can help? You just told me that there were those who could walk the path with me. Are they not there to walk with you?"

"I have done too much and made too much noise. It would be a danger for any of them to help me now. So, how much for my horse?"

Cahey takes in what Mickileen has said and looks at the horse. "I cannot afford such a beautiful horse."

"Tell me what you have with you to spend and the horse can be yours."

The men make a deal. Cahey pays Mickileen, who holds the horse's head gently in his hands, then he turns and walks away. Cahey watches him leave until the crowds engulf Mickileen and Cahey is left alone holding his new horse.

13

The ride back to Galway after the Ballinasloe fair is uneventful yet restful for Cahey. The immense numbers of people and animals and all the mixed sounds make Cahey happy for the silence on the return trip. The fair had a carnival atmosphere with performers, arguments, races, games, and the opportunity to meet new people and to learn about new things. He is so full of thought that he never calls for Michael to relieve him. He drives the horses in the front wagon until the darkness begins to brighten. He can make out the bushes and trees on either side of the road now and does not have to depend on the moonlight to guide him. He drives for hours, not feeling the hard boards of the wagon as he sits, not hungry or thirsty, just thinking about what Mickileen shared with him. The troubles in Ireland seem to Cahey to keep on coming and he is watching as people he meets have to make quick and life-changing choices to survive.

As the morning comes, Michael sits up. "Where are we?" He rubs his eyes and looks out over the sides of the wagon.

"Almost back," says Cahey.

"You didn't wake me."

"It's fine; I have a lot on my mind and would not have been able to sleep anyway."

"Well, you need to stop and give me a stretch."

They pull off the lane and Michael dashes into the trees. Sheila yawns and sits up. Pádraig does not even turn in his sleep. Sheila asks, "It is light. Have we been asleep all the way?"

"I do believe so," says Cahey. He takes a sip of water from his canteen.

Sheila looks about. "Ah, there is the peace of the countryside that is so nice to remember when the city gets too busy, isn't it now?"

"Yes, I like the quiet. But the river where we are rushes past so swiftly that often it blocks out the town noises."

"Not where I live. Above the alehouse, it is noisy late in the night and then there is major work to be done the next day with cleaning and preparing for the night. Always noise."

Michael returns and Pádraig awakens with a huge yawn. Michael starts to get up into the wagon with Sheila but calls to Pádraig, "Would you like to drive the wagons back into town?"

Pádraig is excited. "Would I!" He crawls past the empty barrels and into the driver's seat next to Cahey.

"No, let's trade the horses so they can have a rest from finding the way," says Michael.

Everyone agrees, and the wagons are traded out with Pádraig sitting up in the front wagon ready to drive into Galway.

"I'm going to sit up with Pádraig since he's in charge and I'm in charge of him," says Sheila.

Michael nods, and Cahey joins Michael in the back wagon.

"And why don't you ride your new horse?" suggests Michael.

Cahey takes his cap off and wipes his forehead. "You're just full of ideas this morning, aren't you?" But he likes the idea a lot. He hops down from the wagon, unties the new horse from the back of the wagon and climbs up. This horse stands much taller than Colleen and has energy pulsating from her muscles. Cahey has to learn to give her a loose rein or she will toss him right over her head. Horse and rider prance next to the wagons. Cahey tips his cap to Pádraig. "I'll see you at the stables."

Cahey takes off on the horse. At the next opening in the meadow, he turns the horse into the hillside and they gallop over the ground covered with the morning dew. They reach a stone wall and the horse glides easily over. Cahey almost whoops outloud again. He has not had as much fun riding a horse since he and Micil rode in the countryside that day at the beach. It's October and though they have been writing, Cahey would like to see her. He has to wait two more months before she is back at the telegraph training; two long months before he sees her again. He has been getting things organized in his mind as to his future. He has built up the number of horses being used at the stables. Seámus has been good to his word, and Cahey has advanced in working with the horses and in owning the horses and carts used for some of the deliveries. His wages have increased accordingly, and with the employee room and board, Cahey has been able to save just about all of his wages. He now has four horses and two carts, plus he runs the odd delivery using Colleen. Twelve horses are used at the distillery stables at the present. To make his plan work, he needs to purchase eight more horses. If all goes according to plan, he can make four more purchases in the spring at the Spancil Hill fair and finish with the other four in October at Ballinasloe. Then maybe he can afford a cottage and ask Micil's papa for her hand. He chooses a path, keeping the river in sight and rides across the hillsides toward Galway dreaming of having Micil on the back of his horse and smelling her lavender.

Cahey arrives at the stables and introduces Seámus to his new horse.

"And where is my son?" Seámus looks to the entrance of the compound.

"Soon, Seámus, soon. He is in good hands and has grown two feet since you saw him."

Seámus laughs. "I knew it would be so. He's eatin' us out of house and home as it is, so he must be growing something. What have you named this horse?"

"Ah, I haven't thought about it, but I think I will name her Lavender."

"Some name for a horse. Seems like you have been missing the lady in Labane."

"That I have, Seámus, that I have."

"Good thing you have a letter waiting for you then." Seámus pulls it out of his apron pocket and hands it to Cahey. The letter smells of lavender. Cahey wants time to read the letter so he stuffs it in his jacket pocket and gets to work helping Seámus brush down the new horse and get her fitted with a harness.

Not long and the wagons come rolling into the compound yard. Cahey looks over his shoulder and sees Pádraig looking all grown up driving the horses into the yard. It seems to Cahey as he watches, that Seámus stands a bit taller as he waits to greet his son. Sheila gathers the parcels purchased from the fair to give to Mrs. Kelly, and then, with Pádraig walking beside her, they both move on home. Seámus continues to stand and watch as they leave, and Cahey realizes how much he misses his own papa.

14

Days go by quickly when there is work to do. Cahey has learned along the way from men who have been working at the distillery for many years that 400,000 gallons of whiskey are produced there annually. As the only legal distillery operating in Connaught, the company proudly also displays on their label: As supplied to the House of Commons. There is a lot of work for Cahey and the men at the distillery.

One morning, though, Cahey learns about a job the men at the distillery cannot do. He sees a dozen small lads being ushered into one of the preparation rooms for the distillery.

"What's going on with the lads?" he asks Michael as both of them watch the young boys all in a line go into the distillery.

"Don't you know that they bring the lads to fix the tiles?" explains Michael.

"Lads to fix the tiles?" Cahey is baffled.

"Come on, I'll show you. It's quite a story, one you can tell your children in the future. Tell Seámus we'll be right back."

The two men go through the doors following the lads into the building. They proceed up two flights of steps, then in an outer room, the lads take off their shoes and stockings and are handed what looks to be long metal sticks. The boys are instructed by the overseer.

"Lads, some of you have been here before; some, this is your first time. The Worcester tiles are perforated and must be opened to allow the air to circulate properly and to reduce the possibility of fire. Over time, these holes get stopped up with some of the grain particles. Since the tiles are delicate, size is important, thus having you lads come in to help out is great. What I need you to do is to take a tool, like this, and unstop all the holes in the tiles. Just push the grain through until all the holes are open. Understand?"

The lads nod and then dutifully line up to file through the door and into the tile area.

Cahey is curious. "How long will it take them to do this? It is a big area."

The overseer smiles. "Yes, it is big, and the lads will tire quickly because it is not fun, but they will manage to get it done in four or five hours."

"Are they paid?"

"Of course, they are paid. We give the money to the school and they disperse the coins to the lads."

"Which school?"

"The one near the workhouse."

As they return to their jobs, Michael shares a memory. "The lads cleaning the tiles remind me of a book my papa read to us in the winter around the fire; it was one of Charles Dickens' books, *Oliver Twist*. Have you heard of it?"

Cahey has not heard of the book.

"Ah, it's a great story about a young boy, an orphan, who falls in with a bad lot and things go terribly wrong for him. He has to do things he doesn't like to do, much like these lads. In the end, though, he finds his real grandpapa and lives quite grandly. Great story."

Cahey makes a mental note to ask John if he has a copy of *Oliver Twist*. Though Cahey did a lot of chores on the farm growing up that he did not enjoy doing, and those chores made him know that he did not want to be a farmer for the rest of his life, he hopes the young boys will have a better future than living near the workhouse and opening tiles at the distillery. There is a growing need to learn more inside of Cahey. Since he returned from the horse fair, he feels the urgency to catch up with topics he has had no idea about. He is practicing his writing through letters to Micil; he is practicing his numbers through keeping up with his horses, the hours, the amount due for shelter and food and caretaking for them; he needs to now practice more of his reading. He did read Kickham's book and can see why so many homes in this part of Ireland own a copy; it is all about the rural Ireland he grew up in.

The next night over at Seámus' house, he asks John about which books he has. John doesn't have many and what he does have is poetry. So, the next free time Cahey has, he goes to the bookbinders to see what is available.

He walks into the shop and begins to look about. The tall shelves have many books including Dickens' book, *Oliver Twist*. Cahey takes down copies of *Tristram Shandy*, Dean Swift's letters, *Paradise Lost*, *Gulliver's Travels*, *Captain Freney the Robber*, *Life of Redmond O'Hanlan*, and finally a book entitled *Life of Lady Lucy*. He has many choices. Then he sees the pamphlet written by Thomas Davis and Charles Gavin Duffy on the Young Ireland Movement for one shilling. The books he has been looking at cost from three shillings down to sixpence. He settles on the pamphlet and *Oliver Twist*. As he pays, the shopkeeper eyes the pamphlet.

In a lowered tone of voice, directed only to Cahey's ears, the shopkeeper says, "Do you know there is a reading room down the street where you can get other reading materials and maybe some of the newspapers as well."

The shopkeeper has captured Cahey's interest. "Where down the street?"

The shopkeeper looks both ways around them before telling Cahey. "It's the third house from Abbey Lane on the Main Street side. It is occupied by Mr. James Young, who is the librarian, bookbinder, and custodian. He is also a boot and shoemaker. Stop in for a visit. You might find something there."

Cahey thanks him and decides to go the long way back and pass by the address. The shops and storefronts along the way give him the excuse to look at all of the addresses and not be looking for just one. He finds the place easy enough and sees a man in the first-floor shop working on a pair of shoes. The double doors are wide open to allow for a breeze.

"Hello," Cahey calls out to him as he approaches.

"Good day, sir. What can I do for you?"

"I understand you have a reading room."

The man holds the shoe he is repairing but stops his work to look at Cahey. Then he looks out at the roadway. Finally, he asks, "Ah, and who has been telling you this?"

Cahey lowers his voice and steps a few feet closer into the shop. "The shopkeeper at Hynes tells me there might be material I could read." Cahey senses that the man is evaluating him.

"What is your name?"

"Cahey Ó hArrachtain. Are you Mr. Young?"

"Yes, James Young." James takes a few more seconds to evaluate Cahey and Cahey waits for him to finish his thoughts. Cahey knows how much trouble there has been and how guarded people must be about certain subjects. Cahey is about to thank him and move on his way when James says, "The room is open for meetings and readings on Friday evenings. You are welcome to visit and if it is to your liking, we could set you up as a member."

"How much is the membership?"

"Half a guinea."

"Thank you, sir. Thank you very much." Cahey moves toward James and shakes his hand.

As he goes down the road back to the distillery, Cahey feels a bit excited about his new adventure in reading. He has never done anything like this. Though he has read one book already and now owns a book and a pamphlet, he is aware of what he does not know. And as his transportation business grows, he sees the need to be able to read and write effectively to handle his business and to advance his future, which is why he came to Galway in the first place. Now that he has met Micil, he is hopeful.

15

F riday after work, Cahey prepares to go to the reading
room. He has no idea what to expect. He has read the
pamphlet and has started the book. Soon he finds his
way to Abbey Lane. The shoe shop is closed, but he sees some
men entering the shop. He follows. They go up a back stairway
and enter a cozy room on the south side of the building away
from the street. There are two small windows high up on the
wall to offer more privacy but also light. Tables are under them
with lamps for the evening readings. Chairs are scattered around
the room and another table at the other end of the room has
three chairs behind it. Pamphlets, newspapers, leaflets, hand-
bills, and books cover all the tables. Cahey sees James and takes
his cap off and shakes hands. James has changed out of his boot-
maker's apron and has a plaid shirt on with his work pants and
boots. The other three men in the room are all in work clothes.

"Hello, I see you have come again."

"Yes, I want to see what you have." Cahey looks first at
James and then at the pamphlets and newspapers on the tables.

"You are welcome to browse. We do plan on having a

meeting when more of the men arrive, so look around and see what there is to read."

Cahey thanks him and heads over to one of the tables. He passes two of the men on his way and he nods a greeting to both. On the table is a stack of newspapers: *Galway Vindicator, Galway Express, Galway Independent, The Connaught Journal, Connolly's Weekly Advertise, The Nation,* and the *Irish Independent.* He picks up one and starts to read. As he finishes the first page, he hears James call out to the men present, "Hello, can we take a seat and get started?"

The men find chairs; Cahey sits at a chair nearest one of the smaller tables. James and two other men are at the long table with the three chairs.

James stands. "In an effort to be completely transparent to those of you who are members, I want to introduce a young man who wants to know about what we have here to read and what our meetings are all about. We are always looking for able-bodied men who can help our causes. So, Cahey, stand up and introduce yourself. Where are you from?"

Cahey is hesitant. This is new and unexpected, but he stands. "Good evening. My name is Cahey Ó hArrachtain and I come from Mannin Bay in Connemara."

"What brings you to Galway?" asks one of the men sitting at the table up front with James.

Continuing to stand, Cahey looks at him and answers, "I came to find a job and I have; I work at Nun's Distillery with the horses and deliveries."

The men nod and murmur welcome as Cahey sits back down.

"Welcome to you, Cahey." James continues, "As business goes, we have several things to report and talk about. Tonight, we would like to inform you of the Plan of Campaign. William O'Brien, editor of the *United Ireland* newspaper wrote the piece and it appeared on the front page of that paper on 22 October. I will read it to you now."

James reads loudly and precisely. The men find chairs or lean against the tables. The plan, conceived by Timothy Healy but organized by Timothy Harrington, secretary of the Irish National League, with William O'Brien and John Dillon, is to secure a reduction of rent where tenants feel overburdened as a result of a poor harvest. If a landlord refuses to accept a reduced rent, the tenants are to pay no rent at all. The rents are then collected by campaigners who bank them in the name of a National League committee of trustees and are to be used to assist evicted tenants who have risked eviction in hope of fair rent negotiations.

As James finishes, the men are loud with their comments. One man stands and says, "We must stand together and support this plan."

James calms the men down with his hand gestures. "There is more. I am afraid. The very next day, the Irish National Land League was proclaimed an unlawful association." He picks up the news item to read out loud but stops and says, "After we've come so far? Don't you remember the outpouring only two or three years ago now?" He picks up another newspaper and holds it up for all to see. "Here is the report from the *Connaught Telegraph*, April 26, 1879. They reported an estimated 15,000 to 20,000 people came to the meeting. The article reads:

'Since the days of O'Connell a larger public demonstration has not been witnessed than that of Sunday last. About one o'clock the monster procession started from Claremorris, headed by several thousand men on foot—the men of each district wearing a laurel leaf or green ribbon in hat or coat to distinguish the several contingents. At eleven o'clock a monster contingent of tenant-farmers on horseback drew up in front of Hughes's hotel, showing discipline and order that a cavalry regiment might feel proud of. They were led on in sections, each having a marshal who kept his troops well in hand. Messrs. P.W. Nally, J.W. Nally, H. French, and M. Griffin, wearing green and gold sashes, led on their different sections, who rode two deep, occupying, at least, over an Irish mile of the road.'"

Cahey is listening to every word being read. He did not know about the demonstration. He could see the procession from James' reading. He could hear the noise of so many people gathered together for a purpose. The description intensifies what Cahey can see in his mind's eye.

" 'Next followed a train of carriages, brakes, carts, etc. led on by Mr. Martin Hughes, the spirited hotel proprietor, driving a pair of rare black ponies to a phæton, taking Messrs. J.J. Louden and J. Daly. Next came Messrs. O'Connor, J. Ferguson, and Thomas Brennan in a covered carriage, followed by at least 500 vehicles from the neighboring towns. On passing through Ballindine the sight was truly imposing, the endless train directing its course to Irishtown—a neat little hamlet on the boundaries of Mayo, Roscommon, and Galway.'

"Now what is happening," James continues, "is that Lord Salisbury's Conservative government has declared the campaign to be an unlawful and criminal conspiracy. Parnell, unable to prevent it, persuaded O'Brien to confine it to only the estates upon which it was operating. However, the campaigners had moral support from the Catholic Archbishop of Dublin, William Walsh, and from the Archbishop of Cashel, Thomas William Croke. A complication for the Church is that it has lent money to larger Catholic landlords, such as the Earl of Granard in Longford, who cannot pay their mortgage payments to the Church when receiving no rents."

The men are outraged that there is resistance to the plan and are loudly expressing how they feel when James finishes. He quiets them down again. "Okay, men, our job is to get the word out. We need to let people know what is happening. Each of you are a captain for a certain area, we can get some pamphlets made to pass about, but we need to explain the Plan of Campaign to the people, there will be other estates being challenged like Clanricarde's in County Galway, right here in our backyard. Now, let's decide how to do this."

The meeting evolves into who will be going where and reading and when. They discuss and plan every detail. Cahey sits and listens. He pretends to read the newspaper, but he is fascinated by the talk. Even when folks were dying back in Mannin Bay, he did not hear men speak so passionately about what people need to know.

During the planning, James comes over to where Cahey is sitting. "Well, what do you think?"

Cahey lays the newspaper down on the table. "I am ignorant of so much. I did not know any of this. You hear a few rumblings during the workday, but we live and work in the distillery compound so we don't mingle out with folks that much."

"I understand. But do you want to be a part of this? We need every man."

Cahey stands up so that he is next to James. He does not want to appear uninterested; he understands why James is asking for his help. "I cannot say yet. I feel I must educate myself and learn about the issues. What you have shared tonight makes me want to jump up and say yes immediately. I have never witnessed such passion among men. But I find I must listen and learn before I say yes to something that may change my life for good or bad." Cahey is looking around the room at the men gathered, then he looks directly at James. "Are you willing to allow me that time?"

"Of course. But know that these are issues that will demand loyalty once plans are in place. We cannot have people observing and not participating for long. The issues are too important, the losses are too great."

"I understand. What would it cost for me to come and read for several weeks so that I can be better informed?"

"Nothing, *a charra*. We will not turn an able-bodied man away." With that James shakes Cahey's hand. "Stay and read a bit more this evening, we will be talking a while longer on our plans."

Cahey thanks James and looks at the other pamphlets and posters scattered on the table. The pamphlet is written by the editor of *The Nation* newspaper. In the pamphlet, the editor urges members of the Young Ireland Movement to raise political consciousness of the people. He suggests that copies of *The Nation* be given to newsrooms and temperance societies to be placed in their reading rooms, and to the Repeal Wardens to be read aloud at weekly meetings. All people must hear the news and must be informed. The editor writes that the politics of the people must influence newspapers in spreading revolutionary ideas. The effectiveness of the propaganda drive depends on a literate populace. He urges that people must be taught to read. And Cahey knows that the Irish have high illiteracy, especially among the Irish speaking and laborers both in the field and in the factories. The writer's words make sense to Cahey. He is aware of his own limitations based on his lack of education and lack of knowing the issues.

He takes his leave from the men, who are still planning, and heads back to the stables. The walk takes him down Main Street to the Wolf Tone Bridge. He crosses the river and sees the expanse and the fast-moving water. The power of the river always amazes him, yet he is also buoyed by how man has been able to harness that energy to provide work, food, and power. He continues to walk up the roadway. It is late. He has not been out this late from the compound except a few times with Michael listening to music. As he nears the turn into the last lane before he gets to the distillery compound, he sees a man step out of the shadows.

"Who is there?" Cahey pauses and peers into the shadows. The man approaching him says nothing. "Who are you and what do you want?" repeats Cahey.

The man steadily moves toward Cahey; his hat is down over his forehead to hide his eyes and to keep his face in shadow. There is little light since the moon is in its waning stage. Cahey speaks softly. "If it is money you are after, I have none. If it is to give me a good scare, then you have succeeded." The man continues to approach Cahey. As he gets even closer, Cahey can see that he had no intention of stopping. Without thinking, Cahey runs head first into him to knock him over, but the man braces well and pounds Cahey with his fists until he falls. Then he kicks Cahey harder after he is on the ground. Cahey cries out as a boot kicks his side not once, twice, but three times.

Cahey hears a voice. "Who goes there?"

The kicking stops and Cahey recognizes the voice of one of the guards at the compound. "Are you all right? Is it you, Cahey? What happened?"

Cahey gathers his strength and with the help of the guard makes his way into the compound. The guard tells him that he did see someone move away from Cahey into the shadows. Cahey has no idea of who might want to hurt him. People have warned him that being connected with the reading rooms or his stance during the singing at Ballinasloe might be trouble for him. He needs to think about how he can learn about issues that have become important to him and not get beaten up.

16

Cahey tries to explain to Seámus in the morning that he is fine and that the man who attacked him must have thought Cahey was someone else or the man is a crazy man. So many are hungry and have lost their homes, families, and livelihood; it is enough to make a man crazy.

Seámus wants to report the assault to the police. "The police are here to help everyday citizens, right? The police have a thousand men in Galway to protect the citizens and to work with the government."

Seámus tries to reason with Cahey. "The police are more than just 'mind the law' enforcers. Yes, there are those who butt the heads of offenders, but they try to keep the streets safe. They also take the census, compile agricultural numbers, undertake surveys for different government offices, report contagious diseases, and act as the eyes and ears of the government."

Cahey laughs and then winces because his ribs are sore from the attack. "You know a lot about the police. How come?"

"My brother is a policeman. He's a good man."

"Well, if it happens again, I'll talk with your brother, but for now, I'm fine and need to get back to work."

"You'll do nothing of the kind. You need to rest today. Don't you have some accounts to do? Some type of work with your finances?" Seámus has gotten into the habit of teasing Cahey about his growing number of horses, and though he teases him, Cahey realizes that Seámus is also proud of what Cahey is accomplishing.

"I need to learn more about feed costs and how those calculations are made. Do you think the clerks would allow me to ask questions and learn a bit today?"

"Go ask. The worst they can say would be 'no' and you have heard 'no' before." Seámus laughs and goes off to do his work.

Cahey finds it hard to stand but manages. The men in the sick box stables help to gird his ribs with cloth to make it easier for him to heal. He stands and makes his way inside the warehouse door and into the clerks' offices. A man, with his clerk jacket hanging on his emaciated body, looks up at Cahey. "What can I do for you?"

Cahey catches himself staring at the man. "I'm Cahey Ó hArrachtain. I work with Seámus in the stables."

"Yes, I have seen you about the yard." The young man is sitting behind a huge wooden desk stacked with papers, ledgers, and ink wells.

"I was wondering if you or someone here could help me understand how to keep accounts for the feed of the horses and care for them, if I could look over someone's shoulders and learn."

Without a breath and without looking at him, the young man says, "No. Sorry."

Cahey listens but doesn't want to hear "no." Seámus is right that he has heard the word "no" before, but he is not feeling like hearing it today. He is sore and moving any part of his body is painful. Where did this man get off being so rigid? So, he stands a bit taller and asks why not.

"You come in here and want a free education, right? I have worked in this job for years learning the systems and keeping the books and you walk in and want to look over my shoulder? Like it is so easy, you can learn it right away!"

Cahey turns red, not from embarrassment this time but from anger. "I simply asked you a question; I do not need your lecture. I do not need your help." Cahey turns to leave, baffled by the young man's response.

The young man is not finished. He continues talking to Cahey in a harsh tone. "What do you know about need?"

Cahey slowly turns back to the clerk. In a soft, even voice he says, "I understand need. I have lost my entire family. My papa is dead of broken pride and killed himself on a hillside in the Maumturk Mountains. My mum died of the fever after giving us what there was to eat and not eating herself. My two sisters are lost forever in domestic work in Dublin, and God knows where my brother is in the army of the British government. I am here. I am alive. I am learning every day how to survive, with or without your help." Cahey turns to leave.

The clerk stands up quickly. "I'm sorry. Please forgive me. There is so much misery in my own life; I forget that others have their stories as well. Please," he says as he motions for Cahey to return and sit in a nearby chair.

Cahey pauses.

"Please."

Cahey turns and looks at the clerk. "Shall we begin again?"

"Yes, let's. I'm Colm Mullins. You have told me your story; here is mine. Bear with me. My story is longer to explain than yours, and while all of my family is alive, we have had needs too."

Cahey sits as Colm begins his explanation. Colm is from the Weir at Kilcolgan and explains that the Weir is named for an old wall built across the tidal basin of the Dunkellin River. Fishermen trap salmon and gather oysters from these beds. The Hookers, as they are called, the Galway Bay Hookers, are broad black hull boats with thick masts and white or rust-colored sails. These boats, common in the Claddagh district, are used to ferry turf, cattle, and beer. Cahey knew of them because they also brought the barley to the quay that they used in the distillery. The boats, as Colm explains, bring the turf in from the bogs of Connemara and the seaweed from the Aran Islands. Farmers bring their horse carts out to the Weir to buy the turf for their winter fires and seaweed to fertilize the land. With so many people coming and going, three of the nine houses at the Weir had liquor licenses. His papa had one of these houses, but the decline in the oyster population and the decline in shipping because of the new railroad meant that his papa lost his business. There are eight children. Colm is the oldest and only one who has found work. His wages must feed ten people.

Being the oldest in his family and having been told he had to take care of his family, Cahey completely understands the burden Colm is under. Cahey's papa had made him promise to take care of the family should anything happen. Cahey remembers asking his papa, Richard, questions when they were working together out in the fields. Why farm? Where are their relatives? Why stay on the farm if it cannot feed the family? Richard gave short answers. "The farm gives him hope," he said. "Every year is a new year." Their relatives came up from Galway; he had no idea where they were. As to the last question Richard paused and shook his head, running his fingers deep through his scalp, almost pulling out lumps of his hair. "I may have made a mistake staying on this farm," he said. Cahey sat still waiting for Richard to continue. He had wondered why they stayed when so many of their neighbors had left. "I've made a lot of bad choices." He paused for a long time and

Cahey did not interrupt, then he said, "I have few skills to get by on other than farming."

Cahey gritted his teeth. He had not heard this from his father before. Then Richard said in a voice so quiet that Cahey had to lean in closer to hear his father, "All of you would be better off without me." Cahey took a deep breath; he could not bear to hear this from his father.

"What would we do without you?" he said.

"You would figure it out. You have always found a way to get things done."

"Yes, and what about mum and my brothers and sisters?" Cahey has been told that he must take care of the family if anything happened to his papa. Richard made him promise and now that promise is a reality.

"Our biggest gift is to be able to figure out how to survive. You know what you must do," his papa had said.

Cahey did know. He just didn't like it; but he knew. And, he knew what it meant to be the oldest.

After the introduction, Cahey makes a deal with Colm. "If you teach me more about keeping books, I will pay you to keep my books from my growing transportation business."

Now it is Colm's turn to stop and listen to Cahey. "You will pay me to keep your books?"

"Yes, I don't have a lot of money, but I hope to increase the number of horses I have, and with that increase, it is taking more and more of my time to learn how to keep the accounts correct, especially when I don't have the training, as you point out." Cahey looks into Colm's eyes. "Will you take me on?"

Colm accepts and Cahey sees a transformation in Colm's face. The crease on his forehead relaxes and he looks more like the young man he is than the older one his body forces him to be.

The two men begin. Colm gets up and moves the chair next to his so that Cahey can see how he posts the accounts. He explains some of the accounting principles to Cahey, who listens all morning long. Though Cahey has learned a lot about what transpires at the distillery, by lunchtime, he has a headache. "This work is tedious and requires more thinking than I am allowed in one day."

Colm smiles at his new colleague. "When do you want to start on your books?"

"I am in a healing stage right now and hope to do some catch-up work in the harness room today, but I think I can be free tomorrow. You don't work on Sunday, right?"

"Sunday would be fine," says Colm, and then asks, "Would that be before Mass or after Mass?"

Cahey forgets that he has not been to church since he left the farm and even then, just on special holy days. The church was a long walk away and the farm chores often came before going to church. His papa did talk with him about God and what it would take to be a decent man in this world. His mum would remind them of what being good children meant; they did say a blessing before meals.

"Your choice."

"You have the horse. If you came out to the Weir early, we'll go over the accounts and then you can go to Mass with us. We have Sunday lunch after Mass and you can stay and then come back into Galway."

"How far is the Weir?"

"About five miles."

"You walk that every day?"

"No, I take one of the boats across the bay unless the weather is bad; then I walk it. But the boats don't run on Sunday."

Colm gives him directions: look for the old stone bridge, cross the bridge, and go until the road is no more. His house is the last one before the wall.

17

A majority of the people in western Ireland are Catholic, that is what Cahey knows. He remembers one of the local priests, who did stations in his area, was upset over a traditional wake and the crossroads dancing, among other more rural traditional beliefs of fairies and banshees passed down for generations among the families of the Maumturk Mountain people. Cahey's folks did not go to the stations, but he has gone with neighbors. The stations are day-long events where the priests visit a local village to say Mass and to hear confessions. This event includes tea, singing, storytelling, music, and step dancing. He only went when neighbors included him. He has been to Mass on holy days.

Early on Sunday morning, he awakens to the idea that he is going to church. He puts on his best shirt, then gathers his records for the accounting and stuffs them in his rucksack. He almost forgets, but he returns to his room for the kale he had Sheila find for him at the market. He decides not to saddle Colleen. The pain of lifting the saddle is too much; he uses a bench to get astride his horse. His ribs need time to heal. He rides down the road to Kilcolgan, slowly so as not to jar his body. Locating the stone bridge, just as Colm had said he would, he meanders down the narrow roadway and sees the oyster beds. The tide is just coming back in; half of the oyster bed is not under water, but the other half is covered with water. At the end of the road, he sees Colm standing, waiting for him. They wave and as Cahey gets closer Colm moves down to meet him.

"Welcome to the Weir."

"Glad to be here; thank you for inviting me."

"Come, let's get some work done before the family descends on us."

Cahey slides slowly off his horse and ties her to a post. Colm leads Cahey to a side room of the farmhouse, a shed where Colm has set a table, two chairs, and a lamp.

"My office," Colm says.

Cahey produces his accounting records, and the two men sit down to figure out how to set up Cahey's business accounts. They are bent over deep into their discussion when Cahey is aware that someone else is in the shed with them. He looks up and sees a small lad in a nightshirt standing by the doorway. Colm sees him too.

"Cahey, meet my youngest brother, Paul."

"How do you do, Paul?"

Paul does not answer but goes over to Colm and tugs at his sleeve.

"What do you want, Paul?"

"Mum says there is tea if anyone wants it." And with that he dashes out the door.

Cahey laughs and they continue to work. Then there is another person at the door. This time it is a young girl who looks to be about age ten.

"Yes, Sarah?"

"Mum says there is tea if anyone wants it." And she dashes out the door.

Colm looks at Cahey. "We'll have no peace until you meet the family. Come on."

They enter the farmhouse from the rear door through the kitchen.

"Why didn't you bring him in through the front door instead of coming through the back?" says his mum as she tidies her hair and straightens her apron.

"Mum, this is Cahey Ó hArrachtain. Cahey, these are my brothers and sisters."

He rattles off their names, and Cahey knows there is no way he will remember. So, he simply nods and says to all of them, "Happy to meet you."

Then Colm's mum ushers him to sit down and have a cup of tea. Cahey is about to sit when he remembers the kale. He jumps up, dashes to the shed, retrieves the bag of kale and returns to the kitchen. "I forgot to give these to you when I first got here, Mrs. Mullins. I got a friend to get these for you at the market." He presents the bag of kale to her.

She thanks him over and over and as the two men sit, she pours tea and chatters about the house not being as clean as it should be. But with ten people in the house, it can never be clean," she says.

Cahey nods and drinks his tea. Soon Mrs. Mullins scatters the brothers and sisters. "You must get ready for Mass. Go now, go. These men have work to do." With a smile and a sweep of her hand, she has dispersed the children to another room to get ready and gives leave for Cahey and Colm to return to the shed to finish their work, which they do with a thank you and a "we'll be ready to leave when you are."

The men finish their accounting ledgers. Colm assures Cahey that he has all the right records; the amounts just need to be put in certain columns for what is spent and what is taken in so that it all makes sense. He will have the ledger sheets ready for Cahey next week and they can begin.

Cahey is excited about this new venture with Colm. They agree on a percentage so that the accounting will be fair; as Cahey's business grows, so will Colm's. Together they shake hands and hear Mrs. Mullins calling them for Mass.

When the two men go out to the front of the house, Mr. Mullins is there. He is a sullen man, bent with age and worry. He has little to say to Cahey who notices that Colm bristles at his papa's treatment of him. As they walk together, the eleven of them over the hill and down the road to the church in Kilcolgan for Sunday Mass, Cahey makes a few comments to Mr. Mullins about the area, but there is no response. Then Colm whispers to Cahey that there is usually no conversation going to Mass; one must prepare to be spiritual.

As they approach the church, Cahey sees many other people walking to Mass. The men tip their caps to the Mullins, the women nod their heads, and the children look at their feet. Inside the church, Cahey finds himself positioned between Mr. Mullins and Colm. The service begins and after much recitation and singing, the priest stands and presents his sermon. He speaks in both English and Irish, but mostly in Irish since the majority of the rural people in western Ireland, especially in the area surrounding Galway, speak Irish. Colm whispers to him that he speaks occasionally in English because the government authorities feel that the Catholic priests are inciting their congregations when they are speaking in Irish, so they insist that they speak in English when one of the government officials is in the congregation. Cahey looks about the congregation to see if he can spot the official. There is one man who looks out of place because he is sitting alone and has better quality clothes on, something one would buy from a draper in town, not handmade. Cahey nudges Colm and directs his gaze to that man. Colm shakes his head no; he whispers, "That's Mr. Riley. He is one of the farmers for the big estate across the road." Cahey continues to look about but then he catches what the priest is saying. The priest is talking about James Daly, an Irish nationalist who supports the tenant farmers' rights and founded the Irish National Land League. Cahey remembers reading about Daly and hearing the accounts he wrote as editor in the *Connaught Telegraph* newspaper when Cahey visited the reading room in Galway. Now here is the priest talking about this same Daly.

The priest says in Irish, "After being released from jail, Daly published in his newspaper the following: 'Truly is the dawn of freedom appearing—truly the emancipation of the tenant farmers of Ireland. The south is awakening, slowly but surely.'" Then the priest says in English, "After much thought and vision, Daly has revised his views on land reform by saying: 'We must support farmers, but we must work within the system for all farmers of Ireland.'"

With that statement the Mass is over and the benediction allows the people to leave. Mr. Mullins heads out immediately. Colm and Cahey follow but Mrs. Mullins has people to greet. Cahey stands with Colm and his father while the children run and call to their friends. A young woman, petite, wearing a navy and white striped dress with a matching trimmed hat, walks by. She looks at Colm and smiles. Cahey notices that Colm smiles back but then turns red when he sees that Cahey has been watching. Finally, Mrs. Mullins appears, chattering away to her husband about what she has heard and they begin the walk back to the house.

"What did you think about Mass?" asks Colm.

"The priest gave me much to think about."

"So, you are a religious man after all," says Colm.

Cahey thinks a minute—he feels he must figure out what being religious means. There seems to be much politics in choosing to be Catholic or Protestant. Many of the people he knows in the rural area of Mannin Bay remain silent rather than choose to be outwardly religious because of how political religion has become. What he does say to Colm is: "Being spiritual always includes reflection."

With that the two men walk back to the house in silence.

Lunch is basic praiseach, a gruel made of oatmeal and water, but this time Mrs. Mullins adds the kale Cahey had given her so the praiseach had a tangy juice. There is stampy as well and everyone is in good cheer, except for Mr. Mullins, who eats his praiseach, drinks a cup of tea, and leaves the table. Cahey looks over at Colm, who is looking at his bowl and not his papa's empty chair.

After lunch, Cahey and Colm settle on how Cahey will give Colm the reports. Colm will record them and give them back to Cahey for keeping. All of this will be done before and after work so that it will not interfere with their regular jobs. A shake of the hands and the deal is made.

The air is crisp as Cahey mounts Colleen to ride back into Galway. The ride always gives him time to think. He is still a long way from meeting his goals. He still needs to buy more horses, but he feels the expense of Colm will allow him to focus on the horses in the stables and make sure they are well kept and groomed and the carts are in good condition, and maybe he should be thinking about adding to his business. The talk of the railroad taking the shipping business away from the oyster bay and ruining Mr. Mullins' business makes Cahey think he must find additional ways to make his future so as not to rely on one type of income. Then he has an idea. He clicks to Colleen and off she speeds. As they gallop down an empty roadway for a Sunday afternoon, Cahey puts together a plan.

18

"Seámus, I have an idea."

Seámus laughs out loud. "Why am I not surprised?"

"I talked with some guys over at Ballinasloe Fair and they were telling me that some of the distilleries bagged the draft from the distilling process and sold the draft to farmers for their milk cows. The draft was sold for £5:10 a ton. How has the distillery been getting rid of the draft?" Without waiting for Seámus to answer, Cahey continues, "Don't you know they have just been throwing it away? That's what I learned from the accounting clerk, Colm. So, if we organize a way to bag the draft, hire a couple of guys to do the bagging and loading, get the word out that the draft is good feed for the milk cows or for a piggery, we could do something good with the leftovers. Farmers are always looking for ways to increase their milk production and to reduce the cost of feed for cows and pigs, especially in the winter."

Cahey pauses and Seámus is silent. Finally, Seámus looks at Cahey. "That's a brilliant idea."

"So, who do we talk with?"

"I think you need to go right to the top."

"To Mr. Persse?" Cahey has never spoken with the owner of
the distillery.

"Why not? It is his business. I'll go talk with the clerk in his
office and see if we can get a meeting. You get all your numbers
together."

"I'll need to talk with Colm. We will need a couple of days
to get things organized."

"Okay, we'll see what happens. But if this takes place, I want
to be part of the hiring of the men, I think I do a pretty good job
at that," he says as he claps Cahey on the back.

Cahey meets with Colm who agrees to stay late the next day
to help organize the material they may need for the proposal.
Cahey suggests that he just stay over; there is always an extra
palliasse they can pull into his room and he can bunk in with
Cahey, now that Cahey has his own small room. Michael is
nearby in the room next to Cahey's.

The next night after dinner the two men go out to the
back shed. Cahey sees several sawed-off tree stumps and a
couple of boards from the cooper's scraps. It takes the two of
them to get the stumps up the stairs and into Cahey's room.
Colm gets two stools from his clerk's office and Cahey goes
back to the shed for the two boards. Pulling the palliasse into
the room is easier than they anticipated but Cahey realized
that they should have moved it into the small room first.
Finally, they have a make shift office set up. The real work
begins. They figure out what it would take to purchase the
bags, how much draft would fill a bag, how many men it
would take to fill the bags and load them for the farmers, and
consider how much it would cost to promote the venture in
the newspapers.

"I have no idea what that would cost," says Colm. He is
making myriad notes in his book as they talk.

"I can stop in Hynes bookbinders to ask," says Cahey.
"Surely, they would know. And, since the company will make

some money off this, maybe the company will pick up the promotion cost for the new business."

Colm thinks that is a brilliant idea and leans over to add other figures to the sheet.

At last, the two men lean back from their work. "Do you think we can make money doing this?" asks Cahey.

"From what I figure, the draft is free, no cost, so we factor the cost of bagging and loading, then subtract that from the £5:10 other people are selling the draft per ton and that means we can make a seventy five percent profit."

Cahey is ecstatic but Colm quiets him. "Hold on, the company will want a cut, you will want a cut, and your accountant will want a cut."

"And I agreed to let Seámus hire the workers."

"So Seámus will get a cut. We need to figure out the percentage we can take to pay you, me and Seámus, so that when the company suggests a figure, we know if we can do it for that or not."

Cahey claps Colm on the back. "I knew I hired a good accountant. Okay, how do we do that?"

The men continue to talk and finally have a proposal they feel will work. They have a variation of the least percentage they can accept to make it profitable for them and the best percentage they can hope for, the one they will start with should there be any negotiations. Pleased with their work, they agree to go to sleep and go over it again first thing to make sure they did not forget anything.

Cahey finds sleep is difficult. He tosses and turns. His room has a window, but it is dark. He has not heard the early bells for the compound workers to wake up. He is nervous about the proposal. He thinks it is a good idea, but if Mr. Persse doesn't like the proposal, they will have to scrap the entire plan. He finally falls asleep and dreams. In that dream, he replays the time he had to leave the farm early in the morning when he heard the landlord outside. The dream seems to go on and on. He heard shouts that woke him. Knowing that the eviction notice was on the door when the brothers and sisters returned from burying their mother, Cahey prepared for his departure, but he had to make sure his brother and sisters were gone before he could leave. He made a promise he will keep. His sisters and brother left late in the day with a group of travelers they had seen many times in the years as they passed through the area on their annual pilgrimage. The travelers were going past Dublin to the south coast and would escort Cahey's two sisters and brother to Dublin. The sisters wanted to get jobs as domestic servants and his brother would enlist in the army. Once they left, Cahey felt it was too late in the day to start his journey to Galway, where his papa had told him that their family was from and where the travelers had given him directions by drawing a map in the dirt on how to get there. Cahey hid his boots under a bush behind a wall and his packed rucksack further along the wall in a thicket.

He had gone to bed fully dressed and upon hearing the shouts outside, he pushed out through the back window to creep quietly behind a stone wall until he was some distance from the cottage to where he had hidden his boots. As he sat in the early morning twilight to put on the boots, he turned and saw that the landlord had set fire to the cottage. A blaze burst out of the window he had just left. The fire in his dream awakens him with a jolt and he stifles a loud gasp at watching the cottage he had lived in for eighteen years burn.

As he laid on his palliasse with sweat covering his arms and legs, remembering his dream, he glances over to see if Colm has been awakened by his noise. There did not seem to be any movement from Colm, and Cahey could hear Colm's soft snores. Cahey takes a deep breath. He knows it is a dream. He also knows that, in reality, he was able to make his way to where he had hidden his rucksack, his horse's saddle, and then finally to the back of the meadow where he had tied his horse. And he knows he escaped. Cahey lies awake for some time but then does go back to sleep. When he awakes and sits up, he finds Colm dressed. He has reviewed the figures one more time. Morning has come and both men remember that they did not allow for the promotion costs. Cahey will see to that right after work.

Work goes quickly; there is always a lot to do with the horses, the carts, taking care of the deliveries, helping unload and load, repairing a harness. Seámus is called to the office. When he returns, he tells Cahey that Mr. Persse will see him at ten in the next morning and asks if he ready.

"I have one more piece to put in and plan on getting that done right after work. Yes, I will be ready."

"Fine, I will tell the clerk. Oh, and a letter came for you."

Cahey gets a whiff of the lavender scent before he even sees the handwriting. This letter is a couple of days late. She is never late writing him. He goes over to a bench and tears into the letter.

My dear Cahey,

I can call you dear, can't I? This letter may be late, I am sorry, there has been much to do here that has stood in the way of me writing to you. I write now to tell you that I may be delayed in coming to Galway after Christmas. There is nothing to be done about it, I am sorry. I would love to see you and to feel the wind in my hair riding behind you on Colleen. That is what you are calling her now, isn't it? I will write more later when I have time; but I write now because in writing to you I feel you are here with me and I can see you through my words. I must go for now. My love to you,

Micil

Cahey holds the letter gently. She is not coming? He thinks there is more than just what she says in the letter. He has a sick feeling inside, a feeling he has not had since he found his papa on the hillside in the rain. He goes quickly to find Seámus. "Christmas is next month, right?" Seámus agrees. "Do we have time off during Christmas?"

"Yes, the distillery is closed for three days; the day before Christmas, Christmas, and the day after."

And before Seámus can say another word, Cahey dashes away.

The clerk at Hynes Bookbinders is helpful and gives Cahey the newspaper contacts, what the bookbinders would charge to create a handbill to promote the business, and what kind of time it would take to get it all done.

The next morning, Cahey and Colm add the promotion figures into their proposal. Colm feels Cahey should go alone to the meeting since it is his idea. At precisely ten o'clock, Cahey enters the clerk's office for Mr. Persse. He is offered a chair but is too nervous to sit; he paces instead.

Finally, Cahey comes into the harness room where both Seámus and Colm are waiting for him. The two men look at him, but Cahey does not give them a clue as to how the meeting went.

"Well?" they both ask at the same time.

Cahey pauses then looks at both men, "We need a name for our new venture."

The three men throw their caps about, shout and whoop, clapping each other on the back; Seámus gives them both a big hug. With much posturing on all their parts, they finally settle down and agree to meet on Friday night to begin drawing up the details for the hiring, for the purchasing of bags, and for a name. Cahey tells them that Mr. Persse wants to start right away, since the holidays are approaching; it is already November and farmers will need to buy winter feed. He's willing to take on the promotion costs, and the percentage fell in the middle between the good and what they would accept with the idea should it be successful, the percentages could change in their favor. Cahey is pleased and sees this as an opportunity to expand and to build a future for Micil and him. He asks Colm how he feels.

"More money for the family," he says.

Seámus adds, "The extra money will help educate my children."

Now they must name the venture.

19

After work, Cahey goes to his makeshift office in his room. Though they had to return the palliasse and the stools, Cahey leaves the makeshift desk but positions it so he can sit on his palliasse to work. He begins his longest letter yet to Micil. He tells her about the new venture, the excitement expressed by Colm and Seámus, and how they have to jump on it right away because Mr. Persse has given the go ahead. He still plans on buying four more horses so he can have eight at the stables and then buying four more in the spring to be able to run the entire stables from his horses and his carts, relieving the company of that part of the delivery business. Finally, he tells her about his dreams for them, how this will allow him to speak with her papa, if that is good with her. He misses her and has a surprise for her. He signs it, 'Love to you, Cahey.'

As he leaves to put the letter in the post, he runs into Michael. "I don't see much of you except during our workday; how have you been keeping?"

"Ah, my friend, I am off to help Sheila tonight at the alehouse. It seems her papa has come down with the croup and she needs some help. Why don't you stop in? I'll even buy you a drink and you know if I buy it there are no strings attached. Plus, there is something I have been meaning to ask you. But you'll need to be sitting down and have at least one drink in you before we talk."

The men laugh and Cahey agrees to stop in for a drink.

Cahey goes to Hynes Bookbinders where he knows he can post his letter this late in the day. As he enters, he notices a crowd around a middle-aged woman. People are talking to her and the stranger is smiling but saying little. Cahey skirts around to the back of the crowd and sees the shopkeeper. He deposits his letter and his coins.

"Who is that?"

"That is Lady Augusta Gregory."

"Really? From Coole Estates?"

"The very."

"What's happening? I know a scholar who frequents her Sunday sessions, but I have never met her."

"She's setting up a reading for her new poet, Yeats."

Cahey nods to Lady Gregory and finds his way out of the store and back to the alehouse. Though it is evening, it is early and the alehouse is not crowded. Cahey heads to the bar and sits. Michael comes from around the bar and joins him.

"You look like you know what you are doing here," Cahey says.

"When you have put time in at a place like this, you do get to know how things work."

Cahey sees Sheila who enters the pub from the outside courtyard, ignores several requests for ale and comes right over to Cahey and Michael. "Have you asked him yet?"

"Not yet. He's not had his first drink." Sheila moves quickly behind the bar and fills a mug with ale. She puts it down in front of Cahey. "Hope you'll drink this one." And she swishes off to serve the other customers.

Cahey takes the mug and begins to sip the ale. "Okay, what's the question?"

"Will you be best man at my wedding?"

Cahey nearly spits the ale out. "What is it you say?"

"I asked Sheila to marry me and she said yes! We're going to be married!"

Cahey claps Michael on the back, "Of course, of course I'll be your best man. Let's drink to that!"

In front of Cahey, Sheila adds two mugs for them to toast.

"Here's to a happy couple!" They drink, they laugh, and they hug. "When are you planning it?"

"Well, next month is Christmas so we were thinking of getting married just before so we can have a few days off together. Winter is busy here at the alehouse. With nothing going on and the weather bad, people come in and drink and play cards or chess. Sheila's papa has not been getting on so well, so we figure if I marry into the family, maybe Sheila and I can run the alehouse. Her father seems to think it is a good idea."

Sheila leaves to serve customers and Michael shares the details of the wedding, something simple, no church wedding, but a minister, Sheila's papa insists. "So, we might have it out in the courtyard then we can have a reception with just family and a few friends here inside. That's what we've been thinking."

Cahey tells Michael that all of their ideas are brilliant and he's excited for his friend. He finishes his ale, gives Sheila another hug, and goes off to think about how his own wedding might be.

20

First task on the agenda for the men involved in selling the draught is to name the business. Colm and Seámus look at each other. Colm speaks up. "We think it should be 'Ó hArrachtain Services' since it includes the horses and the selling of the draft."

Cahey laughs. "Gentlemen, who could say my surname? We'd be out of business in a fortnight because no one would admit that they couldn't pronounce my name."

The men had to agree that it was an interesting name to conquer.

"What about calling it 'Irish Services'? That way the English would think we call ourselves after our country and the Irish would think we call ourselves after our country and everyone is pleased. Neither will figure out that they both think the same thing. We can speak both Irish and English and can promote other ventures when they arise. What do you think?" asks Colm.

All agree that the name of the new venture is 'Irish Services.' Cahey is the co-owner with Mr. Persse on the draft side of the business; Colm and Seámus are coworkers. Now the real work begins.

With the scholar John's help, Cahey creates a broadbill to be printed at Hynes. Mr. Persse makes a few adjustments and then it is ready to be printed and distributed. Seámus gets word out to a few of his men that he will be hiring two or three workers for bagging and loading. Colm puts the finishing touches on the paperwork with copies of the figures and Mr. Persse signs off. Within two days, they are ready to go. They prepare a corner of the compound yard where the workers can load the wagons. They are planning on only loading one day a week on Mondays when the work week is starting and cattle and pigs need feed.

The advertisement goes out. The Monday coming up will be the first day of the draft sale. Cahey, Colm, and Seámus are ready. Just before the gates open to begin the morning, one of the guards comes over to them. "Sirs, you need to come with me." He leads the three men over to the gate house window. "Look out," he says. They look out at the road. There are wagons lined up down the roadway. In fact, there are wagons so far down the road that they can't see the end of the line. The three men stand back and look at each other. Cahey is the first to speak, "What have we done?"

Seámus answers, "We have started a business. Shall we get to work men? Open the gates!" He prepares to help guide the wagons to where the two men he hired will load them with the draft. Cahey will collect the monies and record the inventory sold, and Colm will get the records later to post with the monies to distribute to the people involved. The day goes by in a blur. They run out of draft before they run out of wagons. Farmers at the end are disappointed so Cahey gives them a certificate number they can bring the next Monday to be first in line.

With the number of customers and the demand for the

draft, Seámus and Cahey decide they must reconsider where they are loading and how they get the wagons back out of the compound so the other deliveries and pickups will not be disturbed. It is a nice problem to have, they think.

November passes quickly with the new draft sales, letters being written back and forth between Cahey and Micil—though Cahey notices that the letters he receives from Micil are short letters, she is still writing—and then Michael grabs him to discuss wedding ideas. Time is passing quickly. He gets up in the morning, works all day at the distillery, works late at night on his studies, on reading, on his new business venture, on writing to Micil—he is busy, but enjoying his work and his friends but missing Micil.

Michael pulls him aside just before the end of the day. "We have decided to have the wedding in two weeks, on Saturday afternoon with a dinner in the alehouse afterwards. Is that good with you?"

Cahey assures him that this is good, but his face says otherwise.

"You do have a Sunday suit, don't you?" When Cahey looks away, Michael laughs. "Well, it looks like you better get off to the tailors quick." He laughs again and claps Cahey on the back. Cahey looks away and turns bright red.

The next evening, he is off to the tailors. He finds the shop that Mrs. Kelly recommends and enters. The tailor greets him, asks a few questions on the occasion for the suit, and then measures him in every possible direction—under his arms, around his neck, down his pants leg—inside and out—around his waist, wrists, chest, and thighs. Then the tailor shows him fabric. Cahey has no idea. The fabric samples begin to all look alike. He asks which fabrics are most often worn all year. The tailor suggests three samples: a subtle tweed, black, and a dark grey with thin pinstripes. Cahey chooses the grey. The suit will be ready for a fitting the following week. Cahey pays the tailor for the material and will pay the full amount when the suit is completed. He leaves with a sense of satisfaction; he will soon own a suit, his first suit. Maybe he should buy a hat as well; then again, maybe not. He will wait and see what the suit looks like.

21

Saturday morning of the wedding and Michael is too nervous to tie his tie. Cahey is no help but luckily Colm has stayed overnight and knows how to tie one. The men are to wait at the stables for Seámus and Mrs. Kelly, who will go with them to the alehouse.

"Quite a procession if you ask me," says Cahey to Michael who is now pacing back and forth across the compound. "How do you like my new suit?" Cahey attempts to model the suit for the amusement of Michael, but Colm is the one who laughs most.

"You would think it is your first suit of clothes," teases Colm.

"It is."

"Oh, my, I'm sorry. It fits you so well; I thought you knew what you were doing."

"Never assume that, *a charra*, never assume. I went to a tailor that Mrs. Kelly recommended. He built this suit just for me. And cost me a bloody fortune, Michael, a bloody fortune!"

Michael ignores Cahey and searches down the road for sight of Seámus and Mrs. Kelly. "Here they come."

The five of them march down the road together.

One of the musicians Cahey recognizes from the music at the pub meets them at the front door and takes them around the building and into the courtyard through a gate in the alley wall. The outdoor courtyard is bright and cheerful for a winter day. Though a brisk wind has pushed them up Main Street, inside the courtyard the wind is still. Bows of greenery are above the doorways and gateways. A new arbor stands at one end of the courtyard. "Sheila has wanted a garden out here so now with the arbor she can start one and it will be nice," says Michael. Garlands of greenery also cover the arbor as well; as some holiday ribbons in green, red, and white are tied to catch the wind. Michael introduces the group to his sister and her husband, who came up from Ennis for the wedding. Michael's mother is too ill to travel and his papa died when he was a boy. The other three people are friends of Sheila's papa, people Sheila has grown up knowing. And then comes in the minister, a quiet man who nods to the people standing about and moves over to the side of the courtyard beside the arbor and stands.

Just as they were beginning to wonder what to do, Sheila and her papa, Mr. Lowry, appear in the doorway of the alehouse. Sheila is glowing and dressed in a long white chiffon dress. Her hair is down and a wreath of flowers is on her head. She is holding a bouquet made from the same type of flowers. Mr. Lowry, in a suit that fit him ten years earlier and now is left unbuttoned and stretching at the sides, holds his arm for Sheila to tuck her hand under and they walk slowly to the arbor and to the minister. Michael and Cahey hurriedly get into position at the arbor with the minister. The wedding begins.

After all the pledges and vows are exchanged, the minister says, "You may kiss your bride." Michael gives Sheila such a long kiss that the men tease him to give her air. Then the minister says, "I present to you, Mr. and Mrs. Michael O'Flaherty." Michael's friends shout and congratulate the couple; everyone is in good spirits.

Mr. Lowry gets everyone's attention, "It's cold out here and there's a good fire in the other room with food on the table." As the wedding party moves into the alehouse, they find tables are pulled together to make one long table at the side of the room. Tablecloths are layered over the old wooden tables with vases of flowers and lovely tea pots decorating the center of the table. Platters of food are laid out down the table. "Sit," says Mr. Lowry, "sit and enjoy."

The wedding party guests eat, drink, and share stories. Mr. Lowry insists on keeping the glasses topped off with ale. As the guests and wedding party settle in and get comfortable after a big meal, the four regular musicians, the ones Cahey recognizes from the *ceilidhs*, move over to a corner of the room. They give a brief fiddle intro and begin to play. Guests move their chairs about and stand up to dance. Much partying takes place in the alehouse that evening. Even Seámus and Mrs. Kelly get out on the floor for a slow dance. After midnight, Cahey and Colm are helping Mr. Lowry tidy up the alehouse. Everyone else has gone including Michael and Sheila who disappeared up the stairs to many cheers and bawdy jokes.

"You fellas go on; there's morning when I can finish up in here," says Mr. Lowry.

Cahey and Colm take their leave with many thanks and good wishes. It has turned cold in the night. They shiver in their suits and pull their caps low and tie woolen scarves around their necks. Little is said going back to the compound until they are almost back and Colm speaks up.

"Do you ever think you'll get married?"

"Yes, I do. I plan on asking Micil's papa for her hand when I surprise them next week for Christmas. We have three days off so I decided to ride down to Labane Village."

"Ah, good for you.

"What about you? There is that pretty young woman who smiled at you at church that day."

Colm's scarlet face gives him away. "Yes, well, I have known her since we were little. Her papa owns the hardware store in Kilcolgan."

"Okay, so what about her?"

"Cahey, don't you see that marrying someone right now with all the responsibilities I have is totally out of the question? I can barely feed ten much less eleven, and if we want a family, then there's that, too."

Being hungry and having responsibilities changes one's choices. Cahey definitely understands that, but he also understands that a pretty young woman like that will not wait for the right guy. He just hopes that his business ventures will help Colm and will also help him build a future with Micil.

22

There is a lot to prepare before he heads out for Labane Village. Cahey wants to share a bit of the holiday spirit with his new friends. He has given a lot of thought as to how he could thank them for being a part of his new life. He and Colm meet right after work. Colm's mother has sewn two bar aprons and Colm tells Cahey that this project has given his mother the idea that she can sew for other people. Most of the children are older and sewing money will help contribute to the family coffers. Colm is pleased and so is Cahey. The aprons are splendid. She even embroidered Sheila's and Michael's names on the front. Colm gets a pen and ink set from Cahey and teases that it's not so much a gift as it is an investment in the accounting end of Irish Services.

"What? Can't I give you something you are constantly using?" but Cahey shares a grin with Colm that there might be a tie-in with the business. "Maybe this will sweeten the gift." He passes the cookies he had gotten from the company baker to Colm for the family.

Colm has brought Cahey a bag of oysters from the Weir. "Merry Christmas, Cahey. And since you won't be joining us for

Mass on Christmas Day, I share with you what we say when we leave Mass, 'Glory to God in the highest, And on earth peace, goodwill toward men!'"

Next, Cahey goes to the Kelly household. He has saved a variety of fruits and nuts from the dining hall to give Mrs. Kelly, who hides them in the pantry for Christmas morning. The book Cahey brought, *Tristram Shandy*, could be started that very night in front of the fireplace. Cahey shares the oysters, and Mrs. Kelly immediately puts them in a pot on the fire to prepare for Christmas dinner.

Cahey walks over to Seámus. "I have a gift for you, I have seen you borrow this from John, so I guessed you did not have one of your own." Cahey watches as Seámus unwraps the new Bible. Seámus looks up at Cahey but does not say anything; there are tears in the big man's eyes. He opens the cover of the Bible where Cahey has inscribed: "To a man who has taken me in and treated me like his own, I am forever grateful, Cahey Ó hArrachtain, December 1885."

As Seámus sits thumbing through the Bible, Mrs. Kelly walks over to the decorated tree in the corner and picks up a long package. She hands it to Seámus and stands next to him. Seámus passes it to Cahey. "Please, open it now."

Cahey unties the ribbon and takes away the wrapping. Inside is a wooden plank with an elaborately engraved title: Irish Services. "I thought you needed something for your office." Cahey reaches out to hug the man he has included as family.

Dinner is served. To celebrate Christmas with Cahey, the children have produced a play for him and have written it all down and illustrated it so that he can have a copy of it to take with him. He is delighted and watches every scene from the chair moved closer to the fire. As he prepares to leave and go to the alehouse, Mrs. Kelly gives him rhubarb jam to take to Micil. Cahey is at home in the household that is warm not just with the fire in the fireplace but with the friendships that have developed.

Cahey hurries through town and arrives at the alehouse to see Michael and Sheila are busy serving customers and Mr. Lowry is seated at one end of the bar sharing story after story with whomever will listen. He is enjoying not being on his feet and yet still being a part of the business that he has grown for all these years. "Welcome, young man, welcome," he shouts out to Cahey, who takes off his cap and waves it at Mr. Lowry.

"Good evening, Mr. Lowry, you're keeping well, are you?"

"Very well, thank you, now that I have some decent help around here." He laughs but Sheila glowers at him.

"Decent help has always been around here, if you just looked about you." She swishes a bar towel at him and he laughs again. She comes from around the bar and ushers Cahey to a table in the corner. "You need to be as far from him as possible if you hope to have any conversation with anyone tonight."

Michael appears by her side with a mug of ale for Cahey. "Here go you, *a charra*. How have things been keeping you?"

"Good. I am riding down to Labane to see Micil tomorrow evening after work and wanted to come by and wish Christmas joy to the two of you."

"And a merry Christmas it will be for us. We'll have two days of no work!"

"Two days? We get three, don't we?" Cahey is suddenly nervous.

"Yes, the distillery gives us three days, but the bar never closes except for Christmas Day. However, Mr. Lowry is giving us the day after off so we can have a two-day holiday."

"Yes, and before I forget, I have something for you two." He pulls out the package containing the aprons and hands the package to Sheila. "Go ahead, open it, it is for both of you."

Sheila carefully unties the ribbon and removes the cloth

wrapping. She holds up one of the aprons, the one that says "Michael." Michael grabs the other one that says "Sheila." "I want to wear Sheila's."

But Sheila grabs it out of his hands, "No, this is mine and this is yours."

They put on the aprons and prance around for Cahey to admire.

Michael speaks up first, but Sheila dashes off behind the counter while he says, "We have a gift for you, too."

Sheila returns with something hidden behind her back. She and Michael stand side by side in front of Cahey. Sheila holds out a bar mug. On the mug is Cahey's name. "For when you come; you have your own mug and can drink as much as you like," says Sheila. "That way you'll be owning it and not owing anyone."

Cahey burst out in laughter. "What a great gift!" He admires the lettering that Michael says is Sheila's talent.

Soon, though, they hear Mr. Lowry. "Customers are wondering where their next mug of ale will come from."

"We have to go. Stay and have as many drinks as you like." And they were off working the tables and pouring ale from behind the bar.

Cahey does not stay long; he is too excited about getting to see Micil. He bids them farewell and returns to his room. He places the jam, more cookies, and a journal for Micil in his rucksack. Then he sees the photo of his papa and mum on their wedding day. He has propped it against the wall at the end of his make-shift table. He looks at the man and woman in the picture. He can see more of how he looks like his papa now than ever before. He puts it in his rucksack and, without changing clothes, lies down to sleep.

23

Morning comes, and though he swore he would never be able to sleep, he did. Now he must rush about and prepare for work. A day cannot go any slower for Cahey than that workday. At every hour he thinks it will be time to ride, and it is not; he has more hours to go.

Finally, the day is over. He grabs his rucksack, whistles for Colleen, says his Merry Christmas greetings to Seámus and the workers, and rides down the road. He is cold but is bundled with a heavy jacket, wool cap and scarf, and has a blanket over his legs that he has tucked underneath him to keep the chill out. He rides until the December cold gets to him. Then he dismounts to walk with Colleen for a while and get warmed up. He can hear his boots crunch on the frozen roadway but the exercise warms his legs. Though the walking slows him down, he wants to arrive when everyone is getting up for the day, significant for starting a new day together.

The dark is still around him when he comes into the Labane Village and approaches Micil's family farmhouse. In the winter, the light is short in the day. As he gets closer to the house, he sees Micil's papa returning from the barn with a pail of milk. He stops when he sees Cahey and waits for him to dismount.

"I see you have come."

"That I have, sir."

"And not too late, I hope."

"What do you mean?"

"Has Micil not written you?"

"Yes, she has written me, but I do not know what you are speaking about and you are making me nervous. Is she all right?" Cahey doesn't wait for his answer and pushes pass him to enter the house. He does not see her in the kitchen. He goes through the room and enters the bedroom in the back. Micil is in bed. Her eyes are closed. Cahey stands silently; he does not want to startle her by awaking her suddenly. Her papa comes in behind him. "She has been sleeping hard like that for a few days. She has the fever her mother had." Cahey looks at him. "What? Why didn't someone tell me?"

"I thought she had written you and told you she was sick."

Cahey moves slowly to the side of the bed and kneels. He reaches out and takes one of her hands and softly caresses the top of her arm. She turns fitfully in her sleep and then opens her eyes. "Cahey, am I dreaming or is it you?"

"I am here, Micil. I am here. Why didn't you tell me you were ill?"

"I didn't want to worry you; with your new business and work. My papa has been taking good care of me."

Cahey holds her hand. She drifts back off to sleep. He turns to her papa, "What can be done?"

Her papa turns away. Cahey follows him into the other room. "What can be done?"

"The doctor says unless the fever breaks nothing. I change out the cloths on her forehead and try to wipe down her body to keep her cooler. She needs to sip water as much as possible, and the doctor left some medicine that she needs twice a day, in the morning and in the evening." He pauses and sits in front of the fire. "And I pray."

Cahey looks about him; he feels as though he has no air, no air to breathe. He rushes outside and sees Colleen standing where he left her in the cold. He goes over to her and leads her to the barn where there is shelter from the cold and a little hay for her to eat. He takes his rucksack and blanket off her and attempts to brush her down but instead leans his head against hers. He is silent. Then he gathers his things and heads back into the house.

The first thing he does is put more water on the fire to heat. He grabs another large pot and puts the cloths used to cool her forehead into the pot. When the water boils, he pours it onto the cloths and steams them well. Then he takes the pot, tosses the water outside and drapes the cloths on the pot in the cold wintry day to cool.

"We need to change her bed clothes," he says to her papa. Together they move Micil from one side of the bed to the other replacing the linens and then moving her to the other side and tucking them in. Cahey takes the used linens, moves them all outside. He builds a fire in the pit and puts a caldron with water over the pit. When the water is hot, he puts in the linens. With a pole, he moves the cloths in the boiling water much as he did with Muirghein in the fishing village. When he thinks about how long ago that was, it seems like centuries but was only last year.

When the linens are cleaned, he drapes them over the clothesline Micil used so often growing up in this house. The wind and cold will knock the water out of them. He gets fresh well water and grabs a cool cloth as he enters the house. Micil's papa is back sitting in his chair by the fire, worn out with the worry and with the nursing he has been doing. Cahey goes into the bedroom and puts a cool cloth on Micil's forehead. He sits by her bed, and when she wakens even so slightly, he holds a cup to her lips and tries to get her to sip the water. All day. he sits and gets new cloths and cleans the used ones. Late in the evening, Micil awakens. Cahey has his head gently on the mattress by her side but is holding her hand. He senses that she is awake and sits up to look at her.

"There you are my dear Cahey. You are here. It is not a dream."

"No, Micil, it is not a dream. I am here."

"And what about your work? Are you missing work to be here? That's why I didn't tell you. I didn't want to be a bother."

"It's Christmas. I have a holiday. I am not missing work."

"Ah, Christmas, and I have not had time to bake or cook anything special."

"Not to worry, I brought cookies from the kitchen at work."

They talk about work and the farm, when she got sick, why she did not write him about her sickness.

"I knew your mother died of the fever, and I was not feeling so sick that you should come and sit by my bedside."

"So, should I not have come?"

"Oh, no, I am so pleased to see you. You look grand, Cahey, really grand."

"I have something I want to show you." He retrieves the photo of his parents from his rucksack. "These are my parents. Mum and Papa Ó hArrachtain, meet Micil, the woman I love." He continues. "The family has been told about Agnes and Richard's meeting, how Richard swept her off her feet at a farm fair when there was lots of dancing."

Micil looks from the photo to Cahey and back again. "What are they about in the photo?"

"This is their wedding day, and the horse was my mum's dowry."

Micil is silent. She reaches out to touch the photo. It is too heavy for her to hold in her weakened state, so she takes a finger and outlines the figures of his mum and papa. "You favor your apa with your red hair and build, tall and slender, and you have his face."

"I do, don't I?"

"And your mum, what was she like?"

His mum, Agnes, through all the shortages, managed to sew, cook, and prepare food for winter storage and find roots, herbs, and berries to add to their food stores. She gathered wild mint leaves with their fragile blue flowers for their tea. His papa teased her as being "his short Irish lassie." She did not complain but would keep looking, making, or inventing anything they might need. She found a way to make things work.

"Sounds like you take a lot after your mum as well with all your business plans."

Cahey has not really thought about that but senses that Micil, even with her eagerness to hear about his family, needs to rest. "I have talked too much; you must rest."

"But I want to hear everything. I want to remember everything."

"Ah, that is why I have brought you a special gift."

"A gift? What is it?"

Cahey rummages deeper into his rucksack and brings out the wrapped journal. He starts to give it to Micil but remembers her weakness. "Here, let me unwrap it for you." He lifts the leather-bound journal up and shows it to her.

"Cahey, it is so beautiful."

"It is to write all your wonderful thoughts. I love getting your letters, but one day, and I hope one day soon, you will be near me and the letters will not be needed, but your wonderful thoughts will be."

Micil takes the journal and cradles it against her chest. "I want to write in it now."

"Now?"

"Yes, please. Give me the pen and ink over by the window seat."

Cahey fetches the pen and ink. He props her up a bit on her pillows and opens the journal to the first page. Micil takes the pen, dips it in the ink well, and writes. She leans back on the pillows and breathes deeply. "There."

Cahey takes the journal and reads what she has written. "I love you, Cahey, with all my heart and soul, Micil, Christmas Day, 1885." He leans over to kiss her cheek. "I do think you should rest now."

Micil smiles. "Leave the journal on the bed. I want it near me." She closes her eyes.

All night, Cahey sits by her side. Her papa comes in and tries to relieve him, but Cahey will not let him. In the morning, Cahey must have drifted off to sleep. He wakes up and raises his head from the mattress next to Micil. He looks at her and his heart pounds. She is so still, too still. He reaches out and touches her cheek; she is cold. He calls for her papa. They see she is not breathing. Her papa bows his head and prays.

Cahey makes a sound, a sound that starts off like a low moan and crescendos to a horrible wrenching sound that comes from deep within him. Micil's papa tries to console him, but there is no consolation; there is no way to take the grief he is feeling and make it all right again.

24

The funeral is quick. No one wants the fever. The parting from all that is Micil leaves Cahey without voice. He has nothing to say to anyone. He gathers his items and places them in his rucksack. He sees the journal where someone had moved it to the window seat. He takes the journal, wraps it gently in the cloth, ties it together, and places it in his rucksack next to the photo of his mum and papa. He nods his head to Micil's papa and whistles for his horse. Colleen saunters over from the watering trough. He must get back to Galway.

The cold ride back to Galway gives him time to think. It is morning when he reaches the compound, time to be at work. Seámus, the first person Cahey sees, walks over and grabs the horse's bridle. Cahey dismounts.

"How are you keeping?" asks Seámus.

Cahey looks at him, takes a deep breath, and says, "Micil died yesterday of the fever." He takes his rucksack and blanket off Colleen.

"Go put your things away. I'll take care of Colleen."

Cahey nods and heads for his room.

Before Seámus can get Colleen brushed and out to pasture, Cahey is back. "Take some time, lad. We can handle today; it will be slow today with everyone getting back."

"Thank you, Seámus, but I need to be busy. I need to work all this anger I have out of my body before I seriously hurt all the people who have caused this hunger, this fever, this insanity in Ireland, the people I feel are responsible for killing my Micil. I need to work."

Seámus nods and the day starts. Word passes quickly to Michael and Colm and to the rest of the workers in the compound. No one knows what to say to Cahey, but before an hour is out, his friends all have on black arm bands. By the end of the day, the entire work crew at the compound has on black arm bands.

Finally, Cahey notices. "Seámus, what is with the black arm bands?"

"The men want to show you they are with you in this."

If Cahey had tears, now would have been the time to show them. He has none. They are buried somewhere under his anger.

25

In the weeks following Micil's death, no one dares ask Cahey how he is keeping on. People work around him and give him the space he asks for. Colm gives him reports and invites him out to the home place for the weekend, but each invite is turned away. He has much work to do, he says. Michael and Seámus get the same response.

Months pass and another year begins. The evenings for Cahey are full of reading, learning about how to maintain his business, and staying up with the current events of the day. He frequents the reading room and joins so he can attend meetings and read the books and pamphlets. He even gives a try at writing his own essay on what it means to be Irish. He gives it to James for a readthrough. Then one evening he sees the journal he had given Micil. He has not opened it since bringing it back. He picks up the package, unwraps the journal, and opens up the cover. He reads: "I love you, Cahey, with all my heart and soul, Micil, Christmas Day, 1885." Sometime when he was sleeping, she wrote: "I'll be listening for you."

It takes all night for the tears to stop. The next morning people who work around him did not even speak to him. They simply let him be. He is silent for a week. Each evening after work he goes to his room and stays there until the next morning. At the end of the week, late in the night, there is a knock at his door. "Yes, come in."

James Young is standing in the doorway with his hat in his hand.

"We need you," says James.

"To do what?"

"We need you to write about what is happening in the Woodford area."

"Why me?"

"Because it needs to be someone they do not know, someone who has a powerful need to right wrongs, someone who has learned how to be passionate with his words."

"And you think I am that person?"

"Yes, we all do. I read your essay on what it is to be Irish to the men at the meeting tonight. I was hoping you would be there. The men were deeply moved and want you to be a part of our next plan, and that is to record what is happening in the Woodford area."

Cahey is clearly baffled. He doesn't know whether to accept this offer and move on with his life or send him away and allow himself to grieve and to hurt.

Then James says the one thing that makes Cahey consider the offer. "We have been listening to you, and we like what we hear."

Cahey looks at him. Both men are silent. Then Cahey says, "Please, sit down, let's talk."

The two men talk for a while and agree to meet again the following evening with several of the other men in the reading room group. James leaves with a nod of his cap and shuts the door behind him.

Maybe this is where he should direct his passion, toward righting wrongs. He looks back through several of the pamphlets he has and reads more. Cahey knows about the potato blights. He witnessed the heavy rains that came and destroyed any food crops growing above the ground. He knows that the rents are due even if there are no crops. All of their crops—barley, milk from the goats, wool from the sheep—were turned over to the landlord, who never seemed to think it was enough; leaving little to feed the family. He saw Richard change and age with the years of worry, fatigue, and debt. He saw Agnes die of the fever. And he read the eviction notice on their door. Finally, sleep overtakes him and he dreams. In the morning, he remembers his dream of riding across the hillside with Micil behind him. There is a definite scent of lavender in the room.

26

I n the months to follow, Cahey learns about Lord Clanricarde. He reads an article in the *London Times* about how "Lord Clanricarde has treated his tenants with incredible baseness." What Cahey learns is that within two years' time, Clanricarde collects £47,000 from his properties just outside of Galway. There has been a drop in the value of livestock and the tenants have applied for a reduction in the rents. Clanricarde treats the applications with contemptuous indifference. The tenants agree to resist Clanricarde's demand for payment in full.

The tenants of the Woodford area had a "Plan of Campaign" and put it into action with vows made by each man to honor the plan. Clanricarde, however, calls for more than 500 troops to enter the area and evict the tenants. The people in the area barricade the houses listed for eviction and make them into little fortresses. In the reading room, Cahey reads the newspaper account calling them "Saunders' Fort." This fort is garrisoned by twenty-five young men including a young man named Tommy Larkin. These men are arrested, treated as criminals, and sentenced to terms of imprisonment with hard labor for six to eighteen months.

In the overcrowded Kilkenny gaol, an epidemic breaks out and Tommy Larkin falls ill but is neglected. He dies in prison without a priest, doctor, or family member. When his body is taken home for burial, thousands line the funeral route in what the press calls one of the greatest public demonstrations of sympathy and solidarity ever recorded in rural Ireland. Tommy Larkin's papa finds an eviction notice at his house after the funeral.

Cahey identifies with the story. Finding his father on the hillside and knowing that his father died alone has filled him with grief. He was there when his mother died, but there was no priest who could come and no money for a doctor. Even so, being with Micil when she died has not eased the grief he feels.

27

Michael stops by to talk with Cahey. "You have missed all the *ceilidhs* this summer and now that little Cáit is here, you must come. You are her adopted uncle; you must come and celebrate her first birthday with us. Will you come this Saturday night?"

Cahey agrees but hastens to say he cannot stay long. Michael nods.

Before leaving for the alehouse on Saturday evening, there is a loud knock at Cahey's door. Without waiting for a reply, the door opens and two men in long dark coats, quality coats, not ones the workmen wear, enter the room.

Cahey does not stand but says, "What can I do for you?"

The men say nothing but start poking about, looking through his clothes hanging on pegs on the wall and then the stack of books and pamphlets at the end of his worktable catches their eyes. One of the men approaches to look at the book titles and Cahey speaks up. "Who are you? And what do you want?" He stands but at the same time takes the edge of the quilt on his bed and throws it over the pile of books. "Stay where you are. I demand that you tell me who you are and what you want."

The shorter of the two men says, "We hear that one of Mr. Persse's employees has been writing about the Irish. We hear that employee is also spending time with James Young. We believe you may be that employee. Are we correct?"

"You cannot enter my room and go through my belongings. You have no right."

"We're sorry, but this is the property of Mr. Persse and he has given us permission to search this room. If in our search we find nothing that suggests you have been involved with Mr. Young, who by the way has been arrested for illegal activities against the government, and if we find no writings that would indicate you are writing about the Irish revolutionaries, then you have nothing to fear."

Just as Cahey is about to say more, Seámus hurries into the room. He sees the two men. "I told you fellows that Mr. Persse would never grant permission for someone to go through one of his employee's rooms. I just talked with Mr. Persse and he verified that he has no idea who you are. I suggest that you leave immediately. I have called the guards to lead you out."

Seeing that Seámus is a big man and that Seámus has his boss' word against theirs, the men tip their hats and back out of the room. Just as they are leaving, the man who spoke before looks at Cahey. "We are watching you." And they are gone.

Cahey is still standing and feels his heart pounding in his chest. He listens as Seámus, who is out of breath and leaning against the doorway, explains that the men stopped by the harness room to ask where was Cahey Ó hArrachtain's room. They said that Mr. Persse gave them permission to come into the compound and seek Cahey out. But Seámus knew that Mr. Persse would never give permission like that to strangers; he's been working for Mr. Persse for years and knows he respects his employees too much to do that. So, while the men were looking around in the harness room, Seámus says he hurried over to the office and the clerk told him that Mr. Persse was still there and since it was urgent, please go in and ask Mr. Persse directly. Seámus was right about what Mr. Persse would say and hurried back to the harness room to have the men leave. He didn't see them there so he came up to Cahey's room.

"Thank you," says Cahey, who still has not moved.

"Are you all right?"

"Yes, but I have a few things I need to take care of." With that Cahey moves the quilt and begins to gather his papers as Seámus leaves him.

Cahey gathers the books and pamphlets that have anything to do with reform or revolution and tries to think how he can hide them or destroy them. He remembers his tour with Michael on that first day and thinks of where fires are used in heating the mash. He thinks he remembers which building that is. He wraps the materials with a cloth and makes his way to the building at the end of the compound nearest the river. The door is locked. He goes to another side door and it too is locked; but as he is about to turn around, one of the compound guards comes through the door. He recognizes Cahey and nods to him as Cahey nods back then moves quickly through the doorway before it closes. When he gets to the furnace, the grate has been left ajar; he tosses his books and pamphlets into the fire and exits quickly the way he came.

Immediately, he leaves for the alehouse; but rather than walk, he whistles for Colleen. She comes to the pasture gate. Without a saddle, he mounts her and they gallop through town to the alehouse.

Sheila stands holding little Cáit when Cahey walks over and swings them both around in his arms. "What is making you so playful?" Sheila asks when he stops swinging them. "This is not like you."

"It is my niece's birthday; can't I be playful?"

Cahey sees that the birthday party is in full swing with plenty of ale and music. Little Cáit is passed from one person to another until she has no idea who is holding her and breaks into a loud wail. "Here, here little one," says Michael, when he rescues her. "Don't cry, your papa is here, don't cry."

For a moment, Cahey feels his loss of family and Micil more than he has in months. He sees how happy Michael and Sheila are that they have little Cáit. He will not have this kind of happiness, not now at least. At the moment, he has more serious worries on his mind, like people trying to link him with the Fenians and with James Young.

"What's on your mind? You seem a hundred miles away," asks Michael, bouncing Cáit in his arms.

"Nothing, nothing at all. Though, I do want to talk with you. Do you have a minute? Can we go out into the courtyard?"

"Sure, let me give Cáit to her mother."

The two men take their ale and walk out into the back courtyard.

"What's up?"

Cahey tells him about his visitors and how Seámus rescued him and how he has destroyed all his books and pamphlets. Michael is relieved.

"So, they have nothing to peg you with."

"Well, I did write an essay on what it means to be Irish and I did give a copy to James Young, and James did read it at the meeting. My name is not on the essay, but James did attribute it to me at the meeting and all the men have been talking about the essay."

"Not good."

"No, not good; they have arrested James. So...I may need to leave for a while?"

"Where will you go? Where will you be safe?"

"I have an idea that I may go to Dublin and check on my sisters and brother. I can probably find my brother in the army;

hopefully he knows where the girls are. I have to think about it, though I need to think quickly; these men will be back."

"Okay, but you know Sheila and I will do anything."

Cahey remembers his talk with Mickileen, "No, you are to do nothing. I do not want you connected in any way with my work. Well, except I need you to run my business while I am away."

"Yes, of course, I will."

"I will only be gone until things quiet down—hopefully Seámus will understand and hold my job for me. You do have help. Seámus and his son, Pádraig, run the draft business; you know all about my horses in the stables; and Colm does all the books. But I just want someone to be on top of all the pieces, and since you are my best friend, I would feel comfortable with you running it. Make whatever decisions you need to. When I am settled, I will notify you as to where I am."

The men clap each other on the back and then Michael hugs Cahey. "Keep safe, *a charra*, keep safe.

28

There is a clerk from the main office in the harness room when Cahey comes down to work on Monday morning before he has had a chance to talk with Seámus.

"Mr. Persse would like to see you."

"When?"

"Now, I believe. Yes, now."

Cahey gives a questioning look to Seámus and joins the clerk to go to Mr. Persse's office. "Please wait here while I verify that Mr. Persse is ready."

He does not have time to sit down in the outer office before the clerk is back. "Mr. Persse will see you now."

Cahey enters the office. Not only is Mr. Persse there but so is the gentleman Cahey had met at Spancil Hill, the lord of the manor who had given a wager that won big money for Cahey in his horse race.

"Thank you for joining us, Cahey. I hope all is fine with you and you are keeping well?"

"Yes, sir, Mr. Persse, everything is fine."

"I believe you have met Mr. Sona Lynch before but have not

been formally introduced."

"Yes, sir, I do remember talking with you at Spancil Hill."

Mr. Lynch nods to Cahey and extends his hand. "Good to see you again, Cahey Ó hArrachtain."

Cahey reaches to shake his hand when Mr. Persse stands.

"Cahey, Mr. Lynch has come to ask for help. Since the request has to do with horses, I asked Seámus for recommendations and learned that you might consider the offer. When I mentioned your name to Mr. Lynch, he remembered meeting you. Since his business is with you and only you, I am not needed in this exchange except to introduce you. Please hear what Mr. Lynch has to say and let me know what remains to be done. With that, gentlemen, I bid you good day; I must catch a train to Dublin for a meeting." And with that Mr. Persse retrieves a satchel and leaves the room.

Cahey continues to stand with his cap in his hand.

"Please, let's sit and talk. I will be straightforward with you."

"Thank you, sir."

Mr. Lynch explains that a man by the name of William Kissam Vanderbilt has built a major horse exchange in New York City. Mr. Vanderbilt, through his agents, has identified Shire horses as a new addition to the American market. Mr. Lynch explains that he and Mr. Vanderbilt have met several times in France at various horse races and Mr. Vanderbilt is aware of what the Shire horses can do from their conversations, not specifically as a racehorse but as a major work animal for the American market. Other Shires have been shipped to America, but Mr. Vanderbilt wants the best and is assured that Mr. Lynch can provide him with the best.

"However, I do not want to ship four Shire horses to Mr. Vanderbilt without a proper person to assure their safety, health, and timely arrival. That's why I came to ask Mr. Persse if he had suggestions for an escort since the horses will leave from Galway. When he mentioned you, I was interested in talking with you, Cahey. I saw from the race that you understand horses; I gather from what Mr. Persse has said that you may have an interest in chauffeuring my horses to America and guarantee they get to Mr. Vanderbilt safely. Mr. Persse regards you highly. Your trip will be paid along with all expenses in New York for the time you need to settle the horses. This may give you time to make other decisions on what you may want to do. So, what do you think of my proposal, Cahey?"

Cahey feels there is nothing to think about. This is perfect and better than perfect, absolutely legitimate and will even be affordable. Cahey pauses before he speaks. "Mr. Lynch, you give me great credit where no credit is needed. I thank you for your offer. I appreciate the support Mr. Persse has offered me during my employment with Nun's Distillery. When would you want to ship the horses?"

"Right away; the horses are ready, but the shipping line to New York is overwhelmed. Therefore, the agent has arranged transport on the Allen Lines to get the horses to Boston where there is a train with a box car for the horses to get them to New York. Does this work for you?"

"Yes, sir, this works. Who will I work with to get the details for the transport?"

"I will have my agent work with you."

"Thank you."

"Thank you, Cahey. I love my horses and appreciate anyone who knows a good horse. I tell my workers every day, 'If a horse is not working for you, then it is your fault and not the horse's.'"

The men shake hands and walk out together into the compound yard.

"The agent will contact you," says Mr. Lynch as he gets into his carriage and drives away.

Seámus comes out of the harness room and sees Cahey. "Well?"

"I'm coming to dinner tonight; we need to talk."

29

Dinner is a joy with the children showing off all they are learning and Mrs. Kelly produces her best carrot and coriander soup with nicely baked brown bread. The two men go out into the yard to talk.

"You know of some of the problems, yes?" Cahey asks.

"I know the men coming looking for you is not good."

"Right, well, I have agreed to take four Shire horses over to America. It will give me a chance to think through what I need to do."

"I understand."

"I have asked Michael to oversee the business. You and Pádraig are running the draft business and Colm knows all the book work, but I figured one person needed to be in charge, and since he is freer in the day than the two of you, Michael it is."

"I agree with your choice. I can do the draft, but with the other work I need to do, I really can't take anything else on."

"Good, so we are agreed."

There is a silence. Seámus has been a major family figure to Cahey and now Cahey is going so far away. Cahey feels the pain of the separation already. "I will write. You know I write regularly. You have posted many a letter for me."

Seámus smiles. "And will you come again?"

"My heart will always be in Ireland."

Next, Cahey has to talk with Colm. He asks if he can wait a bit after work and talk with him.

Colm comes to find Cahey in his room.

"So, when are you leaving?"

"What? I don't even get to tell you? How do you know? Does everyone know?"

"No, I guessed. I have known you a long time. I know that you have some difficulties right now and I saw the accounting sheets for the new venture between Mr. Lynch and Mr. Persse with getting the horses on the ship. I also saw the entry where the company doctor gave you a vaccination. I just put it all together."

"I leave as soon as the agent contacts me and all the arrangements have been made. I have asked Michael to be in charge of our business. I have talked with Seámus and Michael and they know what to do. I would like for you to continue being the chief accountant and business officer. I will bow to what the three of you tell me and will give you how to reach me when I know. Sorry for the short notice."

"I understand."

"Plus, I would like for you to house Colleen. She likes being ridden and I think that might help you get back and forth every day. Any feed and care will be part of the business expenses, okay?"

Colm grinned. "Thank you. And since you are leaving, you need to know that I have been going out with the young woman you saw at the church."

Cahey grins and claps Colm on the back. "Well, that means we have to fatten you up. Let's go to the alehouse to celebrate." Both men head out down the road looking forward to an evening with friends.

Michael and Sheila are pleased to see them and seat them at a table on the side. Sheila fills Cahey's special mug. Though the men are offered as much ale as they want, neither man is a drinker. Soon, however, the four musicians appear and there is music. Sheila sticks her head next to Cahey's. "Since you aren't drinking, you might as well dance with me." She drags him out to join a quadrille and they dance faster and better than they have ever danced before.

When they finish and the two men say their good nights, Sheila steps in and whispers in Cahey's ear, "There has to be a girl out there for a man like you. Please keep looking." She kisses him on the cheek and they wave goodnight.

30

The rucksack is a bit heavier than it has ever been in Cahey's travels. He has decided to take his keepsakes rather than leave them for someone in Galway to hold for him. He has several books plus food items Mrs. Kelly has prepared, the illustrated play the children gave him, Micil's journal, his parents' photograph, his suit, the sign for his business, and his mug that Michael brought to him. He decides to wrap the food items in a separate parcel since they will be consumed during the voyage. The saddle and quilts brought from the farm will remain with Colleen, thus Colm will have them.

Earlier in the day, Cahey meets with Mr. Lynch's agent at the ship to be introduced to the horses and to go over information Cahey needs to keep the horses safe and healthy during the voyage. Cahey learns that the horses have been exercised and worked hard for the past two weeks. They need to be tired for the journey. They have been given no food or water that morning and their back shoes have been removed. Cahey will need to have those replaced once he is in New York.

Down in the ship's hold, Cahey follows the agent to see

where the horses are stalled. After several stairwells, Cahey forgets the turns and hopes he will remember them when he has to come alone to take care of the horses. Alex, the ship's staffer who is in charge of the area where the horses are, will also maintain the stalls and notify Cahey if anything needs to be addressed regarding the safety of the horses. Alex is a seasoned ship staffer who has transported many horses. He is the one who helped the agent load the horses so he shows Cahey how slings are in four of the stalls with another four stalls reserved for when the horses need to be moved to clean the stalls. He will help Cahey pull the slings under the horses and secure them so that in calm weather the horses could put their weight on the sling and sleep. In stormy weather the slings are not to be used and Cahey will need to be here to calm them. All other times, the horses will be secured with only a canvas collar and two ropes, one on each side. Alex points out that the stalls are wider to accommodate a horse wanting to lie down in the hay cushioning on all sides of the stall. Though Alex will clean the stalls, Cahey should keep the horses' feet thoroughly clean and rub their legs daily.

Fresh air is a must to prevent respiratory disease of the horses and the ship has air funnels on the top deck that forces air through ducts to the bottom holds of the ship. Cahey knows the horses need water and food, but Alex explains that they will need at least twelve gallons of water a day to keep the animals in minimal condition to allow food to pass through their intestines correctly. Alex shows Cahey the storage area where they have fifty forty-two-gallon barrels of water, thirty-two fifty-pound bags of horse feed, and ten gallons of pig oil for the care of the horses' feet and legs. Preparation for the welfare of the horses has been well thought out and Cahey is relieved that someone on board will assist him in the maintenance of these horses.

The ship inspection tour is over, and Cahey returns to the

distillery to pick up his belongings. He looks about the room he has lived in. Though it is not like the cottage at the farm, it has been his home. Everything is as he found it, but he looks one more time to be sure. He turns and leaves the room. He has allowed time to walk to the quay to meet the tender that will take him out to the ship. In the compound he sees Seámus at the door of the harness room. He has said his goodbyes but calls out, "Save my place." Seámus nods and raises his arm in a wave.

Though parting with his friends is difficult, the hardest parting is leaving Colleen. He walks to the pasture gate and whistles. Colleen saunters over in her usual gait. He runs his hand gently through her forelock and caresses her muzzle. In Irish he tells her that he'll be back to ride her on the beach and for her to be happy with Colm and his family. He steps away from the gate and picks up his rucksack. As he walks away, he hears Colleen whinny loudly. He continues to walk without looking back.

As Cahey approaches the roadway, Michael is sitting in a cart waiting for him. "I drove you into the compound that first day; I plan on driving you out." Cahey climbs aboard, claps Michael on the back, and the two men drive down to the quay.

There is a lot of activity at the docks. People are getting into various tenders to be ferried out to the ship. There are suitcases, trunks, parcels, boxes, crates, and children running about with men and women in full traveling gear standing, waiting to board, hugging other family members and friends. Many of the people are crying as families are being torn apart with hopes of being united again. Cahey jumps down from the cart; Michael gets down, too. Together they walk over to the agent, and Cahey takes the paperwork needed to ship the horses. A big hug from Michael and the two men part. As Cahey walks over to join the queue to board a tender, he hears his name shouted out in a booming voice.

"Cahey Ó hArrachtain, is that you?"

Cahey stops and when he turns, he sees King Ryan Ó Ruad-háin from the fishing village. With him are his grandson, Séan, and Sophie, the girl in the village with the raven hair. Cahey steps quickly to where the three are standing to shake Ryan's hand.

"Hello, yes, King Ryan, how have you been keeping?"

"Good enough, but not as good as you, I hear you got a job right away in Galway and things have been easy for you."

"I don't know about easy, but how did you hear?"

"Ireland is a small place; everybody knows everybody. I hear things all the time."

Cahey looks at the two young people beside Ryan. "Séan and Sophie, you two are all grown up! I can't believe my eyes."

Sophie blushes while Séan ducks his cap but stands a bit straighter.

Cahey is confused. "Why are you here? To see someone off?"

"Actually, we are leaving," says Séan, and pulling Sophie close to him. "There is no new work for fishermen anymore. There are opportunities in America. There is land to be had and jobs, I hear. We have been reading about it in letters sent back to us from other friends of the fishing village who have already gone. So, we are going to start our lives in America."

Cahey looks at King Ryan, who is looking away and seems not to be pleased with the decision. "I see."

"And you, Cahey, why are you here?" asks Sophie.

"As luck will have it, I am your traveling companion."

Ryan puts an arm around Cahey's shoulders. "That is good to hear, that you will be going with these young people, but is it to stay?"

"I have no idea. I am taking four Shire horses over for Mr. Lynch of Spancil Hill for a new venture in New York being produced by a Mr. Vanderbilt. It will give me a chance to see what options are in America."

"Ah, I see. Well, the best of luck to you and to these obstinate young people."

The agent calls out to Cahey. "You must board the tender now."

Cahey grabs his rucksack and food parcel, shakes hands with Ryan, and the three of them, Cahey, Séan, and Sophie, board the tender. Cahey looks up on the shore and sees Michael has paused and is watching Cahey as the tender moves away from the shore. Michael raises his arm high over his head. Cahey does the same. Once he boards the ship, the first thing he wants to do is to check on the horses from Spancil Hill.

PART II

1887 - 1904
"All the future looked to him as beautiful and dim
as the mists that fill a mountain glen under the morning sun."
from "The Boyhood of Finn MacCumhal"

31

I rish journeys across the sea are less frequent in 1887. The main emigration waves have passed; therefore, few ships pass through Galway, as Mr. Lynch's agent has explained to Cahey. The ship he is on originated in Glasgow. As soon as the Irish passengers board, the SS Hibernian will leave for Boston. Cahey is on board with 222 other passengers. He has been placed in the intermediate level of accommodation, which he did not expect. He had planned to be in the steerage with other laborers and domestics like Séan and Sophie. Upon boarding, Séan and Sophie are led to a far stairwell. They say farewell for the time being, and Cahey assures them that as soon as he is settled, he will come to find them.

Cahey follows the porter to the intermediate level of the ship.

"Where is your trunk?" he asks.

"No trunk; everything I need is in my rucksack."

The porter shows him the room, gives him a schedule for dining, and gives him the shipping company's provisions: a mattress, pannikin to hold a pint and a half, plate, knife, nickel-plated fork and spoon. The agent has thought of everything, which Cahey is thankful for since he did not plan well for what he might need. Now what he needs is to check on the horses.

Though he had been on board to see where the horses have been stalled, Cahey cannot remember where the stairwells are to get him to the horses. He goes down one and realizes there is no next level. After several wrong turns, he finally locates the deck master's office down below and checks out a horn lantern arranged with special permission by the agent for Cahey to be able to see in the hull of the ship. He gets reminder directions on where the horses are boarded. As he enters the stall area, he sees the horses are jittery but fine. They quiet down as he begins to talk while he brushes them down. It is quiet in the hull of the ship. Cahey hears only the horses and the creaking of the ship. He notices a movement that he had not felt earlier and he hears the ships horns announcing their embarkment. The horses bend back their ears at the sound of the horn, and Cahey is happy he came when he did to settle them down. There are no other animals traveling on this trip, so says Alex; that is good for Cahey since the horses are nervous. Additional noises might really spook them. He does not know these horses but he understands that they are nervous; so is he. He will need to know their personalities in order to get them safely to New York. Alex had shared the checklist posted for each horse as to when they are fed, watered, cleaned, legs massaged, and feet cleaned. Cahey looks it over to see if anything needs to be done. All seems to be in order, so he will simply brush them and get to know them. As he brushes, he studies them.

The stallion of the four is jet black with a white blaze on his face and four white feathered, stocking feet. He is solidly built with an aloof attitude. He manages to tune out the circumstances that may alarm others. He appears to keep the other horses in a spirit of cooperation. Cahey is pleased that the stallion has such a personality; it will make the handling of the four horses easier. Two of the mares are chestnuts; they have reddish brown body color with black manes and tails, but their lower legs have white feathered stockings. Both of these horses are social animals and are always interested in whatever is happening to the other horses. Cahey finds them looking and nodding at him as he goes about brushing one or the other. The final horse is also a mare and is a chestnut but has a white stripe on her face. She appears to be the youngest of the four and is also a social horse. Cahey has worked with other types of horses, challenging ones and fearful ones. He is thankful that Mr. Lynch picked these horses to make the trip confirming Cahey's notion that Mr. Lynch knows horses along with also being generous. Both traits motivate Cahey to do a good job with the horses in his care.

As he works, he remembers the horses he has had to leave behind. Lavender, who Cahey has enjoyed riding, is now part of the horses used to deliver ale. He must remember to ask Michael when he writes to ride Lavender occasionally. Maybe Michael could take Cáit riding and introduce the child to horses early. Cahey misses Colleen the most. She is in good care with Colm, but she has been part of his life both on the farm and as a start to build a transportation business.

After taking care of the four Shire horses, he bids them goodnight and returns the horn lantern. Returning to his accommodations is easier than when he arrived. He now has a sense of the stairwells and directions of the hallways. Idle time has never been something he has had to deal with so he assesses his rucksack items and company issued provisions, which doesn't take long. There are few people in the intermediate section so the two sets of beds in his assigned room are all for his choosing. There is a chair at the side of one of the beds. He sits down, then stands right back up. He is curious as to what the ship is like. He goes exploring, starting at the top deck.

As he walks along the corridor in the salon area, several porters are in one room, loading trunks for a passenger. Cahey can see through the open door that the room is large with a lofty ceiling. A lantern cupola hangs from the center of the ceiling and he notices other side lights. The white ceiling is paneled and has gold moldings. The wood in the room is highly polished. All the chairs are upholstered in rich crimson velvet. The salon area is much richer than the intermediate area. The porters exit the room and shut the door.

He follows the porters down the hallway and out to the deck. Passengers are dressed for dinner and are promenading on deck prior to being invited into the dining room. He has never seen so much finery, lace, and dress suits. He stares a bit too much because one of the stewards comes over and suggests that he goes to the deck below where the intermediate class passengers can exercise before dinner.

Cahey is restless and wants company. There is time before his scheduled dining time. He goes down to the steerage and looks for Séan and Sophie. He sees them huddled together on one of the beds. Séan is telling a group of children in the steerage section a story. Though there are electric lights in this section also, all the bunk beds and clothes hanging on the bedframes create a cocoon type of atmosphere for the people in steerage. Cahey cannot see the children's faces, but he can see how still they are as they listen to the story. The first night Cahey had stayed with Muirghein, Ryan, and Séan in the fishing village, Ryan told them a story of the Fisherman's Son and the Gruagach of Tricks, since Cahey had exaggerated and told Ryan that he had raced his horse and won when actually he had only practiced with the horse and his papa was the one who raced. The story Ryan shared was about a magical race where the son was a horse and how he was able to return to his father as his son. Now as Cahey listens to Séan telling a story, he hears the same inflections his grandfather had used to tell a story.

Cahey perches on the end of one of the bunk beds and

listens to Séan, who is telling the story "The Boyhood of Finn Mac Cumhal."

"In Ireland long ago, centuries before the English appeared in that country, there were kings and chiefs, lawyers and merchants, men of the sword and men of the book, men who tilled their own ground and men who tilled the ground of others, just as there are now. But there was also, as ancient poets and historians tell us, a great company or brotherhood of men who were bound to no fixed calling, unless it was to fight for the High King of Ireland whenever foes threatened him from within the kingdom or without it. This company was called the Fianna of Erinn.

"To the present day in Ireland the Fianna of Erinn live only in the ancient books that were written of them, and in the tales that are still told of them in the winter evenings by the Irish peasant's fireside."

The story continues and Cahey listens to Séan as he describes the people in the tribe and then sets up the conflict at the battle of Cnucha, near the city of the Hurdle Ford, which is the name that Dublin still bears in the Irish tongue. Cahey remembers as a boy when he first heard this story at the fireside in the middle of winter, how vividly he could picture the Treasure Bag of the Fianna, which was a bag made of a crane's skin containing jewels of great price, and magic weapons, and strange things that had come down from far-off days when the Fairy Folk and mortal men battled for the lordship of Ireland.

Séan tells how the boy has many adventures while learning the arts and exercises. How the young man finds like souls who banded with him to hunt and live in the forests. These banded men fight with enemies and leave with spoils including a bag of riches that is turned over to the elders who have been weakened and hidden in the forest. Every face in the bottom of the ship is tuned into the story. Séan is a gifted storyteller.

When Séan finishes the story, not only the children but all

of the steerage passengers are listening. Séan has his grandpapa's gift and is able to share it with those like Cahey who appreciate the oral tradition of storytelling. Cahey admires Séan's ability to remember the stories and to make them come so alive with different voices and different pacing.

Cahey has heard the story since being a boy. He is impressed with how Finn finds "like souls who banded with him." Cahey's early friendships were few since he spent most of his time with his family. Though his brother is close in age, they were so different in their approach to learning and interests that he was closer to his papa than his brother. The story also gives Cahey thought about the bag of treasure; to him the bag of treasure has to be Finn's gifts: things he could always count on to get him through life. Cahey thinks about his own bag of treasure. He names the tangible things: a suit of clothes, a few books, his parents' wedding photo, the business sign from Christmas, and the bar mug with his name from Michael and Sheila. Can he get through life's trials with only these? What about the intangibles? What about the memories of his family and of Micil, his knowledge of horses he learned from his papa, and how to work hard and diligently? It was Micil who suggested that he learned how to grow a business from his mother. She could always work things out and figure out how to help the family survive. That is until she got sick and Richard lost hope. Neither of them could survive alone. Now as he crosses the ocean to America, Cahey asks himself what is in his bag of treasure and whether he can find like souls, other people like Michael, Sheila, Seámus, and Colm, to share with him this life he has yet to figure out?

"Time will tell," he says out loud, "time will tell."

Séan sees Cahey and waves. Cahey nods back. At least there will be entertainment on board to make the voyage manageable, he thinks.

32

Days on board the ship gives Cahey cabin fever. He is aware that he cannot just get on Colleen and ride away. He feels restricted for the first time and does not like it. He spends the time he is not with the horses pacing on deck, the intermediate deck, since the stewards now know who is traveling at what level. Sometime early in the voyage, he decides to get more exercise by walking quickly. He is walking fast on the deck. He looks out at the ocean and the waves and walks even faster. Almost at a jog, he passes a door and does not see a man standing beside the door. Deep in his thoughts and moving quickly, he knocks into the man who loses his balance and falls to the deck. He is holding on to something tightly.

"I'm sorry, I did not see you," Cahey says.

Lying flat on the deck, the young man says, "Obviously. What were you looking at that you did not see a man standing here?"

Cahey, without thinking, tells the truth. "Nothing, actually, I was in my thoughts."

"Oh, one of those." The young man stands with Cahey

reaching out a hand to help. As he adjusts his jacket, he now begins to inspect a camera he is holding for any damage.

Taken aback, Cahey asks, "'One of those,' what do you mean?"

"One of those thinkers, the intelligentsia," says the young man not even looking at Cahey but looking to see that his camera is intact.

Cahey laughs at the thought. "Your assumption is incorrect," says Cahey. "I hope you are not injured."

"I'm fine, and luckily my camera is all right too."

Now that he knows the man is fine, Cahey is curious. "A camera, do you take photos for fun or for a livelihood?" He has not seen a camera like this one.

"For a livelihood. I can retouch photos as well."

"Retouch?"

"Yes, if the photo has aged and is fading, then I can help restore the image."

"Ah, well, as long as you are all right."

"Yes, thank you, I am fine. Just watch where you are thinking." A small grin softens his words.

Cahey turns to walk away when the young man calls to him, "Sir." Cahey turns around and the young man snaps a photo. "Thank you."

Cahey stops, then he steps back towards the young man extending his hand a second time. He realizes that he needs to be reaching out to others if he has any hope of getting through this voyage. "I am forgetting my manners, I am Cahey Ó hArrachtain from Mannin Bay."

"And I am Frederick Davidson from Glasgow."

Cahey nods toward the direction he has been walking and together the men begin to walk around the deck, slower this time. Cahey notices that Frederick's curly hair is full, almost shaggy, and dark brown, but he has a well-groomed beard. He's tall enough that he has to duck down through several of the passageways on board the ship. As they walk, they discuss their plans of what they will do when they get to America.

Frederick has a job lined up with a photographer in New York City. Cahey tells him about taking the horses to Vanderbilt's American Horse Exchange in Manhattan as an errand for Mr. Lynch. He leaves out the reason why he rushed to leave Galway. He will have to know Frederick better before he shares his problems of being identified as a rebellious Irish. As they talk, Cahey remembers his photo of his parents. Frederick is interested and asks to see it. They proceed to Cahey's room in the intermediate section. Frederick points out that he is down the passageway. As Cahey retrieves the photo from his rucksack, Frederick sits on the chair with Cahey sitting on the side of his bed to study the photograph displayed between them.

"Amazing," says Frederick. "I haven't seen one of these in a long time."

"One of what?" asks Cahey.

"It looks to be a ferrotype."

"A what?"

Frederick explains that he learned in a photography class that a French man by the name of Louis-Jacques-Mandé Daguerre in 1837 invented a way to take photographs. These are called daguerreotypes. They have a mirror-like quality and are placed in cases made of wood covered with tooled leather or embossed paper. They are expensive. Other, better, easier processes developed in the 1854 are called ambrotypes. Though these photos are produced as negatives on glass, they are then backed with a dark material or black paint and the image appears normal. They too can be in photo cases.

"Seeing that these earlier versions are one of a kind and take fifteen minutes to process, the likelihood that this photo is either one of those is not probable," he says.

Frederick studies the photograph. "It does, however, look to be a ferrotype. They are cheap and easy to use, often taken by itinerant photographers who referred to them as tintypes because of the tinny feeling of the material. Looking at the photo of your mum and papa on a horse, and the tones of the photo, I would say it is definitely a tintype." He pauses and looks up at Cahey, "however, tintypes were produced in England by William Kloen but not popular and widely used in Ireland until the 1870s. When did your parents get married?"

Cahey is speechless. He has been told all his growing up years that this was his parents' wedding photo. He was born in 1868. Could this be their wedding photo? He does not know what to think. He tries to remember exactly what his parents told him and could not come up with much.

"My parents never told us a date of their wedding," says Cahey and takes the photo from Frederick.

Frederick is quick to say. "I am just telling you about the photographic image and its development. I learned it all from teachers and pamphlets; they could be wrong."

"I see," says Cahey, but he really doesn't see. He is confused as to why his parents made it seem as though it was a wedding photo. He is momentarily distracted when Frederick begins to demonstrate what his camera is capable of doing. As he learns about cameras, Cahey is also wanting to learn more about Frederick. He turns their talk to how each are getting to New York, since the ship docks in Boston. But then Cahey remembers the horses and that he needs to go tend to them; Frederick joins him.

When Frederick sees the Shire horses, he immediately wants to photograph them, but the light is bad down in the hull of the ship with only one horn lantern; he will have to wait until the ship docks. It's now Cahey's turn to teach Frederick about Shire horses.

∽

Later, after dinner, Cahey goes to seek out Séan and Sophie. He finds them talking with a group of young people their age, but when he arrives, they break away and invite him over to their corner.

"How are you keeping yourselves?" Cahey is perched on one bed and Sophie and Séan are on the other.

"Sophie has been a bit queasy from the ship swaying so, but we are fine. And you, are you all right?"

"Yes." Cahey pauses. He is unsure how much he should share, but he has known Séan and Sophie since first leaving home and he knows their village families so he accepts them as friends. He tells them, "I have learned some information about my parents and do not know what to think about it. I met a photographer from Glasgow, and I showed him a photograph I have of my parents on their wedding day with a horse. This photographer tells me that based on the type of photography it is, the photograph may have been made after I was born."

Cahey looks so distressed; Sophie looks at him then laughs out loud, her raven hair falling back from her face. Cahey is even more confused by her laughter; his face shows his confusion.

"I'm sorry, Cahey, but you did say you were from Mannin Bay outside of the Maumturk Mountains, yes?"

"Yes, that I am."

"And, your parents were rural Irish people, right?"

"Yes, that they were."

"Then everything is just as they said it was. Many Irish did not marry formally but lived together in marriage. When they could afford to be married, they did get married. So, the horse may have afforded your mum and papa to finally get married after you were born."

Cahey listens to what Sophie says. It makes sense to him. "Thank you, I understand now why they never gave me a wedding date." Séan and Sophie smile at each other and Cahey looks at them more closely. "Are you married?"

They laugh. "Yes, immigration would not let us come together if we had not had the marriage ceremony and could prove it." Sophie throws back her hair and meets Seán's look with her own eyes. This look, this one glance, is clear as to why they married. Who would have thought that these two, who were so young when Cahey first met them in their village, would marry and now be going to live in America? When he was in their village, he thought their future and all of the villagers would be in that village. He has a lot to learn about people's futures, including his own, and how they can change so quickly.

33

As the shoreline of America appears, Cahey spends the time calming the horses. They are tired and restless. He rubs their legs and has Alex help him with the slings so they can rest. Now that there is a lot of activity on the ship and with the horns frequently sounding, Cahey needs to be with the horses. Frederick asks if he can stay with Cahey since all the passengers have to be cleared for immigration before the horses can be taken to shore. The two men have spent their time together during meals and exercising on deck. Frederick has frequently come with Cahey to brush and massage the horses. Since they will be arriving at the Boston port of entry, officials will come aboard and clear the passengers on the ship before anyone can leave. Each passenger must have a vaccination certificate, identification card, and immigration ID cards or ID tags. Fortunately, Mr. Lynch's agent prepared all the paperwork for Cahey.

Cahey left word with Alex to alert him as to when they could disembark with the horses and he stays down in the hold with the horses. Time moves slowly for the immigration procedure to clear 222 passengers, many of whom speak only Irish and not the English, Danish, and German languages the immigration officers are prepared to speak. Alex comes down to ask if Cahey can help with the Irish translation. When Cahey arrives at the hall where the passengers are being processed, he sees lines and lines of people. He agrees to translate but has the officials recruit Séan and Sophie as well to help with the translations. The three of them sit at different tables with the immigration officers, and Frederick documents their work by taking multiple photographs. Several hours later, though tired from translating and wanting to leave the ship, Frederick insists on taking a photo of just the three of them before their lives are forever changed when they disembark on American soil. He takes two so that Cahey can have one and Séan and Sophie can have the other, to be forwarded to them when developed.

The agent for Mr. Lynch has booked Cahey into a hotel near the train station in Boston that has a stable to house the horses until the train departs the next morning. Carefully, Cahey and Alex load one horse at a time into a sling that is on the lower deck. As the horse is lowered with a pulley system to the dock, the two men exit and race down to the dock to unload the horse from the sling. Cahey recruits Séan and Sophie, who have disembarked, to hold the horses. Frederick stays with the horses waiting on the ship to be loaded onto the sling. Finally, all the horses as well as Frederick and Cahey are off the ship and joyful to be on firm land. Sophie does an Irish dance on the dock with the horses as her audience.

Sophie isn't the only performer on the dock; the horses are getting a lot of attention. Having been in the ship's hold for weeks, they have a lot of energy and are prancing and moving about while still tethered to a post. The huge Shires have been groomed by Cahey so their coats are in top condition, but the horses must be guided to the stable for the night. When the young couple and Frederick decide to join Cahey since he is the only one with a hotel booking, Cahey is relieved. The more people who know how to guard the horses, the better and easier it will be to move them down the street. Séan and Sophie are to meet up with other Irish fishermen, friends of Ryan, but Séan must send word to them about their arrival and can tell them to meet at the hotel. With parcels tied to the horses, the four split up with Cahey and Séan holding two horses each. Frederick walks on the far side with Cahey and Sophie does the same with Séan to create a buffer between the horses and other people on the street. The stable is easy to locate as it is next to the hotel with a fenced in field where Cahey releases the horses so they can get some exercise. The horses race around the circumference of the field and frolic up and down through the grass. Cahey watches them and is relieved that none of the horses seem to have suffered from being in the ship's hold for so many weeks. Their exercise time will give Cahey a chance to check into the hotel.

All goes well. Things are where the agent said they would be and all the expenses have been paid in advance. The hotel clerk, a young man who looks only at Sophie, agrees to let Frederick join Cahey in the room, but Frederick must pay extra for meals. The hotel has a telegraph service and the message is sent to the fishermen friends. Parcels, trunks, and rucksacks are stored in the hotel room.

"Now that everything has been arranged, I think we should see a little bit of Boston, don't you?" suggests Frederick. Cahey agrees but has to put the horses into their stalls first. They go by the stable to take care of the horses. Three of the four horses come to Cahey quickly. The stallion decides to stay in the field. Cahey settles the three horses into the stalls and gives them feed and water. He returns to the field and watches as the stallion backs away from him and turns around and trots to the far side of the field. Cahey knows the stallion must be hungry. He goes back into the stable and gets a bucket of oats. Out in the field, he whistles to the horse and shows the bucket of oats. The horse snorts and paws the ground but does not come close to Cahey. Slowly, Cahey puts the bucket down on the ground and walks away. The horse pauses, looks toward Cahey and then looks towards the bucket. Soon he approaches the bucket. As he puts his nose into the oats, Cahey walks slowly towards him and talks as he has all the weeks in the ship. The horse remains calm and continues to eat. Cahey is able to put a rein on his bridle, and with the bucket as a lead, guides the horse into the stable. Now all four are secured and being fed and watered. The three friends have leaned on the fence and watched. Now they are ready to see Boston.

The streets are busy with horses, carriages, and bicycles. There are shops, pubs, offices, and houses. They feel good walking about after being on the moving ship for so many weeks, but they decide to take a break and have a pint of ale. They enter a pub to find the patrons eager to talk, especially when the patrons discover that the four have just arrived from Ireland. They crowd around asking questions. "How are things with the rents? How are things politically? How are people coping with the stringent rules of the British?" Séan and Sophie offer their village perspective, Frederick has no idea, and Cahey, after all he has been through with his essay on "being Irish," chooses to remain quiet. He turns the conversation to asking them about how it is to live in America.

The men in the pub speak up and tell him to be choosy about where he eats and drinks; not everyone is accepting of the Irish. There are signs on shop doors, they tell him, that say, "Irish Need Not Apply."

A big burly man spoke next, "We see politics as a structure of personalities not principles," he explains, "We direct our political loyalty to those we regard as local leaders." Cahey interprets that to mean the Irish support other Irish.

Labor reform issues are discussed heavily. Spurred by an

industrial revolution coming to America, industries need cheap and abundant labor. "We came for jobs," they say.

Another man, older with white hair, speaks next. "The editor of the *Irish World*, Patrick Ford, has urged Irish laborers to leave the crowded urban areas and take new opportunities offered to the west."

"And you didn't do that?" asks Cahey.

"No, I have family here now and am more settled. That venture is for you younger guys."

Another man speaks. "I joined a union. I think labor reform is happening with the unions, but beware, the unions encourage strikes if no agreement is made at the bargaining table, and there is no money to be made when there is a strike going on. However, there is a bit of sanity." He continues. "The Knights of Labor, a national union with a large Catholic membership and leadership, emphasizes cooperation between the workers and the owners rather than strikes."

And the strikes, they tell the four travelers in the pub, can be deadly. People are ready to fight and fight hard when there is a strike going on, they say. Often there are no friends between the workers and the owners, and should someone who needs a job cross that picket line, beware. "Just goes to show how things can get out of hand when bad feelings exist between people," says another pub patron.

Cahey has experienced how things can get out of hand. He remembers the shadow of the man who accosted him outside the distillery in Galway after his first meeting at the reading room, the men on horseback at the fair who had to stand down when the people sang one of Ireland's national anthems, the men who came to his room to look for books and pamphlets connecting him to the Irish movement, and the arrest of James as reasons he needed to leave Ireland—for a time.

After many toasts and many stories, all four finally bid farewell to their new pub friends and return to the hotel. As they walk and talk about the new stories, Cahey tucks what he has learned into his memory to think about later and consider in light of the problems happening in Ireland when he left, when he had to leave. If so many of the Irish people have left, who is in charge in Ireland to see that the Irish would win the British Home Rule?

———

34

Two burly fishermen are waiting on the steps of the hotel when the foursome return. The round of introductions is hurried; the men want to get back to the shore since they have an early start on the water to fish in the morning. Equally hurried is the gathering of Séan and Sophie's belongings from the hotel room. All too soon for Cahey, the couple is bundled into a cart and pushed off down the road with the two fishermen. Séan and Sophie promise to write in care of the hotel in New York where Cahey is booked. Cahey stands in the middle of the road watching. Sitting in the cart facing the rear, Sophie waves and Séan touches his cap—another parting, another leaving. Though he has made a new friend with Frederick, he misses his Irish connections.

Frederick is waiting for him in the hotel lobby.

"I am going to check on the horses before dinner, will you join me?"

They enter the stable to see a man swinging a lunge whip at the last horse in the stall, one of his Shire horses, the stallion. Cahey runs to the stall, grabs the man with the whip, and tosses him against the opposite stable wall.

"What do you think you are doing? A whip is never used on my horses," Cahey hisses at the man.

"The horse was not allowing me to enter the stall to clean the straw. I was just doing my job." As the man props his arm against the wall to raise himself, Cahey grabs him by the arms and hoists him up against the planks.

"These are my horses and they don't need your attention. You are never to touch my horses again. Do I make myself clear?" The words come out between Cahey's clinched teeth.

The man is struggling to breathe as Cahey has him pinned against the wall with his feet off the ground. "Do I make myself clear?"

The man nods and Cahey drops him. The stablehand swiftly leaves.

Turning to the horse, Cahey enters the stall and begins to talk in a low comforting tone. He switches to Irish. The horse is agitated but gradually calms to Cahey's voice and tone. He turns to Frederick, "Sorry about that."

Frederick sits on a bale of hay. "I'm just sorry I don't have my camera. No one will believe me when I tell them how you handled the stablehand. No one would believe you could have gotten that angry that quickly."

Cahey continues talking with the horse but says to Frederick, "No one hits a horse."

Visits to the other horses indicate to Cahey that they are just as anxious as the horse being whipped. Their eyes are bulging. They are breathing heavily. They are pawing at the stall gates. He talks with each and then goes back to the first one to repeat his path. Finally, the horses appear to be settling down. They still snort and look over their backs at the outside stable door but are quieting down.

"Want to brush a horse?" Cahey asks Frederick and tosses him a brush from a nearby shelf.

"Sure." Both men set to work and comb and brush each horse.

Cahey talks while he grooms the stallion. He shares with Frederick what he has learned about Shire horses. "A good Shire stallion has a long and lean head, averages about 22.5 hands high. They can be black, bay, or grey. They should not be splashed with large white patches though they can have white blazes, stripes, or stars on their faces. The best Shires are not roan," he tells Frederick.

As he combs out the mane and shapes his hands around the horse's ears, he remembers that most Shire horses have slightly Roman nostrils, thin and wide with large, well-set eyes, docile in expression. He describes these features to Frederick. He explains that their shoulders are deep and wide enough to support a collar. They are work horses, he says, and therefore their girth varies from six feet to eight feet with a short, strong, and muscular back. Their coat is fine, straight, and silky. They have good strong characters.

"Okay, that's more than I can remember," says Frederick.

"They are gentle giants," says Cahey. "They are known for their docile temperament and strong work ethic. These particular horses' ancestors came from the Old English Black Horse in the central part of England in counties referred to as Shires."

"I was wondering why they were called Shires."

"But they have a longer history than that," continues Cahey. "In Medieval times, they were used as warhorses. They can carry heavy loads, like a fully armored knight into battle. But now they are used on farms to pull farm equipment and to clear land."

"How did you get to know so much about Shire horses?"

"Remember I worked for a distillery? Shire horses are the breed used to pull the carts we used to deliver heavy barrels of ale."

"That makes sense."

"What's great about them is their dignity. I have never seen it but I have been told that in London Shire horses are used in royal processions. They are called the ceremonial drum horses and lead the Household Calvary, ridden by drummers who work the reins with their feet while holding drumsticks in their hands."

"I would love to see that!"

The two men complete the horses' grooming, fill the buckets with fresh water, and head back to the hotel. At the desk, Cahey asks who owns the stables. He discovers that the hotel and stables are owned by the same person, who also happens to manage the properties, and he would be back at the hotel after dinner.

Dinner is family style with five big bowls of vegetables, a platter of baked chicken, and plenty of rolls. After trying to eat on a moving ship, sitting at a table and having plenty to eat is a delight to both Cahey and Frederick. Before long, the owner of the hotel stops by.

"Hello, I'm Charlie Maddock. I hear you have been inquiring about me?"

"Yes, sir," says Cahey and proceeds to tell him how his horses have been treated in the stable. Mr. Maddock is surprised. The stablehand is new; Maddock did not realize that the stablehand would take such actions. He would tend to it.

"Mr. Lynch's agent suggested that we take good care of you and your horses, I hope this will not be recorded back to him differently."

"I will only say what needs to be said," says Cahey. "Horses are never to be whipped. Mr. Lynch would agree with me on that, I am quite sure."

"But, sir, are you reporting to Mr. Lynch this one incident?"

"Yes, sir, I will."

"I see." And that was the last they saw of Mr. Maddock.

The chamber room assigned to them is small; there is only

one bed. Cahey has slept with his brother for all his growing up years, so he has no problem with both of them on the bed especially since both are tired. They find hooks to hang their clothes and they wash their faces in the basin with water left in the room. The minute their heads hit the pillows both are fast asleep.

35

Morning came too early. They wash in the basin, dress and proceed downstairs for breakfast. Food is plentiful. There are more people in the dining room than the night before. Cahey and Frederick sit at the end of one of the long tables and fill their plates with eggs, bacon, fresh biscuits, and are offered steaming cups of coffee, which they refuse and have water instead. As they leave the hotel, Cahey sees someone at the office window but then a curtain shifts back into place. Cahey claps Frederick on the back and says, "Let's get these horses out of here."

Leading the horses down the road to the train depot is a spectacle. Cahey did not mean for this to happen, but many of the Bostonians have not seen a Shire horse like the four Cahey has brought to America. These horses are huge, broad, dignified, yet serene. People scramble out of the way and peek around posts and trees to get a better look. Several small boys run alongside and ask if they might help with the horses. Cahey thanks them but gives a definite no. He does not need a small boy getting hurt; the horses are a bit skittish that morning but are enjoying the exercise and are prancing along as they walk.

More people are at the train depot. Cahey leaves Frederick holding the horses and he goes inside the depot to confirm the train car for the horses. Cahey comes out of the depot with a railroad man who takes one look at the horses, pulls his railroad cap tighter on his head, and goes back inside. Cahey waits with Frederick.

A few minutes later, the railroad man comes back out with a ledger and a key. He stands away from the horses and tells Cahey quickly, "They'll ride in the last car, the boxcar. We have railing for eight horses so it should be fine." He pauses to look at the horses. "These are giant horses. The train ride is about six hours, give or take. There is a barrel with water and pails for feed if you need it."

He steps away but leads them to the last boxcar and unlocks the door. "The ramp is on wheels. Help me pull it over."

Frederick helps the railroad man move the ramp. The horses are being quite skittish so Cahey stops what he is doing and begins talking to the horses. He asks Frederick to talk to two of them and he talks with the other two. "It doesn't matter what you say; it is the tone they want to hear. Reassure them that this is fine. Remember a horse wants to please. They'll try hard to do what we ask if it appears reasonable to them."

The railroad man comes down the ramp and moves away from the horses. After a few minutes, Cahey hands the third rein to Frederick and leads the first horse up the ramp, ties him to the far rail, and comes back to the door. Each horse follows Cahey up the ramp and into the boxcar. Cahey doublechecks to make sure the barrel has water. The oats are distributed in the buckets and the vents in the side of the car and the doors of the car are opened for ventilation.

"Okay, they are set," says Cahey.

The railroad man hands Cahey the ledger sheet and the

key. "Turn these in to the dispatcher in New York." He takes another look at the horses, turns and quickly leaves. A crowd has gathered outside of the boxcar with people pointing and talking loudly.

Cahey turns to Frederick. "I don't know about you, but I'm thinking that riding with the horses might be the best thing to do."

"Agreed." Frederick walks up the ramp, Cahey shoves it to the side, and Frederick lends a hand to Cahey as he jumps up into the boxcar. They shut the door behind them as a shield against the growing crowd's stares.

Bright slivers of light enter the darkened boxcar through the open vents and gaps in the siding. There are hay bales at one end and these become the reclining seats for the two men. They toss their gear on top and settle down for the ride.

Cahey tucks his rucksack under his head and closes his eyes.

"Did you ever dream that you would one day be in America?" asks Frederick.

Cahey squints up at Frederick without really opening his eyes fully. "No, never really thought about it until it happened."

"Really? Never wanted to start fresh and change everything you knew?"

Cahey thinks a minute about the question. When he was younger and eager to leave the farm, yes, but now he has to answer "no" because all the changes he has experienced have been forced on him. His papa and mum's deaths, the famine, losing the farm, his sisters and brother trying to find their way but going a different path, Micil's death, the threats of harm against him...he has not thought or planned for any of them. "No, I never thought about it."

"I did. My papa and mother are devoted Catholics and wanted me to be."

"Not what you wanted?"

"My faith is fine; I just have problems with the organization of the church in Scotland, which is full of working-class people, including Irish who came into Scotland during the famine years."

"Is that a problem?" Cahey is cautious. His experience with the men in the reading room had taught him that people believed things they heard but had no proof.

"Yes, oh, no, not that they were Irish; it was how the working-class people in the church are treated, like second-class citizens. The middle-class folks run the business of the church with the priests. There are costs for certain seats in the church that the working-class people could not afford. How people sit in the church indicates a person's class and status in society. I have a problem with that."

"I see," says Cahey, and he did understand. He is well-aware of how religion dominates the Irish people and how it separates folks really fast.

"The problem escalated when I fell in love."

"Being a Catholic in love is a problem?"

Frederick makes his own seat on the hay bales. "It is when the person you are in love with is not Catholic and your family is."

"What did you do?"

"I left and here I am in America."

Cahey is stunned. "You left? Where is the girl you fell in love with?"

"Back in Scotland; not to worry, she is to come when I am settled and we will marry here. America is the land of the free, right? We'll be free to worship any way we like."

Cahey is not so sure. Though he wants to ask a lot of questions about being Catholic and the pressure to marry Catholics, he chooses to be quiet. Though many Irish were Catholic in Galway, most of his associates, other than Seámus, did not introduce Cahey to their religious ideology. He did attend one

Mass with Colm, but no one pushed him into attending. Religion can cause its own set of problems, problems that were often too complicated and inherited to solve easily. Cahey doesn't think having or not having religion would have solved any of his problems of why he was forced to travel half way around the world to avoid being hurt or killed for writing about being Irish. It is a lot to contemplate.

36

The horses do not like the starts and stops of the train. Their ears prick backwards when the train whistle is pulled. During the ride, the horses do not eat or drink; they stand and listen. Cahey feels their unease. They are all going to a new place where everything will be different. Cahey has heard stories. Letters from folks living in America were sent back home to Ireland. The stories were about the freedom to work, to learn, to worship. The letters urged family members to join them in America. And then some of the letters told the stories of the tragedies in the mines, in the factories, in the tenements. Other letters were full of wishful memories of Ireland, the music, the rivers, and even the rain. Cahey is not so sure that America is everything people thought it might be.

Cahey has slept fitfully during the long ride. He aches when he is awakened by a particularly long whistle that leaves the horses snorting and prancing at the rails. Cahey sits up and begins to talk with the horses to calm them a bit. Frederick is awake and goes to the door, sliding it back enough to see New York City. The train slows and creeps into town. Though Cahey is talking to the horses, he too is curious and looks out at the warehouses lining the train tracks.

The depot is in sight and the train stops. Cahey gets his rucksack and slides the boxcar doors open. Frederick is right behind him. Cahey sees the movable ramp on the side of the platform just above where their boxcar has stopped. Frederick jumps down and pulls it over to the sliding door. Cahey has tied his rucksack to one of the horses and Frederick's to another to free up their hands to handle the horses. Reversing their loading, each horse is guided down the ramp and tethered to a rail at the side of the platform. Frederick waits with the horses since, again, a large crowd begins to form around the unusually big horses. Once all are down, Cahey turns in the key and documents, thus leaving Frederick to answer questions. Cahey grins as he hears Frederick explain the Shires to the gathering crowd. With the errand complete, Cahey learns that they must take the horses inside the building, one which the two men did not expect to be so huge. As they lead the horses through, they stare at the stairwells, the large hall, the Grand Central Depot, while the people stare at them.

The horses have been a spectacle before, but Cahey is not prepared for the chaos these horses create as they are guided through the balloon shed and down a busy street. Even with his full attention on the horses, Cahey has to constantly watch for people getting in their path, thinking these big horses can stop quickly and not be panicked. A wagon pulling out of a side street in front of them almost causes the horses to bolt. Cahey stops to calm them. Though their journey's end is not far—the American Horse Exchange is located at 50th Street and Broadway and the train depot is at 42nd Street, eight blocks away—Cahey is moving the horses slowly for all of their safety, that it might as well have been eighteen blocks. The trip is lasting a long time. Cahey is tired, the horses are tired, everything is new.

They finally walk the now skittish horses down the street to 50th Street. Though the Grand Central Depot is huge, the American Horse Exchange is even more intimidating to Cahey. The building is three stories high in places, with an open arch in the center of the block that is large enough for a carriage and horses to drive through. Cahey pauses to look at the building.

"What have we done?" he asks Frederick, who simply stares up at the building and says nothing.

Almost in sync, the men tuck their caps deeper on their heads and begin making their way through the arch and into the building. Cahey enters to see a giant oval, 160 by 80 feet, bridged by open truss work, with the perimeter walls made of brick and lined with round-arched windows. He takes off his cap and wads it into his pocket. The first person they see is a grounds man who directs Cahey to the Exchange dispatcher. All of the paperwork is handed over and Cahey signs forms and paperwork that will be sent to Mr. Lynch verifying that the four horses have been received. Finally, with the horses prancing beside him, he is shown where to house the horses.

As he enters the stable area, Cahey sees a place that can house as many as 250 horses. In Ireland, he owns just four horses. The groomsmen offer to take the reins of the horses, but Cahey insists that he and Frederick lead the horses to the stalls. In a quiet area chosen to eliminate any discomfort the horses may feel due to their journey, Cahey takes one horse at a time from the leads Frederick is holding and gets them all in individual stalls. He notices a group of men have gathered and they all seem to be asking how to take care of the Shires.

One of the men, who had been introduced as the stable manager, steps in. "Cahey will be here all week to answer questions on their care. In the meantime, let's get the horses settled and do the other work that needs to be done."

Though the day has been a long one with the travel, there is still much to be done on their first day in New York. The new friends must find where they are lodging.

37

After exiting the American Horse Exchange, Cahey and Frederick look about and see the area near the Exchange is primarily horse and carriage businesses. The area is called Longacre Square. Cahey has been given directions that his hotel is located just down the street on the other side of the train station. The stablehand explain the layout of the city: below 14th Street, the streets are haphazardly laid out. The harbor and ports on all sides of the island grew rapidly; to handle the expansion, with some 500,000 people living uptown between 14th and below 42nd Street, the city has been laid out in grids and numbered up to 96th Street, though in that area there are a few houses, some inns, and scattered country houses but not much else.

The two men decide to locate Cahey's hotel in Murray Hill first and to find something to eat. To find the hotel, they are to pass the Grand Central Depot and at Third Avenue, turn right and go down two or three streets where they would see the hotel. Everything is where they were told it would be and everything is in order. Mr. Lynch's agent has arranged a room with meals and leaves the departure date open for Cahey to decide. The hotel is huge and grand with marble and wainscot trimmings, ornate ceilings, and detail work everywhere, reminding Cahey of the salons on the ship over. The men stand a bit straighter as they walk up the three flights of steps to Cahey's room. Their travel rucksacks are stashed, their faces and hands are washed, and their mission is to find food; they have not eaten since breakfast before the train left Boston. The travels, the horses, the excitement of the stables at the Exchange, and now finally settling in for a week or so make both men hungry. At the front desk, they learn there are four dining rooms at the hotel. The closest is a small one near the front door with a long bar at the back. It is the closest, Cahey puts his hat in his pocket and enters with Frederick right behind. A waitress brings them a menu with four items: mutton stew with brown bread, steak with potatoes, fish baked with greens, and stuffed pork chops with cabbage. They order pints of ale, mutton stew for Cahey, and fish for Frederick.

"So, why don't I walk down with you after our meal to find your place?" says Cahey. "After that train ride, I could use the exercise."

"Good, then you'll at least know how to find me."

"That's right." Cahey pauses while tearing off a bit of brown bread. "I will be here at least a week."

"Have you decided what to do?"

"Not yet. It's a bit loud and busy here, don't you think?"

"Hah, here's a mate talking that's been living out in the hinterland of Ireland for all his life; no wonder the city seems a bit loud and busy."

"There have been so many changes since I left Ireland; it's hard to think that it has only been a month."

"I know. It is a bit of an adjustment, that I'll say."

Cahey eats in silence. The job at the distillery, his friends

and the business interests he has been developing seem so far
away. He can't think about that, for now he has to settle the
Shire horses in their new surroundings and he wants to get
acquainted with this big city called New York.

The men finish. The bill is posted to Cahey's room. They get
Frederick's travel bags and leave to find Frederick's new place of
business and room. They walk west to Broadway and then turn
left to head down to 37th Street. They pass many horse-drawn
carriages as well as horse-drawn streetcars. Corners are busy
with people everywhere. Some are shopping for produce for
dinners; others dodge the carriages and pedestrians as
hundreds of people make their way home after a long workday.
Cahey and Frederick do not talk. There is too much to see and
too much to take in. They look at everything so their journey
takes a lot longer than they had expected. They arrive at dusk.
Frederick knocks on the door and there is no answer. He
knocks again, louder.

A man comes out of the produce market and looks Frederick over. "Are you the photographer?"

"That I am." Frederick takes off his cap.

"You are to go through here and up those stairs. Mr.
Chaney's family and him, they live upstairs and he's already
closed the shop for the evening. I'm to tell you if I see you." He
turns and goes back into the market.

Frederick glances at Cahey, who says, "I'll wait out here
until you know what's going on."

Frederick goes through the passage and up the stairs. Cahey
looks over the produce at the market stall and then leans up
against the building and watches the people going about on the
streets. In the evening glow, the dirt of the day is not as notice-
able on the streets. He can only imagine what these streets
must be like when it rains. He begins planning what he has to
do this next week with the horses when Frederick appears, this
time with a small boy leading the way.

"Cahey, meet John Chaney, the youngest son of Mr. Chaney. They are eating dinner, but he sent the boy with the key to open the shop and let me settle in. We'll get acquainted and get started in the morning."

"Ah, sounds good. Then I'll head back and let you get settled. I will come to see you or get in touch with you as to my plans by the end of the week."

"Yes, I hope so; until then, my friend."

The men clap each other on the back, and Cahey turns to head back up Broadway and away from the only friend he has in New York. As he walks through the streets of New York, he thinks about why he is here. Is he here just to settle the horses and then return to Ireland and all he left? He does have a job waiting and a business started. He has good people handling the accounts. He is not needed to manage the operation—only who will grow the business if he is not there? What if something happens to one of the people he left in charge: Seámus, Pádraig, Colm, and Michael? They have their own families and lives to put together; they should not have to manage his business from afar. As he walks down the street heavily in his own thoughts, he is jostled by a man in a hurry.

"*Tráthnóna maith duit,*" Cahey says automatically.

The man stops. "Speak English to me, man, speak English."

"You ran into me so I wished you a good evening."

"You're Irish, aren't you?"

"That I am, sir," and Cahey tips his cap.

"Nothing's good since so many of you stinking Irish came ashore. You can very well go back where you came from. We don't need more of you here to bring your brawlin', drinkin', and lazy selves. Go home."

And before Cahey can say a return, the man speeds away down the street. Cahey is tempted to run after him, catch him, and give him a good going over, but that would only fuel that man's sentiments that much more. Cahey thinks that this is just one man; maybe he's had a bad day. What does one man know? Still, Cahey thinks, this is America where anyone who works hard can reach the American dream.

38

The beginning of the workweek for Cahey has him feeling nervous and yet excited: nervous because everything is so different and new; excited because everything is so different and new.

Getting dressed, he takes a look in the hotel mirror. His red hair is longer and cannot be pulled under his cap anymore. His clothes, though older are also stained and dirty. He had not noticed any of this earlier before coming into this elegant hotel with the marble and pristine white sheets on the bed and a porcelain-flowered water basin on the side table. He scrubs his face and combs his hair straight back. He pulls out his remaining clothes from the rucksack, including his suit. He hangs his suit up in the walnut armoire in the room. He doesn't know what to do with the other clothes. They need cleaning. He'll have to ask.

As he leaves his room, he sees a maid down the hall.

"Hello, ma'am, may I ask where I might get a few clothes washed?"

"A few you say; how many?" She uses the back of her hand to brush tendrils of black hair hanging in her eyes. She is short,

Cahey notices, like Mrs. Kelly back home, but petite, not full-bodied like Mrs. Kelly. She talks like an American.

"Two or three shirts and trousers."

"Aye, if that's all you have, I can do those for you for half a crown and have them back to you tomorrow."

"Thank you. I left them on my bed in the room down the hall."

"Good enough. What's your name?"

"Cahey Ó hArrachtain."

"Well, I never, with a name like that you have got to be from someplace in Ireland," she says and smiles.

"Yes, I'm Irish."

"Then you better be keeping it to yourself; some New Yorkers don't like the Irish, I should know, my people came from Dublin. I'm Sharon McGee. Here everyone calls me Sharon Mac and I'm fine with that."

"Thank you, Sharon Mac. I'll take your advice." He tips his cap and down he goes to breakfast and the start of work at the Exchange.

"The horses are not eating," explains the stablehand he meets when Cahey goes down to check on them. He should have taken the time yesterday to exercise them, but he had been tired and they seemed fine at the time. He is not that concerned seeing what they have been through, but he knows he can't have four sick horses for Mr. Vanderbilt or Mr. Lynch. He strokes the stallion and checks all four of his ankles. The ankles have healed from the pig oil and sulfur he has applied earlier.

"Where can I exercise the horses?"

"Up in the center of the building there is an arena; horses are walked around the perimeter. You'll see."

Cahey places the reins on one of the horses and leads her

out of the stall and up the ramp to the arena. Groomsmen are exercising other horses. Cahey slowly walks the horse around the oval area. He keeps a shortened rein on the horse so he can be close to her head. He continues to talk with the horse as they walk. Much of what he says is about the surroundings. He describes the other horses, people he sees, what is on the ground, anything that comes to mind. Much of it is chatter and all of it is in Irish, but the horse understands the tone and the intent. After circling the arena for the fifth time, Cahey exchanges the stallion for one of the mares. He does the same thing with all the horses. At the end of each of their workouts, he brushes them until their coats glisten. He sees a basket of apples, which he uses to tempt the horses. He holds one out for the stallion, who sniffs and then chomps down on it. The apples are a treat for all four horses. Stress points are relieved in the horses and they begin to eat the oats and drink a lot of water.

As Cahey cleans up the brushes and feed buckets, he is approached by one of the groomsmen he had met when he brought the horses into the stables.

"You are getting them settled, I see."

"Yes," says Cahey as he refills the water buckets in the stalls.

"We met when you brought the horses in. I'm Peter, Peter LeBlanc."

"Hello, yes, I remember. I'm Cahey." He pauses; he hesitates to give his last name after his warning from Sharon Mac. Peter is muscular and stocky; he could bowl Cahey over in a second. Better wait and see how he feels about the Irish.

"I head up the stables and have been told that you would be about for a week to make sure the horses are cared for properly."

"That's right. Who will be working with me to learn about the Shires?"

"Well, there's me, and I wanted Tommy Berlosconi to work

with us as well. I will get Tommy over in a while. These are giant horses."

"Yes, gentle giants." Cahey looks over at the nearest horse.

"That's good to hear since we have hundreds of horses to tend to every day." Peter looks into the stalls at the horses. "I see you have groomed them and walked them. I will do it with you tomorrow morning. In the meantime, I'll have Tommy come and show you about, where things are and how we do things here; that sort of thing."

"Good, when will that be?"

"Midday, I should say. Go grab some lunch in the canteen and meet me back here at two. The canteen is up the two flights of stairs. Take a left turn and go to the end of the building; you'll see it there. Exchange staff eats for free in the canteen as part of our exorbitant salaries. Tell Danielle, the woman at the entrance, that you are working with me." Peter dashes off to another part of the stable.

Cahey tips his cap and follows the directions to the canteen, a busy place with a line of folks choosing sandwiches and soups off a table. At the entrance is a woman perched on a stool with a notebook. She is ticking off names of people as they go through the line. Cahey gets in line, and when he reaches her, he gives her Peter's instructions.

"So, Peter LeBlanc is sending up people from the streets to eat with us, is he?"

Cahey turns red, pauses, then turns and begins to walk away.

"Wait, I'm sorry. I was just teasing. Don't be so sensitive! Come back."

He turns and comes back to where the woman is sitting. Even with her sitting down, he can tell she is tall. Her brown hair puffed up on top of her head gives the illusion of her being even taller. She sits on her stool with her legs crossed, something no young lady in Ireland would do. Some men might even consider her attractive, but Cahey is too angry to see anything but a lanky, smart-mouthed young woman. "I don't take anything from anyone. I earn everything I get. I am working here for a time to settle some horses. Okay?"

"Okay," says the woman, "okay." She repeats the second "okay" in a quiet tone.

Cahey picks up two sandwiches, gets a cup for some water, and finds a table as far away from her as possible in order to sit. A young man comes over and sits down beside him.

"I am happy to meet someone, anyone, who will give Danielle what she gives out." He reaches out to shake Cahey's hand. "Hey, I'm Tommy Berlosconi. We are to get together after lunch, but I thought now might be a good time to meet, seeing what took place in the line and all."

Cahey barely lifts his eyes to look at Tommy, who shifts a bit in his seat and lowers his hand.

"I saw those gigantic horses you brought in. I can't wait to learn more about them."

That's when Cahey looks at Tommy and sees the young man for the first time. Tommy is skinny and not much older than Seámus's boy back home. He has a sharp straight nose and dark black hair that he has parted on the side. His hair curled tightly all over his head, unlike Frederick's which was full and bushy. Cahey nods at Tommy. "Pleased to meet you."

"Where are you from? They only told me that a man is bringing in some big horses."

Cahey stops chewing and looks at Tommy. "The horses are from County Clare in Ireland."

"Ah, and are you from County Clare in Ireland?"

"Why do you ask?"

"Just making conversation. I'm from Italy, a little village in the south in the region of Campania."

Cahey does not answer him. He just continues to eat. He finishes and picks up his plate and cup. "The horses are waiting." The conversation with Danielle put Cahey in a protective mood and he is not ready to be nice. He puts the plate on a tray and leaves the canteen, not giving Danielle a glance. Tommy hurries behind him.

Peter is waiting for them when they arrive back at the horses.

"I see you've met Danielle."

Cahey looks at Peter but says nothing.

"News travels fast in this place."

Cahey stays silent. "Okay then, let's go over the care of the horses," says Peter.

For the next hour, Cahey goes over all the basics, then he walks around each horse and identifies what makes that horse different from any other horse. This one has a playful streak; this one is tolerant; this one has to be told twice, not because she doesn't want to do it, she just wants to be sure you want her to do it; and the fourth one is all stallion, he wants to control everything. Cahey talks for a while. With no questions from the guys, he forgets that Peter and Tommy are there listening to him and he talks to just the horses. Then he realizes that he might still have the two men listening to what he has to say. He turns to Peter and Tommy to explain but stops—gathered about the stall are a dozen groomsmen listening to every detail Cahey has given about the horses.

Peter speaks first. "Well, I must say, you certainly know your horses."

The other groomsmen nod and agree. Cahey is silent.

"Well, men, back to work. We have giant horses to take care of here," Peter says.

The men scatter. Cahey notices that they look back at him as they leave. He asks Peter, "Did I give too much information? Why do they stare?"

"No, not too much information; I think it might be that they see you have a connection with horses that they don't have but would like to have."

"All they need to do is to listen to the horses," says Cahey.

Peter looks at him and laughs. Cahey's face shows his confusion. Then he realizes that he has spent more time with horses than with people. Talking to just the horses will make people think he is crazy. He has to remember this is a temporary position. Still, there are a lot of different types of horses in the stable. Each horse has a different personality, so it may take a while to learn about all of them.

39

Cahey walks about after his day at the Exchange and he sees all the various horse-related businesses: saddlers, coach refurbishers, harness builders, stables for out-of-town horses, cart builders, and leather goods. He talks with the shopkeepers along the way and learns that the area, teaming with all that has to do with horses, began when a Revolutionary War General, John Morin Scott, bred horses on 43rd Street. Then the Brewster Carriage Company migrated here, and the carriage trade followed along with workers who wanted to live nearby. Cahey appreciates that, having lived on the distillery compound with his long hours. He asks one of the shopkeepers about the name of the area. Being from a farming community, he knows that an acre is how much a horse can plow in one day. A long acre designates that most acres were measured longer than wider because it was hard to turn the horse or oxen and the plow. But how did the whole area become Longacre Square? He is told that London uses the term to designate the area where horses are traded, coaches are built and refurbished, and trade concerning horses and gear take place. The area in New York where Vanderbilt built the American Horse Exchange is the same kind of center for the horse trade; therefore, the area is called Longacre Square, mimicking London.

Cahey looks at the business of horses and realizes that his business back in Ireland has to do with what horses can do and products of the distillery. What is the future of transportation in Ireland and in America? He must think about this.

Wandering about the city, he sees the specialty shops: the Harper and Brothers Building on Pearl Street facing Franklin Square and the Haughwout Building at the northeast corner of Broadway and Broome Street. This building catches his eye. Haughwout is a retailer specializing in cut glass and silverware. Cahey has never seen such splendor; he spends a long time looking at the displays in the window. Cahey is so fascinated by what New York offers that for the first few evenings after spending hours at the Exchange, rather than return to the hotel, he walks about. He finds the American Museum of Natural History and the Metropolitan Museum of Art. He has never been inside a museum before.

On the third evening, Cahey stops by a horse-related business in Longacre Square. There are harnesses and reins displayed just the way he remembers the harness room at the distillery. There are several men talking and examining one of the harnesses. Cahey is close enough to hear them talk. One man asks about the strength of the harness to pull a wagon. The other man assures him that it would do the job. Cahey takes a look at the harness being discussed and silently agrees. The man asking questions decides to wait to purchase and leaves. The shop man hangs the harness back on a wall hook and turns to Cahey. "How may I help you?"

"I am sorry the man did not buy your harness; it is indeed a good one for pulling a wagon."

The shop man looks at Cahey. "You know something about harnesses?"

"I do. I worked at the stables for a distillery in Galway."

"As in Ireland?"

"Yes."

"I see. Well, there is nothing here for you." The man turns and walks away.

Cahey looks at him as he walks away and then quietly leaves the shop. He doesn't want any trouble. He goes to the next shop; before he can ask a question, the shopkeeper immediately says, "There are no jobs for the Irish here." No one asks him what his skills may be or what his experiences have been. One shopkeeper pointed to a sign on the wall: "No Irish Need Apply." Cahey returns to the hotel and stops into a barber shop off the lobby of his hotel to get his hair cut and face shaved.

The week passes in a hurry with Cahey leading many sessions on the horses; exercises, breeding, work habits, maintenance, and health issues. Peter and Tommy are good listeners and ask questions along the way to make Cahey feel they really want to do the best they can for the horses. At the end of the week, he has to decide: go home or find a way to stay and make his future in New York. He is a bit down about not being able to secure a job in Longacre Square so he stops in Peter's office before he leaves for the day.

"Peter, I have a question for you."

Peter has been finishing some paperwork and stops to look up at Cahey. "Yes?"

"You have been helpful to me. I am in no rush to return to Ireland, but I will need a job if I stay in New York. How does one go about doing that? Longacre Square appeals to me. There are many businesses where someone with my experience working around horses might get a job, but I have had no luck. It seems like my Irishness is getting in the way."

Peter puts his paperwork away. "You've asked at the various businesses?"

"Yes, and they point to signs that say 'No Irish Need Apply.' But plenty of Irish are working in this city. How is it done?"

"You need a go-between, someone who will vouch for you and say that you can do the job and will work to prove it."

"I see, and how does one get that person who knows of a job and will also vouch for you?"

"It takes time, is all. You have a solid reputation here after this week and that will get you references. You must just keep asking."

"Thank you, Peter. See you in the morning."

Cahey leaves the Exchange. He has no idea what to do. Mr. Lynch has offered to pay his expenses while he makes up his mind. He does have an income from the Irish Services that Colm deposits and Cahey can draw on from a New York bank, but just this morning before he left the hotel, he gets a telegram from Mr. Lynch asking how things are going and whether he has made any decision on returning to Ireland.

Cahey walks after work among many of the streets he has meandered down all week and finds that he is heading down to 37th and Broadway. He locates the photography studio where he left Frederick and knocks on the door. Frederick pokes his head out.

"Cahey, good to see you, mate. How are you?" He opens the door and pulls Cahey into the photography studio. "I see you found a barber; the style looks more New York."

Cahey smiles. He forgot that Frederick has not seen him sheared and shaved. He is amazed at all the equipment and photo prints covering every inch of wall space. There are all types of box cameras, folding cameras, lenses, and paper with angles and designs. Rather than send most of their work to Eastman Kodak, Frederick tells him that he develops his own rolls in the back darkroom.

"I'm just finishing up some stuff. Come on back and sit."

Frederick dashes to a back worktable and picks up where

he left off before answering the door. Cahey ambles through the shop up front, goes around the counter and through an archway with a black curtain. Frederick motions to a chair nearby. "Sit down, tell me about the horses."

In what seems like a short time to Cahey, he tells Frederick all about the horses, Peter, Tommy, Danielle, his walk-abouts in the city, everything. Frederick listens and works. Finally, he stops, pulls off his apron. "I'm finished. Let's go get something to drink or eat; I'm good with either."

The men exit the shop and Frederick locks the basement door behind him. He knows of a pub just around the corner. When they are settled and have ordered, Frederick catches Cahey up on the photography business. Mr. Chaney, his mentor, is amazing; he is learning so much about the studio shots as well as nature prints. Then he tells Cahey about some of the weird things he is also learning about the business.

"There's this chap down in the Bowery, a Charles Eisenmann, who takes pictures of bearded girls, dog-faced boys, giants, midgets, fat ladies, and other human oddities. This guy is a German immigrant who focuses on freaks of the circuses and sideshows. Eisenmann uses the human attractions exhibited by that circus man P.T. Barnum at his museum on Broadway and Ann Street."

"Why would someone want to do that?"

"No one knows or says. The Bowery is a rough, tacky place with lots of honky-tonks. Perhaps he feels it is a good way to make a living."

"I don't know; makes no sense to me."

"Me neither." Both men laugh and take swigs of their ale. The waitress brings a bowl of pretzels and sits them on the table.

"We didn't order the pretzels," says Frederick.

"Comes with the ale; you can thank the Raines Law for that," she says before sashaying off.

Cahey calls her back. "Miss!" When she returns, he asks, "What is the Raines Law?"

"Prohibition has hit New York, but people still want a drink even on a Sunday. The Raines Law raised licensing fees for saloons and prohibited the sale of alcohol on Sundays, except in restaurants and hotels with ten or more beds. The saloons get by the law by serving meals of pretzels with drinks. Anything else?"

Cahey shakes his head. She turns and leaves.

"Won't make dinner, but it's good for now," says Cahey as he bites into a pretzel. "What else do we need to know about these laws?"

"Mr. Chaney tells me that I have to be careful, that some of these saloons, in order to get around the Raines Law, also have prostitutes working out of the back rooms. It helps the owner pay for the additional licensing fees. This one doesn't seem to have that back room. That's why I feel it is safe to come here."

Cahey is not sure he likes the whole set up of the American saloon; he prefers a pub like the one Michael and Sheila run back in Galway. "So, how is it working for the photographer?"

"I am learning a lot and he's a decent fellow, a family man. He is willing to give me all the assignments he thinks I can handle and lets me shadow him on the others so I can learn. I had hoped to have a window in my room. It is in the back part of the basement and dark as can be without the lantern, but I am out and about so much during the day and at night is when we develop the film and process the prints, so the dark is good, so it's fine. I'm fine. How about you? What have you decided?"

"That's just it; I haven't decided. The week is up and I have a telegram from Mr. Lynch asking me what I want to do. I have walked all over the area and tried to picture what I might do here. There is a lot of horse and coach work in the Longacre Square area, but I have asked and there seems to be no jobs. With hundreds of people arriving every day—I see them as I pass the Grand Central Depot on my way to the Exchange—there might be more people than jobs. I don't know."

"Do you have any ties back in Ireland?"

Cahey pauses. "Well, yes, I have my friends, my businesses, my writing."

Frederick continues, "But do you have family or a girl?"

Cahey looks away.

"I'm sorry. Did I say something wrong?"

"There was a girl, Micil; she loved riding horseback with me on Colleen. She smelled of lavender."

"You're holding back from me, Cahey, and I thought we were friends. Will I be meeting Micil?"

"No. No," he says quietly. "Micil died of the fever."

Frederick looks at his glass of ale. "I'm sorry. I didn't know."

Cahey is lost in his own thoughts. He remembers Micil and for some reason the Connemara Cradle song echoes in his head. As he sits with Frederick drinking his ale, he sings it softly to himself.

"On wings of the wind o'er the dark rolling deep
Angels are coming to watch over thy sleep
Angels are coming to watch over thee
So list to the wind coming over the sea
"Hear the wind blow, love, hear the wind blow
Hang your head o'er and hear the wind blow
Hear the wind blow, love, hear the wind blow
Hang your head o'er, love, and hear the wind blow
"The currachs are sailing way out on the blue
Chasing the herring of silvery hue
Silver the herring and silver the sea
Soon they'll be silver for my love and me."

Cahey shakes the memory from his head, he looks at Frederick. "The people I have loved are gone, my family, Micil. And the friends I have are all growing their own families and future. I will have to start over if I return to Ireland." He takes another sip of his ale. "Well, that answers my question though, doesn't it? I don't have any reason to go back to Ireland at the moment and every reason to find out my future here." Cahey motions to the bartender. "Another round for the table." He raises his glass to Frederick.

Frederick raises his glass as well. "I must say, I am glad you are sticking around." And both men empty their glasses.

Cahey must remember to telegraph Mr. Lynch first with his wish to find a job and stay in New York and then the others when he has something solid to tell them. He'll think of something to do. He can begin his search in earnest at the first of the week. At least it is not the first job he has requested and as Seámus reminded him, he has heard "no" before; he will continue to ask until he hears a "yes."

40

S haron did a good job on the clothes placed in his hotel room. However, now that he has decided to stay, he needs other clothes for New York. He steps out of his room and sees Sharon down the hallway.

"Good evening, Sharon. You're working late tonight."

"Yes, the night girl is sick and so they asked me to stay on for a double. I don't mind; I need the money."

"Here is what I owe you." Cahey gives her the coin. "I thought you might give me some advice. I need some new clothes."

"You're right about that, you are. Those you had me wash, I had to be careful to not put too much scrubbing or else there would be holes in those threads."

"Yes, well, where do I find new clothes, that is, new clothes I can afford?"

"You can afford anything staying in this fine hotel."

"I don't pay for this. My boss back in Ireland is paying and I have to find a job here and move out, so I need some new clothes I can afford."

"Well, that being the case, go to AT Stewart's. You can buy most everything you need there."

"How do I get there?"

"Go to 280 Broadway between Chambers and Reade Streets. It is called the Marble Palace—you'll see why. Oh, and the owner is Irish so he welcomes the Irish." She turns with her cleaning supplies and heads down the hallway.

Cahey goes to AT Stewart's the next morning before showing up at the Exchange. There is a plaque next to the front door: "Welcome to AT Stewart's, offering European retail merchandise at low prices. Free entrance to all potential customers."

Oversized French plate-glass windows showcase the merchandise. The building is unique with a marble-clad exterior. Cahey understands why it is called the "Marble Palace." He buys three shirts, two pairs of trousers, and a solid pair of shoes. He also buys several pairs of undershirts, a pair of long johns, and socks all the same color. Satisfied, he hurries to the Exchange for what should be his last day working with the horses. He arrives out of breath, carrying his packages and rushing through the morning traffic. When he gets to the horse stalls, he is met by Peter.

"There you are. Thought you might be finished with us."

"No, I just had some errands I needed to attend to. Sorry to be late." He places his purchases next to the stall of the Shires, out of the way.

"You are not on my timeclock, so no problem. However, someone wants to see you?"

Surprised, Cahey asks, "Who?"

"Mr. Vanderbilt's business manager, the man who oversees all that we do."

Cahey does not know what to say or to ask.

"Tommy will take you to his office. Oh, and one thing, ask him for an explanation; it is always helpful to know why."

Cahey follows Tommy up the stairs to the top level of the Exchange where all the executive offices are located. Tommy opens the door but motions for Cahey to step inside ahead of him. Cahey enters and immediately takes off his cap and holds it in his hand like a protection in front of his body.

The assistant rises from his desk and extends his hand. "Hello, I am Mr. Vanderbilt's business manager, Roger Malcolm. Welcome. Please, sit down." He motions to a chair in front of his desk.

Cahey approaches the chair and glances back to see that Tommy has exited and shut the door behind him. Cahey sits with his cap in his lap.

"How has your week been at the Exchange?"

"Fine, just fine." Cahey twists his cap in his lap as he watches Mr. Malcolm return to his chair. The business manager is soft-spoken. As he speaks, he steeples his hands and Cahey notices how smooth and white they are.

"Good, that's good to hear." Mr. Malcolm looks at Cahey who remains silent. "Okay, so you are probably wondering why I wanted to talk with you."

"Yes, I was curious at that."

"Everything we have been hearing about the Shire horses has been positive. Mr. Vanderbilt met Mr. Lynch in France and they talked about how these horses could be major work horses in the American agricultural market."

Cahey nods. "Yes, they are hard workers."

"And," Mr. Malcolm continues, "you have demonstrated an unusual knowledge of the maintenance and care of horses which transcends to other breeds, I understand."

"I have been asked a lot of questions about the care of horses while I have been here."

"Right. You have worked with a variety of horse breeds in Ireland?"

"Yes, at the distillery we had every kind of horse pulling the carts. To take care of them, one has to learn what is needed."

"You have demonstrated that knowledge here, so says Peter in his report to Mr. Vanderbilt on the past week. Peter has recommended that we might find a way to keep you at the Exchange. Peter and I have been talking about developing a maintenance and care system for the horses that enter and exit the Exchange. Peter thinks you might be the right person to work with him to finally get that started. Mr. Lynch gives you a high reference. You know our business is one of not only taking care of the horses used in the area businesses, but we also buying and selling horses here at our auctions. Our reputation depends on having healthy horses to sell and not sickly horses. Do you understand?"

"Yes, I do. I think a healthy horse is a good investment."

"Yes, absolutely. Now, what do you think? Could we talk you into staying awhile and not returning just yet to Ireland?"

Cahey can feel his shoulders relaxing and he takes a deep breath. "I think that could be arranged."

"Good, let's talk details." Mr. Malcolm takes up a pen and begins to make notes on his paper in front of him.

Within a few minutes, Mr. Malcolm has outlined the work Cahey would be asked to do, the salary, the benefits, and other details related to the job. He shows Cahey his notes.

"So, will you take us on?"

"I will be pleased to do so, Mr. Malcolm."

"Roger, call me Roger."

Cahey shakes Mr. Malcolm's hand and leaves. As he reaches the top of the stairs, he does a little jig he learned back in Ireland. Then he begins singing a tune, a kick up your heels type of tune he remembers from the pub days in Galway.

"Every person in the nation

Or of great or humble station
Holds in highest estimation
Piping Tim of Galway.

Loudly he can play, or low
He can move you fast or slow
Touch your hearts or stir your toe
Piping Tim of Galway.
"When the wedding bells are ringing
His the breath to lead the singing
Then in jigs the folks go swinging
What a splendid piper!
He will blow from eve to morn
Counting sleep a thing of scorn
Old is he but not outworn
Know you such a piper?
"When he walks the highway pealing
Round the head the birds come wheeling
Tim has carols worth the stealing
Piping Tim of Galway
Thrush and linnet, finch and lark
To each other twitter "Hark!"
Soon they sing from light to dark
Pipings learnt in Galway."

At the bottom of the stairs, Cahey realizes that people are listening to him sing. He tips his hat and with a bright red face that matches his hair, he goes and gives Peter the news and a big thank you. Peter tells him since he has trained the staff to help with the horses and knowing that he is still on Mr. Lynch's time clock, he should take the rest of the day off. Peter reaches out his hand to shake Cahey's. "Welcome to the Exchange."

41

He is too excited to just go back to his hotel but does not know where to go. He drops off his packages and then heads out again. He decides to go around the Murray Hill area. What he sees are huge mansions between Fifth and Park Avenues and brownstones between Park and Lexington Avenues. The stables and carriage houses serving these wealthy families are between Lexington and Third. The neighborhood has many trees and formal gardens. Now that he intends to stay in New York, he needs a place to stay, but this area looks expensive and exclusive. He has to remember, he is Irish.

He returns to the hotel and again seeks out Sharon. He locates her near the lobby as she is just getting off from work. He quickly stops her by standing in her way. As she realizes who is in her way, Cahey says, "I want to go to a *ceilidh*."

"You do, do you?" She has loosened her hair from the bun she always wears and her black hair hangs straight down around her shoulders.

"Yes, I got a job today and I want to celebrate." Cahey knows he is being giddy but he is relieved at having a job and wants to relax—what better way than to hear music?

"Just so happens there is always one on Saturday nights. Come with me down to the Lower East Side; I'll show you a *ceilidh*."

"Let's go."

Sharon turns to go but pauses and asks, "Can you dance?"

"Can I dance? I'm from Connemara. Just you wait, you'll see."

The two of them quickly walk their way down the street. Cahey is full of energy that pulls Sharon in.

"I'm ready for some music," she says. They walk together avoiding others on the busy sidewalks. "Where were you born in Ireland?" she asks.

"Mannin Bay outside of the Maumturk Mountains in Connemara. Do you know where that is?"

"No idea," she says almost out of breath with their quick walking.

"It is a couple of days ride on horseback north of Galway. And you? You are Irish. Where were you born?"

"I was born in America. Mum and papa arrived and I was born almost immediately," explains Sharon. "I would like to go to Ireland one day."

"But you speak Irish; how did that happen?"

"Mum and papa speak Irish at home. That's all we have ever heard inside the home. Outside at school, I learned English. And good that has been, too, or I would never have gotten the job at the hotel. They want English-speaking staff."

They stop on the sidewalk. "We are here," says Sharon.

The *ceilidh* location is a hole-in-the-wall saloon on the Lower East Side. Cahey hesitates at the door. Sharon grabs his arm and gently tugs him inside.

"My papa is playing the melodeon at a *ceilidh* here tonight," she says as they enter into a dimly lit room full of people, who are all talking, drinking, and walking about.

They arrive in time to find a table and two chairs near the dancing area. A quadrille has lined up and the musicians are about to begin. The music notes are quick and the dancers move. The music gets faster and faster, and the dancers twirl and swing, confident of their moves. After that dance, Sharon gets up and whispers something to her papa. He nods and looks up at Cahey.

"Ladies and gents, tonight we have a young man in our midst just coming from Galway. I'd like you to give a warm welcome to Cahey."

Sharon points out Cahey to the patrons and everyone turns and applauds. Cahey blushes but touches his cap in a thank you.

"And I understand that this young man knows the Connemara step dancing and is willing to demonstrate it for you tonight."

The crowd applauds loudly. Cahey is not standing. He simply smiles and shakes his head no. Sharon comes over and gently pulls him out of his chair.

"Do you know Kilgary Mountain?"

Cahey nods.

"Okay, then,"

The music starts and Sharon's papa sings:

As I was a-walkin' 'round Kilgary Mountain
I met with Captain Pepper as his money he was countin'
I rattled my pistols and I drew forth my saber
Sayin', 'Stand and deliver, for I am the bold deceiver.

Musha rig um du rum da
Whack fol the daddy o
Whack fol the daddy o

There's whiskey in the jar.

Cahey dances hard and fast. His feet fly, his kicks are high, his back is straight, and his arms are at his side. He has learned to dance on a door at the crossroads. Connemara steps are all in one area and the dancers don't move around the dance area. He still imagines the area the size of a door. When the tune finishes, Cahey makes a slight bow and hurriedly sits down at the table with Sharon, but the music starts up again with a reel and Sharon grabs his hand and pulls him onto the dance floor. The song is "Strip the Willow" and there are four couples in each set. The dance is repeated until the original couple is back to the top. Cahey wipes his hands on his trousers. But before he can retreat again to the table, the music begins with a military two-step. Sharon is standing in the middle of the floor. He walks to her and puts his arm around her waist and she places her hand on his shoulder. They begin with the heel, toe, heel, toe, walk forward three steps, turn towards each other to face in the opposite direction and repeat the steps. Facing each other, they join hands and bounce on both feet then kick the right foot across the left, then repeat with the other foot. They then polka around the room for eight beats of the music. The dance seems to go on and on. Cahey is tired in a good way. Though he gets a lot of exercise working with the horses and walking around town, this is different exercise and he is feeling how stiff his muscles are. Finally, the dance is over, and Cahey sits down.

"That was fun, and yes, you can dance," says Sharon, leaning with her elbows on the table to catch her breath after all the dancing.

Cahey leans back in his wooden chair and laughs with gusto. It feels good to finally release the stress of leaving Ireland, crossing the ocean, taking care of the horses, and living in a new country. The dancing is good, the music is good, and Sharon is fun. Life is good, he thinks, for now.

During a lull in the music, Cahey leans toward Sharon. She has become his source for information. "Since I am staying in New York, I need a room to let, where should I look?"

"There are few decent places with so many people coming into the city. When the Ninth Avenue train, the El, went into the West Side, it was thought that they would be building decent places for people to live. The whole area had been a farm owned by John Somerindyck, who had once farmed, fished, and hunted on that land. Instead businessmen bought the land and created cheap tenements west of Broadway."

"Okay, that's where I should not look. Where should I look?"

"Look around Murray Hill and see if there is not a boarding house with a room to let where you can also eat your breakfast and dinner and save on cooking." She is quiet for a moment, then leans back toward Cahey so he could hear her over the music. "There's a gent down in the laundry room that was talkin' about someone he knew had a room to let. Shall I ask him the details?"

"Yes, definitely yes," says Cahey. "I walked around Murray Hill this afternoon and though the area is nice, I don't think I will be able to afford it."

"There are areas where some of the mansions have been turned into boarding houses," says Sharon. "I will ask on Monday."

The night ends. They part at the corner and Cahey continues on up to the hotel. He is more relaxed than he has been in a long, long time. New York may be good for him and he thinks he now has two friends.

42

Though it is late in the evening, Cahey telegraphs Mr. Lynch with his new work plans and his decision to stay in New York. He then sits down and writes letters to Seámus, Colm, Michael and Sheila. He dashes off another note to Séan and Sophie, who had telegraphed him as to how to reach them in Boston.

Cahey goes to post his letters. At the hotel desk, he already has a message back from Mr. Lynch congratulating him on his new job and telling him to take his time moving out of the hotel; he owes Cahey a lot for seeing that the horses got to Mr. Vanderbilt safely.

First thing on Sunday morning he goes to find Frederick; he has news to share. As he walks toward 37th Street, Cahey begins to see the city, not as a newcomer, but as a place where he might find his future. He sees the influx of newcomers, immigrants just like him, coming into the city every time he passes Grand Central Depot. He sees the construction going on up above 42nd Street and now Sharon tells him about the new tenement houses being built on the West Side. There is business to be made here in New York and he intends to make some of the business his.

Frederick is out on a photography job with his boss, so says the young boy Cahey had seen that first evening when he and Frederick arrived. Little John Chaney tells Cahey that Frederick is to be back before long and to feel free to wait. Cahey thanks him but says he'll drop back in later to catch Frederick. Touching his cap to the young boy, Cahey swings out into the street and searches for the pub where Frederick and he had been just last week. He does not recognize anything so he goes into another saloon in the Bowery. The minute he steps inside, the raucous nature of the men having a pint on a Sunday morning, playing darts, and hanging with their buddies is suddenly quiet. Cahey pauses at the entrance. The bartender looks up from wiping the wooden bar with a dirty rag. "Hey, Red," he says, "we don't serve the Irish here."

Cahey stands still. The bartender repeats his refusal. "Red, get out of here. We don't serve the Irish here."

Two brute-looking men stand up near Cahey and move toward him. Cahey is frozen in his feet. He doesn't want the men to know he is frightened by them, but he also is taken aback by the hostility he feels in the room. As he pauses, the two men pick him up, open the saloon door and toss him like a sack into the street. Laughter follows him.

Cahey pushes with one hand to stand up and begins dusting off his clothes. As he grabs for his cap that has fallen into the street, a carriage rushes by and squashes the hat under its wheels. Cahey stands looking at the flattened, dirty hat when he hears the carriage driver yell back at him, "Get out of the street!" and sees the driver crack his whip in the air.

"Cahey, is that you? What's happening?" Frederick comes up to Cahey in the street.

"I'm fine. Just fine." Cahey picks up his cap and slaps it against his pants to loosen it up.

"What happened?"

"They don't like the Irish in that saloon."

"I had heard that there are those about. Mr. Chaney has pointed out a few that even I, being Scottish, should not go into."

"Do you have more work to do? I need to walk," Cahey says.

"I'm finished for now."

"Sharon at the hotel and the men at the stables told me about the North Side and the new train area and land ready for development. Let's see what they are talking about."

The two men head uptown. As they walk, Cahey notices that here is a lot of land still open for development. However, near the train tracks at Ninth Avenue, the smoke is dense and the train rumble is loud. The tracks are raised high above the ground on wooden trestles and under the trestles there are meadows much as they must have been before the train tracks were built. As they walk along the bottom of the trestles up towards 60th Street, the barnyard stench is strong. He can see the trains stopping to unload livestock at 60th Street. Though there is a great park stretching many blocks to the north, huge armories line Broadway from 67th to 68th Streets. Then, surprisingly to Cahey, he sees an enormous equestrian school at 66th Street off the great park. With Cahey's experience in taking care of horses, he is pleased to see that horses are the primary means of transportation in New York even with the trains coming into the West Side and to the Grand Central Depot. He stands a minute and looks about.

Frederick interrupts his thoughts. "Let's go eat, I am ravenous."

"Ravenous?" asks Cahey. "You tote a camera around all day and are not in muck up to your knees taking care of horses and you call that work?"

Frederick grabs his friend's neck in a soft choke hug and pulls him down the road to a saloon he knows is safe. They sit at a table near the center of the room and as the smoke and people spin around them, the two men catch up on their plans.

"I've been offered a job at the Exchange," says Cahey.

"That's great news for me, but why wait until now to tell me —we have walked up the West Side and back and you did not say anything!"

"I needed to walk after the tossing on the street and to get rid of my anger."

"I understand, but now that you are definitely staying, this Sunday we need to go out and have a little fun to celebrate being in New York."

"Sitting having a meal with a friend is not having fun?"

"There's just so much to see in New York," says Frederick. "Like the Eden Musée."

"A musée?"

"Yes, a musée," says Frederick. "It's just down the street at West 23rd Street. There are displays, real life size ones made in wax but they look real. There's one of Queen Victoria and a scene from the Spanish Inquisition."

"The Spanish Inquisition was a long time ago. No one who is alive now could have been there to see it."

"This is imagined, Cahey. Think creatively," explains Frederick. "And we don't know, but any number of famous people might show up. They tell me that Sitting Bull has been there."

"Really?" says Cahey.

"Really," says Frederick.

Cahey pauses. "Who is Sitting Bull?"

"Cahey, you don't know anything about America, do you?"

He admits he knows little. He has read only about what has been happening in Ireland through copies of *The Nation* published in America and shared in Ireland. But before he can learn about his new home, he needs to find a room where he can live and begin his life in America. The men finish their dinner. Outside of the saloon, they agree to meet on Sunday to visit the musée.

"I heard it has an admission charge of fifty cents. It'll be the best fifty cents you will spend in New York."

Cahey isn't so sure, at least not yet, but he agrees to go. "Until Sunday."

43

A week passes quickly. He wants to find Sharon to check on getting a room. This is Saturday, and he is getting a bit nervous by running up the bill at the hotel for Mr. Lynch. He returns to the hotel after work and looks for Sharon in the hallways. He should have just gone straight to his room because when he opens his door, Sharon is waiting for him.

"I thought you were going to be forever" is how she greets him. Cahey is taken aback that she should be there, but she does have access to the rooms with her keys. "If you want to see the room, you best come with me right away. Do you have any money on you should he want a deposit?"

Cahey nods yes. He had gone to the bank earlier in the week to make money transfers from Ireland.

As they exit the hotel, Sharon heads south and walks about six blocks, then turns left toward the river. Finally, she stops in front of what must have been a wealthy home. It has all the trimmings of money: the stoop, the columns, the tall windows overlooking a small but well-trimmed front garden.

"Here we are." She goes up the steps and uses the knocker. A short man with quite a paunch opens the door.

"You must be Sharon, come in. And is this the young man I got word was coming by to look at the room?" The man's cadence of speech reminded Cahey of home.

"Yes, this is Cahey."

Both men shake hands. "Come in. I am Thomas. Thomas O'Toole. Come in, let's go back to the kitchen and sit. We'll have a cup-a tea."

Mr. O'Toole guides them through the long hallway to the back of the house. The doors that are open display a sitting room with heavily upholstered couches and divans, as well as a dining room with a long table circled with matching wooden chairs and a large cabinet at the end of the room. Portraits line the hallway. Other doors are closed and have numbers attached. They enter a large kitchen that has two worktables, an oversized wood stove, and myriad pots and pans hanging from hooks dangling from the ceiling like metal carcasses in a butcher shop. A woman as rotund as Mr. O'Toole stirs pots on the stove, clanging lids and tossing spoons back into a pottery dish. She bounces around the kitchen standing on tiptoe to reach dishes in the cupboards and then stooping to pull cutlery out of low drawers.

"Mrs. O'Toole, please meet a new young man just from Ireland, Cahey. Ah, I didn't get your last name."

"Ó hArrachtain. Cahey Ó hArrachtain, ma'am." Cahey takes off his cap and gives Mrs. O'Toole a short bow.

"Well, that will never do," she says. Cahey puts his cap on and takes a step back toward the hallway entrance.

"What are you saying, Mrs. O'Toole?" asks her husband.

"We bring nice young Irish men into this home so they can adjust to this new world. He will not adjust well with a name like Cahey Ó hArrachtain. No one can say it. You know, Mr. O'Toole, how hard it is being Irish in this town."

"Not to worry, we'll change his name. Not to worry. Here, sit at the table and let's get a little information," says Mr. O'Toole.

Cahey pauses. Sharon tugs on his arm and they sit at a table. Mr. O'Toole gets a ledger from a shelf and joins them. "Now, Cahey, let's address the name right away. Cahey. I know —to the Americans it sounds like the letter 'K' and the letter 'A.' So we can write K.A. for your first name." Mr. O'Toole puffs out his chest a bit with the idea for the initials.

"What does the K.A. stand for if someone should ask?" pipes in Mrs. O'Toole from across the room as she takes a large loaf of soda bread out of the oven.

"People don't ask in America," he explains. "It is fine as it is and something he can answer to easy enough, but it could stand for Kenneth or Andrew."

"Or Kildare," pipes up Sharon. Mrs. O'Toole bustles away to the stove and Mr. O'Toole goes on. "Now the last name is more difficult." He thinks with the pen almost touching his lips, which are small on his oversized face. He silently mouths Cahey's last name, over and over, until he says, "I have it: Harrington. That sounds similar, doesn't it, Mrs. O'Toole?"

"Yes, actually, that's quite nice. K.A. Harrington. Quite nice," and she slices the bread.

Cahey looks on and glances up at Sharon, who is smiling and nodding her head as well. "Very nice, really," she says.

Mrs. O'Toole brings over a platter of the sliced bread, a jar of jam, and a dish of butter. She pours tea into four cups. "Do you take milk in your tea, K.A.?"

Over tea, Mr. O'Toole finds out where Cahey is from, his background at the distillery, and his new job at the Exchange. They agree on a price for the room, which includes breakfast and dinner except on Sunday night.

"Mrs. O'Toole visits her sister on Sunday afternoons so there is no dinner served at the house," explains Mr. O'Toole.

There are ten rooms to let. The front sitting room can be

used in the evenings and on weekend afternoons for reading. The dining room is where the meals will be served. Mr. and Mrs. O'Toole live in the rooms down stairs to the right of the front door. There are two rooms to let on the bottom floor with the other eight rooms on the second and third floors. Each floor has a bathroom and must be shared with the other boarders. Cahey nods in agreement, but Sharon nudges him and then turns to Mr. O'Toole. "I think he would like to see the room."

"Yes, yes, of course. Come this way." Mr. O'Toole leads Cahey and Sharon up the front steps to the back room on the first floor. He opens the door to a large room with bed, dresser, a divan under the window, and a large armoire against the far wall. On the dresser is a wash basin with a towel rack. There is even a table with two chairs by the door entrance. The room is immaculate with faded blue willow motif wallpaper, blue linens on the bed, and blue-flowered curtains on the two windows overlooking a back garden. To Cahey, it is perfect, the nicest room he has ever had. He shakes Mr. O'Toole's hand, gives him the first month's rent, and gets a key that works in the front door and another key for the room. He will move in tomorrow.

As they walk away from the house, Cahey thanks Sharon for all her help.

"Happy to help," she says, then she smiles. "I like it that you now owe me and I can collect with my dance card." They both smile, and Cahey is certain he has another friend in New York.

Sharon parts at the street corner; she is going south to where she lives in the East Village. Cahey returns to the hotel to prepare a telegram to Mr. Lynch.

"Staying in NY to work at Exchange. Contact K.A. Harrington at 234 East Houston Street." He pays to have the telegram sent. He goes up to his room to write a few letters. Colm, Michael, and Seámus need to know his plans. They also need to know his new name.

Though it is late on Saturday night, Cahey has a lot to think about. He pulls out his papers on how he thinks about the Irish and begins to write about the Irish in America, at least the experiences he has had being Irish and meeting some Irish folks. He writes long into the night. He falls asleep only to wake up with Frederick pounding on his hotel door. He had forgotten his agreement to go to the musée and now he must settle into his new room. He talks Frederick into helping him move. With only his rucksack and the new clothes, it will be easy. Frederick would then know where to find Cahey. Frederick is disappointed, but he agrees and Cahey is spared going to the musée, for now.

44

At work on Monday, Cahey is cleaning the horses' feet. He picks up one and the horse gives a little shake. Cahey puts down his brush with the intention of giving the horse a little time. He sees Tommy.

"Tommy, you seem to know your way around New York. Do you know where I might find a reading room?"

"Yes, I do," says Tommy. "Several years ago, my sister was part of a sewing class at Grace Church. While they waited for their teacher, one of the girls would read aloud a story from what the teacher thought was a cheap paper. The teacher heard the story and made an offer to loan a book to the girls for one week if they would not buy the cheap paper."

Tommy goes on to tell how the idea caught on with more women teachers interested and five hundred books were collected to loan to the girls. A room at 13th Street was found and was opened once a week for two hours. People came, so many in fact that the entrance was blocked and once there were only two books left in the room. An article appeared in the *Evening Post* about the room and how children and older men along with women from all over the city came to borrow books.

"Seems like many people want to read, even if they can't afford to buy a book," says Tommy.

Cahey is interested—a room with five hundred books.

"No, now they have more than 1,500 books," explains Tommy. My sister took her exams and became an assistant there to learn about how to keep the books and check them out to people."

"Where is this room?"

"On Bond Street, 49 Bond Street. Ask for my sister, Theresa. She works for Ellen Coe, the librarian. It's a great place; it's called the New York Free Circulating Library."

The days go by quickly; Cahey's work expands to include an entire wing of the stables. He is learning new things about how horses are auctioned and how they are bought in America. Many horses pass through the Exchange; the Percherons are being imported as popular draft horses with more than 7,500 horses passing through the Exchange and sold into other areas of America. Cahey's work expands rapidly.

He settles into a routine of living at Houston Street, seeing Frederick for some Sunday dinners, and going to the reading room to find out about what is happening in this new country where he is living.

He reads newspapers, books on early explorations in America, and financial articles on what is happening in America. He learns that the president of the United States, Grover Cleveland, marries Frances Folsom in the White House. This is a big deal in the *New York Herald* with photos and detailed descriptions of the wedding. Cahey explores the city, attending openings of special stores with Frederick taking photos. They go to the opening of the Statue of Liberty, a welcoming icon to people arriving in New York. They missed seeing it being erected since they came into the country at Boston. He and Frederick go to the new Madison Square Garden complex built by architect Stanford White, who is said to have an apartment there. Rumor has it that the building cost three million dollars. They see the boxing and then return there later for the Barnum and then the Ringling circuses. Cahey is amused by Frederick's desire to see many different things but likes having a friend who wants to have fun.

Cahey meets Sharon down in the Lower East Side for a Sunday visit. Seeing the area in the sunlight, he is not impressed. People are living on top of people there. The houses are ramshackle, side-by-side, with filthy stoops and ropes of clothes drying from many windows. Rats run in the gutters, as children with threadbare clothes stand in doorways and watch him pass. Sharon lives with her papa, mother, five sisters and two brothers in three rooms up four flights of stairs. Cahey climbs the four flights of stairs. There is little light in the stairwell. Many of the doors are open to rooms of other residents. Each is as threadbare as the next. When he gets to Sharon's rooms, he meets her mother, who is sewing in the corner with little light. She does piecework for a shop owner. Her papa is at the pub where he plays cards and makes a little extra money singing with his melodeon. Her brothers are out; no one knows where they might be. "They might be in later," she says. She is the eldest girl; five others who look like little duplicates run circles in the front room.

Cahey sits with his cap in his lap and asks about school for the sisters and work for Sharon. There is no school for the sisters; they can't afford the school. All the girls help the mother with the piecework and have only been to school for three years. Sharon actually went to school for six years because the mother was working as a cook at the time and the other girls weren't born until Sharon was nearly twelve. For those years it had been just her brothers and her, and her mother needed her to go to school so she could go to work. But when money got tighter with the larger family, Sharon needed to find something to help out. That's when she got the job as a maid at the hotel.

After a while, Cahey running out of things to talk about suggests that they walk down the street. Outside he offers to treat should they find some fish to eat, maybe shad, and try that new drink a Coca-Cola. Sharon agrees and as they leave the front of the house, Cahey looks up to see all the sisters standing at the window looking down at them.

Cahey and Frederick are having a drink in the pub near Frederick's room. Cahey tells him about where Sharon lives and how difficult it is to see those living conditions.

"We had no money where I grew up, but the cottage was clean and Mum mended our clothes and found ways to make our lives better. Where Sharon lives is dirty and depressing."

Frederick has been to the Lower East Side on assignments for his job. He shares with Cahey what he has heard. "There is a photographer, Jacob Riis, who takes photographs of the conditions in the Lower East Side," says Frederick. "Riis uses graphic descriptions, sketches, photographs, and statistics to describe the people living in the tenements."

"Why does he do this?" asks Cahey.

"Riis blames the apathy of the wealthy for the slums and has said if these wealthy people knew the conditions, they would make changes," explains Frederick. "At least that is what Riis says; therefore, he goes about taking photographs to show others the conditions in the tenement areas and how bad these conditions are for people trying to live there. He uses flash powder to photograph interior views."

"Why does he care?" pursues Cahey.

"He, too, is an immigrant, from Denmark," says Frederick. "He is a police reporter on a beat in the Lower East Side and sees how people are living in the tenements. He wrote a book, *How the Other Half Lives*, and he is one of the earliest photographers to employ halftone reproductions successfully. I have studied his work. He taught himself how to take photographs, and I am learning a lot from what he writes about."

Cahey wants to learn more about why Riis spends so much time trying to right wrongs for others. He thinks he has not seen that kind of social concern for others, but then he remembers how the men banded together in the reading room in Galway to make reforms to the system of rents in Ireland. They used pamphlets and essays to make their points; Riis uses photographic images as instruments for social change. There are a lot of wrongs in Ireland. To Cahey, the issues around immigrants appear to be directed toward him, as he is Irish. But here are people from many different places who have other ideas about issues affecting immigrants in America. Cahey begins to read more about what the Irish who live in America think about. His questions in the reading room lead him to discover that most of the Irish newspaper editors in America had been leaders in the failed Young Ireland's attempted rebellion in 1848 and sought safe exile in America. They wrote about nationalism in Ireland but had little to say about anything happening in America.

45

A new year begins with a fresh snowfall in the city. His time at the Exchange and learning to live in the city has flown by. How so much time can move so quickly astounds him. The months dash by with work and turn into several years with new ideas every day. Now early in January of 1890, Cahey walks through the snow to the Exchange to check on the horses. He sees how tranquil the city can be with a heavy snowfall. No one is on the street. There are no coaches sailing past him with the horses going at a break-neck speed. The street cars are not running. All is quiet. Quiet. The quiet makes him remember. He remembers the wagon ride from Ballinasloe and the quiet with everyone asleep but him, and the horseback rides on the beach with Micil then out into the countryside. He remembers sitting under the trees and listening to Micil tell him stories. He even remembers a song he once sang.

One morning early I went out
On the shore of Lough Leinn
The leafy trees of summertime,

And the warm rays of the sun,
As I wandered through the townlands,
And the luscious grassy plains,
Who should I meet but a beautiful maid,
At the dawning of the day.

He hums the song as he walks in the snow. Soon, in the quiet of the holiday morning, he sings the song out loud. When he finishes, he feels good. He feels Irish, but then he feels sad all in one breath. There is much to see and much to do in New York, but he misses the Irish fields, the river that runs by the distillery, and the friends he made along the way. He misses buying horses at Spancil Hill. He misses all of that. He has also learned through his friends at the reading room that Gladstone's Home Rule bill was rejected. The Finians tell him that Parnell is accused of supporting the brutal murders of the Chief Secretary for Ireland, Lord Frederick Cavendish, and the Parliament Under-Secretary, Thomas Henry Burke in Dublin's Phoenix Park.

Then the Finians tell him that the letter printed in *The Times* in Dublin accusing Parnell was actually forged by Richard Pigott, a disreputable anti-Parnellite rogue journalist, but the damage has been done.

By the time he gets to the Exchange, he is feeling gloomy. Then he sees the horses, hears their neigh greeting, and feels the world he is creating in America. He cannot feel sorry for himself; he has no time to feel sorry for himself. He must be busy creating his future. He plans on checking out the Morris Park racecourse to be opened in Westchester County just north of the city. He is interested in how the horses and spectators might get there. With the new railroads crisscrossing the city, maybe a new rail spur could connect the racecourse with one of the railway stations; that was the rumor circulating at the Exchange.

When he returns to the house on Houston Street, he finds several letters tucked under his door. He goes to the table and spreads the letters out. There is one from Colm, one from Pádraig, and one from Séan and Sophie. He chooses to read Pádraig's first.

Dear Cahey,

I would love to write and tell you that all is well with us, but that is not the case. Papa has been ailing more and more and is not able to do many of the things he has done before. He has no energy and, on a weekend, he sits about reading the Bible you gave him and not wanting to be involved in any of the family activities. He has actually been down in bed for several days last month and unable to go into the harness shop. Papa keeps saying he is fine, but Mother is worried sick and suggested that you need to know how bad things are with him. Hope America is good for you. We would love to see your face on this shore. Business is better than ever. I have taken over most of your accounts from papa and work closely with Michael and Colm. I am sure you are aware of that already. Please don't tell papa that I wrote you about his news. You know how determined he has always been to be the strong person in the family. Write soon.

Pádraig

The letter did not ease Cahey's longing for Ireland. Here is the man who is most like a papa to him not doing well. He walks to the back window and looks out over the snow-covered garden. Strange shapes emerge of plants and shrubs being covered by snow. He thinks about Seámus and all that he had been doing for Cahey's business interests in Galway. Remembering that he had a letter from Colm, he goes back to the table.

Dear Cahey,

I know you have a letter from Pádraig about Seámus and his

health. I wanted to write to assure you that the business ends have been kept up by Pádraig and you have a substantial amount in your account from his good judgment. I am preparing a report for you to arrive shortly after the new year so you will know where your accounts stand. I have every confidence in Pádraig's abilities. He has been trained by his papa, a very competent man, for sure.

On other matters, I am sorry you could not be here for the christening of our second child. He is an amazing little boy. Our oldest loves Colleen with a passion. He asks to ride Colleen all the time when we go to the pasture to check on her after I come in from work. You will be pleased to know that he calls her Colli since he can't seem to get the 'reen' out yet.

As to politics, there is a new party formed which might interest you. It is called the Ulster Unionist Party—something to do with home rule. You may have already heard that Gladstone's bill failed.

Look for the accounts soon.

Colm

Without waiting, Cahey opens the third letter from Séan and Sophie.

Dear Cahey,

I hope all is well in New York. The fishing has been busy in Boston, but Sophie and I wanted to tell you the good news. I have been asked to join a fleet of seamen in hunting whales off the coast. I will be out to sea more often, but Sophie says the extra money and the time I will be at home will be worth it. The babies are doing well. Sophie takes good care of our two little girls. Who would have thought we would have twins? One at a time is what I say. We would love for you to come up for a visit. I know the journey is long and work is busy, but it would be good to see you.

Take care and happy New Year.

Séan and Sophie

Cahey folds each of the letters and puts them back into their envelopes. He goes to the dresser and opens a box where he places the letters, but before he closes the lid, he sees the essay he had written back in Galway on what it means to be Irish. Rereading what he had written that resulted in his having to leave Ireland and come to America has made him even more homesick than before. What does it mean to be Irish? He sits down and begins to write.

46

N ew York in the 1890s is an exciting place for Cahey. Through his persistent reading, he is learning about many new businesses starting every day. The Cathedral of St. John the Divine opens its doors for worship. William Henry Perkin creates the aniline dye and brings mauve color into fashion. New York establishes a ten-hour workday. He remembers the long hours he put in at the distillery and is thankful he lived on the premises. He is not sure he could have had a household to feed and take care of while working those long hours. He admires Seámus for being able to have his family and the work. Thousands of new people are pouring into the city. Changes are happening so rapidly it is hard to know what tomorrow will even be like. With the new railways coming into town and the gas engine automobiles rapidly replacing horse-drawn street cars and coaches, there is a need to diversify. Cahey has built a reputation at the Exchange for being a solid horseman, one who understands what makes a horse work hard for the owner. In that role, he has developed quite a list of clients who use him to evaluate horses, and he assists in training these horses, especially for the new race-course just north of town. He is gaining a reputation for his medical knowledge of taking care of the horses. Cahey sees that horses may not be around to transport people, but he feels certain that people will want to see a horse race.

Along the way, he also has assisted with the auctions that make money for the Exchange. At the auction where horses and cattle are sold, Cahey stands at the back behind the ropes that circle the arena. Many of his fellow stable workers stand with him. They are there to make sure everything goes smoothly. Cahey and Peter are there to verify that the animals being auctioned are of the quality advertised. Heinemann Brothers, the Chicago Horse and Carriage Company, Gold-smith's, as well as Peter C. Kellogg & Company are all present with animals to sell. As the bidding begins, the auctioneer stands behind a podium up on a block at the far end of the arena. Cahey looks out over the men bidding. Some of them he recognizes from photos in the newspapers or from Frederick pointing them out at events since he has made photos of many of them. These men stand out in the arena with their dandy coats and stylish hats, and they all carry walking canes. These canes are used to mark their bids as they raise them in the air. The auction takes more time than Cahey likes to give, but it is part of his job. He does learn that some animals have a higher bid based on the verification that is given from Peter and his assessments.

Cahey's knowledge of the Shires enables him to be in charge of any of the draft horses that come into the Exchange including the Percherons from France. He doesn't know a lot about these horses so he visits the library. He finds out that during the 1600s horses from Perche, the ancestors of the current Percheron, stood between 15 and 16 hands high. These horses were almost completely gray. Paintings and drawings from the Middle Ages almost always showing French knights on gray horses. Cahey knows that this means that the horse has a black skin and white coating. They will turn completely white when they age. He reads that after the days of the armored knight, the emphasis in horse breeding shifted to develop horses better able to pull heavy stagecoaches at a fast trot. Gray horses were preferred because their light coloring was more visible at night. This new type of horse was called the Diligence Horse, because the stagecoaches they pulled were named diligences.

Then one day, Cahey is asked to help with the coach belonging to Vanderbilt's son. He talks to Peter at the Exchange about the request because he has no idea what this is all about, and if he had learned anything from going to the fairs in Ireland, it is to ask questions first.

Peter is helping Cahey massage the Shires legs and explains the Coaching Club. "For entertainment, the sons of most of the wealthy businessmen in New York drive coaches up into the countryside for a day's outing. To create more of a sport and have rules and regulations, three men formed the New York City Coaching Club and came up with the rules."

Cahey is listening in the next stall. "Who is are the men and why did they want to do this?"

"The men are John Scott, Col. William Jay, and Col. DeLancey Kane," says Peter. "Scott has a house on 43rd Street and he is known for breeding horses. The more flamboyant member of the business group is Kane, who has a yellow coach he brought over from England that he calls the Tally-ho; the name caught on so that all road coaches are called Tally-ho." Peter explains that each member of the Coaching Club owns a coach and several changes of horses. Alfred Vanderbilt has seventy-one trotters as well as grooms, trainers, stables, and rented stables along the northern route frequented by these rich sons. Peter moves to the next stall to resume his work with the horses.

Cahey isn't finished. He is thinking that he could see more of the countryside if he went on the ride. "Where does the route go? What is the process?" He has to speak up because Peter is now two stalls away.

"The route goes from the Holland House Hotel on Madison Square to the Ardsley Country Club owned by Frank Gould, twenty miles north. A halfway point is a popular roadhouse called the Old Homestead owned by a man called Stryker, a friend of prominent horsemen in the city."

As Peter seems to be finished with his description, Cahey repeats, "What is the process?"

"I forgot, sorry. The men start out early morning, taking paying passengers for the ride. The coaches are meticulously outfitted since the club has a massive number of rules on every last detail such as where items are to be hung and accepted color schemes to every last detail. The men drive the coaches up to Ardsley, have lunch and drive back to Manhattan. I'm curious. Why were you asked to go? They have plenty of grooms who can make the journey."

"They want me to verify how the horses handle the load, the terrain, and the journey. The men, I have been told were horsemen before they were coach drivers and want only the best care for their horses."

Peter takes his cap off and wipes his face. "Good luck with it then. What day will you be gone?"

"On a Sunday. Not to worry, I'll be here to tend to the horses."

On Sunday, he goes on his first trip with these wealthy young men. Cahey sees the Tally-ho, and as the men stand around, several paying guests arrive. When all have entered the carriage, he is told that his seat is at the top with the driver. Quickly he learns that there is a pecking order to New York society and he is not part of that order. He also learns that money does not stop creativity. The men are always looking for new ways to enjoy a horse-riding experience. They do not limit their ideas to what exists but think of things they haven't tried before. These outings with the wealthy sons of New York businessmen create a desire in Cahey to work harder to make it in this new country. He begins to go on many of the trips and listens to how they plan them and how they discuss them. Though the men do not include him in their lunches nor in any other social event in the city, he is paid well and often asked to join them on their route. They tell him that he is good for business. He always inspects the horses and evaluates the stress put on the horse to pull the carriages for long distances. Additionally, he doesn't feel compelled to go and goes only when he feels he has the time to invest in this new sport. The money he earns is housed in a side business that he calls "Horse Sport." He advises investors on horses to buy for pleasure, horses to race, and horses to use for specific work. The trips he takes with the Coaching Club has given him additional clients and good references.

As his side businesses grow, he learns of Sharon's talent. Though she did not go far in school, she is a natural with numbers. They go to many of the *ceilidhs* on the Lower East Side. This time he invites Frederick. They have several rounds of ale and some pretzels. Other people join them and Cahey wants to pick up the tab. He asks Sharon if she has an estimate of what the bill would be. She takes a moment but then gives Cahey a figure. When the bill comes, she is to the penny accurate. Cahey is eager to find someone in New York who can do what Colm does back in Galway. So, he asks her if she would be interested in learning from Colm how to keep Cahey's books in New York. At first, she says no; her confidence in doing the job, she says, is low. Cahey assures her that Colm will train her and guide her in everything she needs to know. When Cahey tells her that she will earn a percentage of what he makes, she agrees to try. Colm will send her the sheets, and she will keep track of what Cahey spends and what he brings in with any new business. To Cahey, the relationship is business, even though Sharon tries to lure him into a conversation of "will he ever marry?" The conversation never goes further than the question.

Cahey continues to look for ways to grow his business interests. Many people are investing in the railroads. People at the Exchange talk about it every day, but Cahey resists following the Vanderbilt model. He has other ideas of where his strengths may be. What he knows best in New York is how to take care of horses. He thinks that even as the streetcar and railroad take over much of transportation, there will always be a place for horses in sport. He has heard all about the hottest sport in New York: the Morris Park racecourse north of the city. Cahey wants to visit so he can see if what he knows can be used at the racecourse. Accessible by horse and buggy, the racecourse includes a railroad spur being built by the New Haven and Harford Railroad near the Van Nest station to bring people from the city to the racecourse. The track, fourteen furlongs with an iron grandstand, some 650 feet long enough to accommodate 15,000 attendees, opens on August 20th, and Cahey wants to be there.

Opening day arrives, and Cahey with Frederick take the first train up. Though Cahey has been working with several trainers in keeping the horses healthy, his investment is in a clinic of sorts where he thinks he might be helpful during the race in case a horse is hurt. Horses kick other horses, kick themselves, run over horses, and fall into fences along the way. He has his bag of ointments, medicines, and bandages just in case.

As Cahey is looking around, Frederick goes to get a good

look at the track and begins taking photographs. Another train arrives. There is much laughter as a group of six exit the train; all eyes turn to the women. The three women are each in white gossamer gowns trimmed in dark blue or red or yellow with large, matching picture hats, perfect for a day at the races. Each carries a white parasol with matching ribbons trimming the edges. Their hands are casually placed on an escort's arm as they gingerly step from the train and make their way to the stands. Two of the girls have brown hair; the third has blonde hair the shade of golden sunlight. Cahey cannot stop looking at her. She notices him and coyly glances his way but then turns her attention back to her escort. They walk on.

Cahey sees Frederick stop to watch them pass as he returns from the track.

"Hey, did you see those ladies?" Frederick asks.

Cahey says nothing.

"Yeah, I guess you did." Frederick picks up his tripod and dashes down in front of them. Cahey doesn't stop him but watches what he does. "May I take a photograph?"

The ladies laugh and the men shake their heads no; but, the lady with the blonde hair stops. "Of course, you may."

She adjusts her gown and begins to pose as Frederick sets up his camera. The other ladies walk on and the escort pauses but continues also. Frederick takes his time adjusting the camera.

"Where may I send a copy?" he asks when the photograph is taken.

"Send it to 26th and Madison."

"And to whom should I address it?"

"To Stanford White. Tell him it is from Evelyn." She gives him a quick nod of her head, hands him coins from her purse, and joins her friends in the stands.

Cahey stops staring when a young man nearly knocks him down. "Why the hurry?"

"I'm late. I'm to warm up the horses, and I am late." He dashes on.

Cahey knows people are excited. He has heard that Isaac Murphy, a Black jockey, just won the Kentucky Derby and he is to be racing today. People are here for the festival atmosphere, or to be seen, or to bet and make money. Cahey's reason to be here is to greet the riders and groomsmen. These are the people who would recognize if something is hurting a horse and would bring it to the owner's attention; and then, they would refer the owner to someone who might help. Cahey is hoping it will be him. He spends some time talking and working the stalls. There are a lot of stalls, hundreds in fact. It takes him an hour to just glance at all the horses. He looks at the legs, the knees, the hooves, the flanks, the neck, the ears, the mouth, everything that would give him clues on how well the horse is groomed.

As he pauses in front of one horse, a rather stout two-year old, he sees the jockey in the corner of the stall sprawled out on a cot. The young man is pale and not breathing regularly. The groom is brushing the horse.

"Is he okay?" Cahey nods toward the jockey on the cot.

"He says he's fine. I don't know though; he hasn't eaten since yesterday."

"Does he need food?"

The groom glances over at the jockey. "What he needs is another job; this one of keeping his weight down is going to kill him."

"You mean he is not eating so he will not gain weight?"

"Yes, the horse is at the weight limit, so for him to ride he must be light."

Cahey looks at the jockey then back at the groom. "Mix the feed with straw that has stems and walk the horse around a lot. The roughage will help the horse lose some of the weight without damaging what he needs to stay healthy."

The groom looks at Cahey and his bag, like a doctor's bag. Nodding his head the groom says, "Thanks, I'll do that."

Cahey walks on down the stalls and goes to the fence for the first race to begin. He glances in the stands and sees the blonde-haired lady looking at him. She smiles. The race begins and all eyes are on the horses, except for Cahey's.

47

At the beginning of the week when he returns to his room, Cahey finds a letter under the door from Séan. He hasn't heard from Séan and Sophie for a while.

Dear Cahey,

I write because things are bad here. The weather has limited our fishing time. I am trying to find anything I can do to make it here. The fishermen who have taken us in and trained me in the ways of the Boston coast are in just as bad a position. Gale after gale keeps us land side. I don't know how we will get through the winter. The girls are both down with a fever and Sophie has her hands full. She takes in sewing and does all she can to share the burden. If you would be coming this way, this is the time to come. We need a bit of cheering up.

Séan and Sophie

Cahey sits on the bed and rereads the letter. Immediately he grabs his cap and is out the door. He goes to the bank and wires money to Séan with a telegraphed note.

Can't come right away; am sending the train fare I would have spent. Use it for your health and your family's. Stay well my friend. Cahey

He has a meeting to go to that night, so instead of returning to his room, he begins to walk the streets of New York as he often does when he is thinking. He remembers the first time he saw Séan and Sophie and is reminded that a friend's roots of Ireland go as deep as the family roots. He has no idea where his brother or sisters might be. They all lost contact so many years earlier when they went their separate ways.

The meeting has started by the time he arrives. Men are talking about Parnell. Charles Stewart Parnell is seen as one who could unite Ireland, yet the Irish Parliamentary Party split when it was discovered that Parnell was having an affair with Kitty O'Shea, a fellow MP's wife. But something else must have happened; there are a lot of people talking at once.

A bowlegged man stands on a chair. "Listen, men, listen to me." Voices quiet in the room. "Parnell is dead." Men stand silent as the bowlegged man explains. "He addressed a crowd on the Galway/Roscommon border in the pouring rain; a week later, he died. They say he died of a heart attack as he lay in Kitty O'Shea's arms." Men murmur and shuffle their feet as they stand. "The funeral is to be day after tomorrow." The bowlegged man gets down from the chair. Cahey leans against the doorframe and waits like all the others.

A man in the front asks, "What can we do now to unite Ireland?" Silence fills the space. "What can we do?" he repeats with a heavy heart.

One by one, the men mill about the room; some find a place to sit, others simply move to another place to stand. No one is quite sure what they need to do. Cahey crosses the room to seek out an older friend he has had a few conversations with when he is stopped by one of the men.

"Cahey, what say you? You write. Write us an essay to explain how we can unite Ireland. Write it so we can read it loud and clear. Write it so we can feel it down to our roots that pull at us from Ireland." The men in the room pick up the request and there is much agreement that Cahey must write something.

Cahey manages to get over to his older friend. "And you, what do you say to this?" he asks.

His friend nods and smiles. "I agree. Write an essay, my friend; write an essay."

The walk back to his room is a thoughtful walk. If he writes an essay to encourage Ireland to reunite, what would he say?

Cahey sits at his table and stares at the paper and ink. Whatever will he write? He sits until the tea in his cup is cold and the stars are peppering the sky. He sits with the blank paper in front of him. The week passes and every evening he sits at the table with the paper and ink.

At the reading room he learns about Parnell's funeral in Dublin where 200,000 people came. He learns that a wreath of ivy was sent by a Cork woman as the best offering she could afford. The mourners then took ivy leaves and affixed them to their lapels to honor Parnell. Finally, he begins to write.

We, the Irish people residing in America, wish to remember the struggles of so many of our countrymen who have lived through the battles and those who have not. We come together in America to try to determine a way to unite the Irish. Political parties have not been successful. The clergy have not been successful. Fighting with the British has not been successful. And now the death of a great leader may or may not be success-ful. What will it take to bring peace and independence? More bloodshed? More violence? More sacrifice? What will it take? We must think back and remember what makes us Irish. We are Irish because of our birth, our heritage, our traditions, our language. We have deep roots that go back centuries. Though others may conquer our land, our laws, our religion, they cannot conquer who we are. We are Irish to the bottom of our soles. And though the mourners of Parnell wear ivy, let us don the shamrock and lay the foundations for a new Irish land in our hearts and souls. To unite Ireland, we must learn how to live in the present, today, here and now. A united Ireland is wherever an Irish man succeeds. If we work together, the Irish will be strong no matter where he lives.

Cahey finishes the essay. He lets the ink dry and goes to bed. He is to meet up with Frederick early on Sunday morning.

48

Frederick is waiting outside the photography shop when Cahey arrives on Sunday morning. He is pacing back and forth.

"What's up, my friend?" asks Cahey. "I am not late, yet you look agitated."

"I have had a bit of bad news. Let's walk."

The two men turn and begin walking east. Cahey adjusts his stride with Frederick's rapid pace. After a few blocks, Frederick begins by saying, "I have to get out of the dark room in the photography shop. I can't live like this anymore."

Cahey is listening.

"I need a place to live where I can sit inside and share a pint or have friends over for a meal, a real house, something with roots and permanency. I have to get out of that dark back room." He stops and turns to face Cahey. "I do not want to do it alone. What if we went in together to buy a place that we can afford?"

"Well, that sounds fine for now, but what happens to me when your fiancée comes?"

"She's not coming." Frederick keeps walking.

Cahey pauses and Frederick stops. "She wrote me that she has decided to stay in Scotland. She met someone else, she says."

"I see."

The men stand on the corner, not crossing, not even looking, just standing.

"I have been saving up for a place and I want to have a place to continue my life here, but I don't want to be alone with that. If we found a place that we could both afford that would offer each his privacy yet still be a home, that would be nice, yes?"

Cahey immediately thought about Micil. He had wanted just such a place, a place where Michael and Sheila would come, as well as the Kellys, who had been so welcoming to him in their home, but that was long ago. Now all he wants is a roof over his head and a bed to sleep on. But if he intends to stay in New York, he must think about building more than just his bank account. An investment in a house might be just what he needs to put new energies into his staying here.

"Yes, okay. Let's find a house to buy. But let's look on the Upper East Side."

The two men clap hands on their shoulders and walk toward Murray Hill, which was built on the homestead of an Irishman. There are rowhouses there, which may be good. The two men spend the day walking through the Murray Hill streets. Some of the houses have been converted into apartment type places and others are single family homes with servant quarters rented out. Exhausted from looking but still hoping, they chance upon Sniffen Court, a small alley of mews that runs between 36th Street and Third Avenue. Here there are ten two-story brick stables with living spaces above. The stables in the area were often built separate and away from the main houses. One looks empty. Cahey thinks these are perfect. Frederick leans over laughing.

"I should have known that we needed a place for a horse, just in case, eh, Cahey?"

"Yes, just in case." Cahey enjoys the laugh as much as Frederick.

They ask at a neighboring house and locate the broker to find that One Sniffen Court is indeed for sale. Negotiations cannot be continued until the workweek when the banks are open. The broker comes and the men are shown inside. The rowhouse is 3,700 square feet, costs $2,500 with fifty dollars down and the balance payable as rent. The stable area has a wide double door leading out to the alley. Two stalls are on one side and an open area where the cart could rest is on the other. Stairs are up the inside of the stables to the upstairs living area. There are two bed chambers, a parlor, a kitchen with a wood stove and pantry, and a dining room. The house has plumbing and a water closet located between the bed chambers in the back of the house where a hallway had been. Each room has a fireplace. Cahey and Frederick agree, this will definitely work for them. Half the stable area could be converted into a photography studio for Frederick and the other half an office for the two of them to keep their accounts and for Cahey to have a separate place to write his essays. The men are excited when they leave. Cahey gives the owner an IOU to hold the house until the banks open on Monday.

"What say you? Let's celebrate by going to the races. I feel lucky today," says Frederick as he saunters down the alley. And they are off to the Van Nest station to take the spur to the Morris Park racecourse. Cahey wants to feel lucky too; maybe he'll see the blonde-haired woman again.

⁓

The races have started by the time they get to the racecourse. Frederick did not bring his camera so he tags along with Cahey to check out the horses. They walk down the stalls repeating Cahey's previous strolls where he introduces himself, identifies the horse, talks with both the groom and the rider. At one of the stalls the groomsman recognizes Cahey.

"Hello, I see you are checking out our horse. Everything is fine here; her leg has healed completely."

"Ah, I did not know she had been injured."

"Yes, she was kicked by another horse. Aren't you the gentleman who takes care of the horses and makes them healthy again?"

"I have been known to work with a horse and groomsman to assure healthy horses, that's for sure, but I have not seen this horse. How do you know about me?"

"Tommy from the Exchange told me about you and to keep an eye out for you if you should come by. I come in and out of the Exchange checking on horses."

"Who's the horse's owner?"

"Mr. Croker."

Cahey knows who Mr. Croker is and wants to leave quickly. The men at the Exchange have shared information about him. Richard Croker, better known as "Boss Croker," is an Irish American political boss who leads New York City's Tammany Hall. The men were teasing Cahey about being Irish and told him that he should get acquainted with Mr. Croker and all of Cahey's problems would be solved. Cahey knows that would only be the start of major problems, the kind of problems he is trying hard not to be part of. "I see. Well good to talk with you." Cahey turns to leave when he runs head on into a burly man standing just behind him. "Pardon, I did not see you."

"Obviously."

Cahey touches his cap and moves to the side to pass by.

But the burly man stops him. "Aren't you K.A. Harrington?"

"Yes," says Cahey, and Frederick, who had been standing to the side, moves closer to Cahey.

"I'm Patrick O'Neal. I work for Mr. Croker, who is in search of someone to check out his horse. This one was kicked by another horse."

"The groom told me."

"Well, take a closer look. Mr. Croker will be most appreciative." The burly man blocks Cahey's exit.

Frederick starts to speak up but Cahey cautions him back with his hand. "It's okay, I will be happy to take a look."

The groom opens the stall door. Cahey and O'Neal enter the stall. Frederick waits outside and listens as Cahey talks to the horse in a low tone and begins stroking the horse's face and neck. Cahey explains to the horse that he is going to take a look at the injury. He says all of this in Irish.

"Talk so I can understand," says O'Neal.

"It's not you that needs to understand." Cahey leans over and examines the healing leg. He sees that the leg is not quite healed to the point where the horse should run. If the horse gets kicked again, or if the wound starts bleeding from the impact of the race, the horse could have more serious injuries. He stands and ponders what to say.

"Well?" O'Neal is impatient with Cahey.

"I assume that because the horse is here you have every intention of running the horse today."

"That would be correct."

"The wound is healing but is not sound enough to run the horse today. I would scratch the horse and let the leg fully heal."

"Mr. Croker isn't going to like that."

"I have some ointment but did not bring it with me. If you come by the Exchange, I will be happy to give you some to treat the horse." With that, Cahey tips his cap and exits the stall.

Frederick grabs Cahey's arm. "Let's go watch some of the races. Remember, this is our lucky day." The two men go to find a good spot to watch the races but stop to buy a gambling ticket from one of the bookies, just in case it really is their lucky day.

The first race they see is clearly one that is worth viewing. August Belmont's horse, two-year-old Padishah, is a four-to-one favorite. However, Burlington, ridden by Pike Barnes, beats Devoree by a full length, and Padishah is still another length behind Devoree. Burlington earns $8,560 that race. The men are thrilled to see the win since Padishah had been assigned a heavier weight than all the other eight horses in the race.

As they stand waiting for the next race to organize, both men decide to walk down through the grandstand to view the race from the other end. The crowd is loud and boisterous. Men clap other men on the back, laugh, and point to the finish line. Just as the two get midway down the 650-foot-long grandstand, Cahey looks into the stands and there is the blonde-haired woman. She is with a different guy this time. She sees Cahey and smiles. Cahey tips his hat and walks on.

"Are you crazy?" asks Frederick.

"What?"

"Do you know who that is?"

"The woman you took a photo of that we saw before at the races."

"Yes, she gave me an address and a first name. She is Evelyn, Evelyn Nesbitt, Stanford White's mistress."

Cahey turns red from his hair roots to his neck but doesn't break his stride. "Really?"

They watch as the horses line up behind the barrier to begin the race. Cahey reaches out and holds onto Frederick's arm. "Look, there is Mr. Croker's horse. They are running him anyway."

The jockey perches on the horse with his lunge whip in ready position. The bell rings and the horses are off. Cahey watches as the horses move into the turn. The jockey positions his horse in the middle of the pack and they round the bend.

The hill at Morris Park prohibits them from seeing the horses until they gallop around the next bend and aim for the finish line. As the pack of horses round the final bend, suddenly there is silence from the grandstand. One of the horses has gone down and has thrown the jockey headfirst into the oncoming horses. The horses speed by leaving the horse and jockey crumpled in the dirt. Race officials run out to the track. Grooms come to help with the horse. The horse is Mr. Croker's. There is no doubt that the jockey is dead, crushed in the chest by the horses' hooves. The horses move at forty miles per hour and each weigh around 1,200 pounds.

Cahey climbs under the fence and joins the group around the horse. The horse's leg is bleeding heavily; tendons are showing from the gash. Cahey takes control. He calms the horse as best as he can, and then using cloths the grooms brought with them, he ties up the leg and encourages the horse to stand. Cahey guides the limping horse off the field and passes a gurney being taken in to lift the jockey out.

"Serious injuries like this can be avoided," Cahey mumbles out loud to no one in particular.

Suddenly Mr. O'Neal is walking along side of Cahey. "We would like to have your word that you will say nothing to the press about looking at this horse prior to the race."

Cahey stops. "Sir, that would be a lie."

"Yes, but one that could make you a very wealthy man."

"I don't want your money."

"But you need our protection if you wish to continue to work at the racecourse." With that Mr. O'Neal steps ahead of Cahey and greets the press hovering around the wounded horse and groom. Cahey turns and goes back to the grandstand to find Frederick. As he nears the gate, the blonde-haired lady is standing with a woman friend talking with Frederick. Cahey pauses and debates silently whether or not to join them. He steps into their line of vision.

"Cahey, come meet Evelyn and her friend Marie."

Introductions are made and Cahey tips his cap to the women.

"Cahey is an unusual name," says Marie, speaking more with her brown eyes than with her voice.

"Actually, it is K.A.; my friend here just has a Scottish brogue," says Cahey not looking at his friend. He does look at Evelyn and turns to look at Marie when she asks, "Are you the one that people are calling the 'horse doctor'?"

Cahey shakes his head, "I'm just seeing that horses stay healthy."

Suddenly they are interrupted by a young groomsman dashing up to Cahey.

"Mr. Harrington, come quickly. You must help. The horse is wild with panic and pain."

Cahey turns swiftly and follows the groom. He shouts over his shoulder, "Frederick, meet me at the stall."

At the stall, Cahey pushes past several groomsmen and riders to find an enraged horse, kicking and snorting. He walks to the doorway and begins talking to the horse. Slowly the horse stops kicking and just snorts and shakes his head. Cahey moves closer to the horse—not touching him. The horse watches carefully, ears flattened back. Cahey continues to speak to the horse. The crowd is silent, watching the man in the stall. Step by step, Cahey gets closer and closer to the horse, still not touching him. Finally, the horse and Cahey are nose to nose. The horse snorts and backs away. Cahey talks on and steps gently toward the horse; again they are nose to nose. The horse snorts, then when Cahey does not move, the horse puts his head on top of Cahey's head. Cahey begins to stroke his neck and face. In a soft voice he instructs the groom, "Bring me clean cloths, hot water, a clean pan and salt." The groom disappears.

Cahey slowly steps over to the hurt leg and examines the wound. The horse is snorting and his eyes are wide open.

When the groom returns, Cahey ties a tourniquet above the wound to stop the blood. Then he takes the hot water and cleans the metal pan. He pours more of the hot water into the pan and adds salt to make a solution. With another cloth he begins to clean the wound. Once the wound is clean, he takes yet another clean cloth and bandages the wound to keep it clean. He releases the tourniquet. "The bleeding, hopefully, will stop, but the bandages need to be changed and the wound cleaned with a solution of salt and water until it begins to heal. Dry the wound after cleaning. A dry wound will heal faster than one kept wet, but it has to be kept clean." The groom nods.

Cahey turns to find a crowd of people outside the stall with Mr. O'Neal at the front, who tips his hat to Cahey and turns away.

Frederick steps up to the stall door. "We won on the last race," he says. Cahey nods to him, looks back at the wounded horse, then at the back of Mr. O'Neal as he walks away.

"I guess it is our lucky day," he says.

49

During the next months of 1891, Cahey is busy both at the Exchange and setting up the new house. He and Frederick move into the house on Sniffen Court. Cahey is spending time with Marie. In spite of warnings from Frederick, on their train ride back into town from the racecourse, they find themselves seated with Evelyn and Marie. Though Evelyn flirts with both men, Marie corners Cahey for a conversation. Cahey is taken by her dark beauty and the confidence she seems to have that everyone likes her. Somehow, and Cahey is not absolutely sure when it happened, he agrees to have dinner.

Marie is quick to tell Cahey of all the interests she has including being actively involved in the burgeoning New York theatre. She coaxes Cahey into attending theatre openings, light operas at Madison Square Gardens, and then walking in Bryant Park where many New Yorkers walk to be seen. She takes him to the opening of the Olympia Theatre at Broadway and 44th Street. The massive limestone building with its French Renaissance design hosts plays and concerts; the roof garden is a perfect place for a light supper before a performance. In preparation for other outings, Marie talks Cahey into going shopping for some of the latest men's fashions. He soon owns several suits, jackets, and a hat. They attend fashion shows at Henri Bendel's shop on West 57th Street. Bendel, a milliner who is all about what is new and next in fashion, brings Coco Chanel to America from Paris. Marie is always excited about Bendel's shows. Cahey goes to please Marie.

As the men are putting the finishing touches on the office downstairs, Frederick reminds Cahey of Marie's friend, Evelyn, and the people they try to impress. Cahey doesn't listen.

"Marie is charming, pleasant to look at, and knows lots of people, people who are in business and who I need to know to be in business."

"Ah, so this is a business arrangement and not love?"

"What? Love? Don't be silly, Marie can only love herself; she goes out with me because I am always willing. You are the one, Frederick, who always wants to try something new, something different, have a little fun. What are you doing to have a little fun?" Cahey looks squarely at Frederick.

"Nothing," says Frederick. "My friend, who used to go out and do things with me, is busy with someone else."

Cahey sighs. "You can come with us; you are always welcome."

"I thought you were courting her so I didn't want to intrude."

"Courting? No, Frederick, I am not courting Marie."

There is a pause while Frederick places a box of stationary on the desk. "She thinks so."

The men go up the stairs to hang new photographs that Frederick had framed to add to the ones already hung. Cahey is silent as he sees the photograph of his mum's and papa's wedding; the photograph of Seán, Sophie, and Cahey on the ship arriving in Boston; and the one of Frederick's parents back in Scotland, people who have been in their lives. He regrets that he does not have photographs of his Galway business partners or Micil. When they finish, Cahey grabs his cap. "Let's go get food." Frederick is close behind him.

As they walk past Grand Central Depot, they see the newspaper headlines. Every newspaper in New York displayed at the kiosk has headlines in 46-point type, boldly across the top: RAILROADS GO BANKRUPT.

Cahey and Frederick stop and buy the *Herald*. Cahey shakes the paper towards Frederick's face. "Here, this is something to worry about, not whether Marie wants to be courted or not. Who can have a family with times like these?"

"I agree. Hopefully we have enough in the bank to ride out the worst."

"Yes, if the money is there when we need it."

Frederick stops in the middle of the sidewalk. "We can always go back home."

"Maybe you can. I have nothing there but a few friends with lives that are moving along with families and businesses without me. And I have some really tough guys who would love to see me gone."

"What tough guys?"

"Ah, it seems as though I wrote an essay on what it means to be Irish and a guy beats me up and two more came to finish the job, but I got whisked away on bringing the horses over to America."

"That's why you did not know how long you would stay here in New York."

"Yes, that's why."

Cahey is focused on the news in New York. There are twenty English language newspapers in New York at the time, and all of them create such panic that New Yorkers run to take their money out of the banks. The National Cordage Company goes into receivership with 15,000 companies and 500 banks failing. Unemployment soars to between seventeen and nineteen percent of the population. All over the city, people who built glorious Victorian houses simply walk away from them when they can no longer pay for them. These haunted houses stand silent all over town. Some people blame the economic depression on silver with the Sherman Silver Purchase Act and McKinley Tariff. Everyone agrees that things are not good.

Cahey's horse business suffers. No Percherons arrive. People cannot afford to purchase or to take care of these big horses. Bicycles enter the market and horses are being replaced by electric trolley cars and automobiles.

Fortunately, Cahey has diversified his interests; he has invested in the new Coca-Cola product by purchasing a failing chemist shop in Murray Hill where he gets supplies to treat his horses. The shop simply needs more activity so he adds a counter where they can sell Coca-Colas and simple sand-wiches. This purchase also gives him stock in the new company. He doesn't know anything about stock values, but he wants to experiment and this is a good time to invest since prices are so low.

He also keeps his consulting business going by working with owners of racehorses and pleasure horses to keep them healthy. This money keeps them all going during the thin times. As the hours at the Exchange shorten due to the economy and the replacement of horses by electricity, Cahey focuses on taking care of horses and is the first person called upon to diagnose a sick horse, but then the bottom falls out.

Cahey is on his way to work at the Exchange when he hears fire bells and sees people running in the direction of the Exchange. He hastens his steps. As he approaches, he smells why the bells are ringing: the Exchange is on fire. There are 265 horses in the Exchange. Near the building, he can barely move through the crowd. Thousands upon thousands of people are watching the building go up in flames and they hinder the firemen getting to the building. Horses are wild and stampeding through the crowds. Smoke pushes the people back. Cahey tries to get closer but a policeman stops him.

"Can't go in there."

"But I work here; I take care of these horses."

"From the likes of what I see, there will not be many alive for you to take care of. Stand back."

Cahey backs around and when he sees the policeman looking the other way, he dashes through to where the firemen are working. He grabs some rope one of the firemen has dropped on the ground and rushes forward to stop a frightened horse, which rears up and crashes down just inches from Cahey. He swiftly wraps the rope around the horse's neck and guides him over to a safe rail and ties him up. Then he grabs another rope and snags another horse. He continues this until he has nearly twenty horses lined up on the rail, all frightened, all terrorized by the flames and the smoke. He begins asking some people in the crowd to give him scarves. No one will give him one. Finally, an elderly lady with a cane comes to him with hers. "Thank you," he says and dumps the scarf into a bucket of water and ties it around one of the horse's eyes. Once the crowd sees what he needs to do, others volunteer, wetting their scarves and giving them to Cahey to bind the eyes of the horses.

Cahey observes the horses along the rail. There are only twenty. Where are the other 245? He is sure some of them are running through midtown. He saw some of them barrel through the crowd.

The police estimate the crowd to be more than six thousand people. The flames are hot; could the horses get out of their stalls?

At the end of the day, when the flames are out and the building is in ruin, Cahey learns that sixty horses died in the fire. *The*

New York Times reports that through the windows, "crazed animals could be seen dashing blindly about in their terror." Others have been caught and are being held in various locations around Longacre Square. Cahey sees Tommy coming toward him.

"Come to the corner lot in the morning for a meeting," he tells Cahey.

The walk home is troubled for Cahey. He keeps seeing the injured horses. He picks up his pace and gets to the house. Inside he has ointments and medicines to help the horses; his collection for the racehorses when needed. He places as much as he can carry in his rucksack and turns to head back out when Marie shows up at his door.

"I just heard the news. Are you okay?"

"Fine, I am fine."

"Where are you going? You have a cut on your forehead and another on your arm."

Cahey reaches up and touches his forehead. He is totally unaware that he is injured. "It's nothing."

"It's bleeding."

"I am fine. I must go." He dashes down the street leaving Marie at the door.

When he nears the Exchange, he sees people still milling about and takes in the pungent odor of the burned building and dead horses. He moves to where several of the Exchange workers are forming a barrier around the building to prevent looting until everything gets sorted through. Cahey starts down the street to the various stables where the horses are being kept. As he moves along the street, finding horses being held in various stables and yards, he looks over each horse and takes care of any abrasions or burns to the horse. He then gives instructions to each caretaker on how to calm the horse and where he, Cahey, can be reached should they need him. As the evening becomes night, people find him and show him other horses. Many were rounded up from where they ran all over midtown and are being kept in the reservoir in Bryant Park. He hurries over to the park and sees the number of horses. Every bone in his body hurts. His arm is aching from the gash, but he doesn't slow down. He approaches each horse and goes over the horse carefully to see if there are any wounds or burns. The night turns into dawn and he is still treating the horses. As day breaks, so do the skies. Rain comes down in sheets. Cahey is soaked as he heads back to the corner lot for the morning meeting.

Men huddle under a makeshift tent but become silent and move out of his way as he enters. They have heard how he has spent the night taking care of the horses. They guide him to a crate to await Roger Malcolm. As business manager, Mr. Malcolm is handling all the interactions between the employees and Mr. Vanderbilt. Danielle brings in tin cups of coffee and passes them around among the men. As they wait, Cahey begins to shiver.

"Get him a blanket," cries one of the men with whom he has worked. They throw it around his shoulders.

"I will take him home," says Danielle. "He needs to rest." With that she stands Cahey up and marches him down the street. "You have to tell me where you live."

Cahey points the way. As they near the house, Frederick comes out and helps Danielle get Cahey up the stairs and into the kitchen. Frederick heats water and the two of them clean Cahey's cuts, bandage his arm, and then guide him into his chamber where Frederick helps him out of his clothes and into the bed.

~

Cahey opens his eyes and sees that there is light coming into the room. He has no idea what time it is. He moves to get out of bed and feels his body aching. He gently touches his bandaged arm and remembers Frederick and Danielle taking care of it. He dresses and goes into the dining room. A note is on the table from Frederick.

Rest up, Cahey. I'll be back after an assignment. Frederick

Cahey makes a cup of tea and sees that it is late in the day and he has slept many hours. He needs to go and check on the horses. He notices that someone has washed his smoke-filled clothes. They are drying near the stove in the kitchen.

50

For the next few days, Cahey finds Danielle at the house every evening working with Frederick on what they call her catering business plan. Danielle explains that she needs to find a new job, and Frederick tells him how he has pointed out to Danielle that with the Exchange burned and with Mr. Vanderbilt wanting to rebuild, they might welcome a caterer to provide meals for the crews who would be cleaning up the site and preparing it for being rebuilt. They both tell Cahey about Danielle's family.

"My family is from Villefranche-de-Conflent in the French Pyrenees Mountains. They came over to America to start a bakery. Other family members had emigrated and were encouraging them to come. When they got here," Danielle says, "they realized that they could not make the dream of owning their own business happen right away. Papa does work in a bakery and so does my mother, but they never can get the money together to open their own."

Frederick adds, "Danielle is the oldest of four girls."

Cahey gets the message of how the oldest has to help the family. The two of them, while Cahey had been sleeping, talked about drawing up a business plan of how much it would cost to produce meals for the workers and present it to Mr. Vanderbilt's business manager. Maybe he would front the money for the tent, tables, benches, and supplies they need. They think it would be a way to get the most out of the day for the workers.

Cahey smiles for the first time since he experienced the Exchange building fire as he enters the dining room and sees Frederick and Danielle head-to-head over the plan. They tell him that Sharon is to join them tonight and set up the bookkeeping.

"Then I will go and pick up something for dinner," says Cahey.

"Absolutely not," says Danielle. "If I am going to start a catering business, I best know how to cook. I will cook dinner tonight."

Something is simmering on the stove. Smells of food and sounds of conversation fill Cahey with satisfaction, yet longing. Though he and Frederick have hoped to fill their new house with friends who discuss ideas as a way to make their conception of the American dream come to realization, they had no plan on how to do it. There is a knock on the outside door. Cahey rushes down the steps; it is still early for Sharon to arrive.

When he opens the door, he finds Sophie and her twin girls standing with traveling capes and rucksacks. "Sophie, come in, come in." Cahey looks down the lane. "Where is Séan?"

The twins begin to cry. They are little girls, looking just like their mother when she was younger. Sophie stands still and does not enter. "Séan is gone."

"Gone? Gone where?" He shuts the doors behind them and picks up one of the cases.

"There was a storm; he was lost at sea. No one knows what happened; he was fishing with another boat that made it back, but Séan and his boat never washed ashore. I fear he must be dead. I had nowhere to turn. We were barely making it with Séan's meager hauls."

"Come in." Cahey takes the baggage from the twins and Sophie and sits them in the hallway. "Come in and rest. We will figure this out."

Cahey leads the trio up to the dining room and steps aside to let Sophie and the twins enter.

"Frederick, you remember Sophie from our voyage over?"

Frederick jumps up and as he starts over to give Sophie a hug, he realizes that something is wrong. He stops midway. "Welcome."

But before he can ask more, Cahey ushers the twins over. "These are Sophie's twins, Ceira and Caileen. They have just arrived from a long journey from Boston and probably need to rest some before dinner. I'll get them settled in my chamber and then they can join us when they are ready."

With that, Cahey ushers the three travelers into his bed chamber. "I hope this will be comfortable for the night. We will make other arrangements later. Here are quilts and another pillow. Maybe we can make a pallet on the floor."

"Thank you. I will put the girls in the bed for now and join you in the kitchen."

Cahey nods and leaves.

"What has happened?" Frederick is still standing. His face shows how confused he is.

"Seems that Séan is missing at sea and Sophie has no money and nowhere to go."

"Well, they have a place here," says Frederick.

"Are you sure?"

"Of course. We can turn the parlor into a chamber. We don't

use it much anyway. We are either working or in the kitchen or dining room."

"Maybe Sophie could be one of my cooks for my new catering business?" says Danielle.

Cahey stares at the two for a minute when there is another knock on the stable door. He turns and leaves to bring Sharon back with him and to bring the bags left in the hallway. As he explains what is happening, Sophie enters and everyone is introduced. Danielle takes over the kitchen and Sophie pitches in easily. Soon the two of them have prepared dinner and invite everyone into the dining room, including the twins.

As they sit around the table, Cahey surveys his new life and his friends. There is Frederick, who came to this new land with him and who is encouraging Danielle to share her catering idea with the other women. Danielle, who is energized with ideas for her new business, leans heavily on Frederick's expertise. Sharon, who is still working at the hotel but has much better clothes now that she is getting supplement wages from Cahey for doing his bookkeeping, is listening and making a few notes as they talk. The twins sit quietly and eat their stew, looking more and more like their mother than he even thought at first. And then Sophie, her face tired and drawn, the worry filling her eyes, folds her hands and listens.

"Eat up," reminds Danielle. "I have to know if my food is good enough to serve to others."

Dinner is finished and approved, dishes are removed, and the twins are put back to bed. Cahey sits at the dining room table alone with his head in his hands. Sophie joins him.

"Please, sit down," he says and stands to pull a chair out for her.

"Thank you for taking us in tonight. I did not know what to do. I had next week's rent for the cottage and instead of paying the rent, I packed up the twins, we walked to the train station and caught a train to New York. I had the address from your last letter so I got directions from the Grand Central Depot. I was so relieved that you were here when we arrived. I did not know how to contact you. I planned to send a telegram to the Exchange, but the telegraph office told me that it had burned."

Cahey catches Sophie up on all that has happened. They talk about the horses and the rebuilding and the things he is doing along the way. Then Cahey tells her that Danielle asked if Sophie might be interested in cooking dishes for Danielle's catering business.

"I need a place to live and someone would have to help with the twins," Sophie says. "Until that is settled, I cannot help." Tears began trailing down her cheeks.

Cahey reaches out and puts his hand over her hand. "Frederick and I want you and the girls to live here with us."

"Where?"

"We plan on turning the parlor into a chamber. As Frederick points out, we seldom use it anyway. I plan on moving into the parlor to give you and the girls the privacy of the bedroom with easier access to the bathroom. We can get a smaller bed for you and a bed for me. We'll put the chairs from the parlor down in the office on the first floor for a better working space. Plus, you can use the kitchen to help Danielle and the girls can be here with you."

"You make it all sound so simple."

"It will not be simple living with Frederick and me, but it is sensible. We know each other; we are like family."

Sophie cries and Cahey has no idea what to do. Danielle comes in excited about her new business plans. "Please Sophie, will you work with me? I need help."

Frederick is at the door listening to the conversation. Sharon edges around him and announces, "I want the large leather chair from the parlor to be at the desk downstairs. It's the most comfortable chair in the house."

Laughter flows and Frederick finds a bottle of ale. Danielle brings glasses. "We have to have a toast to a new business, new housemates, and new experiences."

There is another knock on the stable door.

"What's next?" says Cahey. "I'll get it." Cahey takes the stairs two at a time. He opens the door to find Marie.

"Ah, you are home. I heard laughter but didn't think you had healed enough to have a party."

"No party, just business friends and old friends. Come up and meet them."

Introductions are made but Cahey notices that everyone disappears. Danielle and Sharon go with Frederick downstairs to finish their planning. They say the proposal should be ready to go to Roger Malcolm in the morning. Sophie exits into the chamber to see about the twins. Marie still stands with her coat and bag.

"Here, please, take a seat. Would you like some ale?" Cahey stands at the side of the table.

"No, thank you." She takes off her coat and places it on a chair with her bag. She sits down at the table. "Well, this is a nice tableau. There are a lot of things going on tonight."

"It does seem that way, doesn't it?" Cahey smiles and begins to stack the used cups and saucers together on the table.

"You seem to have a full house."

Cahey motions with his hand to the chamber door. "Did you meet the twins? They are back in the chamber with Sophie."

"No, I didn't meet the twins. How long will everyone be here?"

Cahey pauses. "Frederick and I have invited Sophie and the twins to stay with us. We plan on refurbishing the parlor as a chamber."

"I see." Marie pauses then says, "Permanently?"

"At least until Sophie can get on her feet and we find out if Séan is lost at sea."

"And the other women?"

"You know Sharon keeps my books and Danielle is developing a business with Frederick and with Sharon and Sophie for that matter."

"Sophie?"

"Yes, Sophie will help cook for Danielle's catering business."

"Oh, I see. Well, do give me a card when they get them made so I can pass them out to some of the people I know who use caterers. They will have cards, won't they? The best caterers do."

"I have no idea, Marie. It is not my business; it is Danielle's with the help of the others. These are difficult times and friends must help friends." He reaches for the ale bottle.

"I totally agree. I just wanted to know the details and where I stand in the order of women."

"Marie." Cahey wants to stop her but she barrels on.

"Well, I have something to share as well." She smooths her skirts and then folds her gloved hands in her lap.

Cahey pours another glass of ale for himself. "Go on."

"I have been asked to be one of the Florodora Girls." She looks at Cahey with a smile on her lips.

There is a pause. Cahey sips his ale and then sits across from Marie. "And what exactly does that entail?"

"Well, there are only six of us in the show at the same time, though there are seventy women total who will be referred to as the Florodora Girls. The musical review is at the Casino Theatre on Broadway. We wear pink walking costumes with black picture hats and carry lacy parasols. The director is looking for women who are about 5'4" and 130 pounds and I qualify, plus I can sing. We sing a song, 'Tell Me Pretty Maiden.' It is supposed to be great."

Marie stops and looks at Cahey, who is staring at her. "What's wrong?" Marie asks.

Cahey shakes his head, sips his ale, and says, "Nothing is wrong, go on."

"Well, the name Florodora comes from the Philippines and is a perfume made from the essence of the Florodora flower. Isn't that wonderful?"

"Yes," says Cahey, with an even tone. "Yes, it is wonderful."

"You'll come and see the show, won't you?"

"Of course, I will. Yes." Cahey takes another sip of his ale.

51

Gradually life at Sniffen Court tumbles into some sort of routine. Frederick is off on photographic shoots during the day and many evenings. Though the economy is bad, there seems to be always something to record, something to remember in pictures so he has plenty of work to do. Sophie is at the house with the twins and she cooks dishes for Danielle's business. She has to have the food ready by ten in the morning, pack it and load it into a cart, and get the twins ready. Most days, Danielle meets her and helps take everything down to the corner lot near the Exchange. Roger Malcolm buys into the business idea right away. He already knows Danielle and her willingness to work; plus, it is a win-win to have food there for his workers. He is on a tight deadline and last winter was not so kind. He needs to get all the walls up so the men can work inside during the cold weather.

Cahey is watching all the comings and goings of his friends. Sharon shows up at the house after work. Most evenings she sits and has dinner with everyone before she heads down to her family's rooms on the Lower East Side. She takes the receipts for the supplies and posts them in the ledgers down in the first-floor office. Danielle gives Sophie any additional receipts so that they are all at the same place when Sharon drops by. Sharon always has a treat for the twins. "Just something I saw on the way over," she says, but everyone knows she has to go several blocks out of her way to the sweet shop to pick things up for the twins. The twins adore Sharon and want to sit with her when she does her books. At first Sophie says no, but Cahey helps move two small chairs into the office so they have a place at the desk. "They can practice their letters and numbers," Cahey tells Sophie, who has to agree as the twins dance down the stairs, asking myriad questions along the way.

Cahey is often out tending horses. He goes to the racecourse on the weekends and takes care of horses there. He works with the newly formed Jockey Club. Mr. George Wetmore started the club and began the national horse show of America in hopes of improving breeding of horses. The Jockey Club becomes the keeper of the American Stud Book. By working with Mr. Wetmore, Cahey has shared his knowledge with members to improve the health of the horses.

He also has a regular route for visiting each horse displaced by the fire. Mr. Vanderbilt has kept on most of his skilled employees like Peter, Tommy, and Cahey. Tommy and his staff see to the feed and grooming of the horses being stabled around the city; Cahey continues his caretaking of the horses.

As the economy improves, so do the coffers of all of the people housed at Sniffen Court. Frederick has an assistant and works with other young men to train them in taking photographs, and Cahey is training several young men at the Exchange to work with the wellness side of the horses. These trainees go with Cahey on his rounds and meet him at the racecourse. Danielle's business flourishes, and she has to take on several more cooks, people they know and trust, to provide food, as well as several servers. Sophie takes care of the house, and Sharon takes care of all the bookkeeping.

Cahey and Marie attend a new restaurant opening up in Little Italy at 53½ Spring Street. Gennaro Lombardi begins serving pizza in New York. The menu offers plain pizza, a pizzaret, and a pizza-bagel. Each cost five cents. Opening night is the night to be seen. Cahey picks her up in a rented coach. Marie is all dazzling in a long green gown with matching hat. Cahey, though in a stylish suit, is overshadowed by Marie. Since her debut as a Florodora Girl, people constantly stop them and ask for autographs; some who have cameras even take their photograph. When they get to the restaurant, there is a long line out front. Cahey pays the coachman and when he turns to walk with Marie, he sees that she has gone to the front of the line. People in line move out of her way. Cahey lags behind.

"Come along, dear," Marie says over her shoulder while smiling at the men gawking as she enters. Cahey follows.

After dinner, Cahey decides they should walk for a while; it is a beautiful clear night. Marie is talking and talking, rambling on about the restaurant. Then she stops. "You are not even listening to me."

Cahey is not listening to Marie. He is far away back in Ireland. He had heard that the Land Act passed in Ireland after so many fights and so many deaths. Many thousands of tenant farmers are now able to purchase the lands they had worked for so many years. If that had happened when he was younger, maybe his papa would be alive today.

"You are not listening to a word I say," repeats Marie.

"Sorry," says Cahey. "Sorry, go on."

"Well, Henri has asked if I would consent to him creating a perfume, a special fragrance."

"Henri?"

"Henri Bendel, you know, the fashion guru."

"Yes, yes, of course."

"Well, Henri asked and I have given it a lot of thought. We have developed an idea for a new fragrance that has the top notes of lavender and geranium with the middle notes of clove and the base notes of sandalwood, patchouli and oak moss. What do you think?"

"Sounds fine."

"We thought we would call it something to do with lavender, maybe Marie Lavender or Lavender Marie." She laughs. "We're not sure yet of the name, but it has to have lavender in the name since that is the top note."

Cahey continues to walk. "Don't call it lavender anything."

"We have to call it lavender something since it is the top note," Marie insists.

"I am asking that you not call it lavender. Pick another scent."

"Cahey, you are being difficult. I can't just call it something else because you don't like it."

"Why not?" Cahey stops in the middle of the walkway and looks directly at her. "Why not?" he asks again.

"Because of the top notes," she says and straightens her hat.

Cahey steps into the roadway and hails a carriage. When it stops, he opens the door. Marie turns and steps inside. Once she is seated, Cahey closes the door and gives the carriage driver Marie's address. Marie leans to the window. "You are sending me home?"

"Yes," Cahey says. "Yes, I am." He does not even watch the carriage leave.

Cahey walks home and goes straight to his box where he keeps letters from his friends and the essay on why being Irish is important. He takes the essay out and rereads what he wrote. He knows that his future is in New York for the time being. Yet he also knows that to be Irish in America he has to agree with *The New York Times* article that reported on Theodore Roosevelt's new book, *History of New York*. Roosevelt said that the citizens of the United States need to be Americans without prefix, "not Irish-Americans or German-Americans but pure, simple Americans."

Cahey knows what he needs to do. He takes the essay down to his office and prepares yet another essay on being Irish in America.

52

The next day, Cahey, with his essay in hand, goes to the American Irish Historical Society. There is a meeting scheduled for organizing a new Irish group called Sinn Fein, Gaelic for "we ourselves." As he enters the meeting room, he sees that the room is packed with people from all over New York, men whom he has met at the racecourse, at the Exchange, and at various outings with Marie. They nod and touch their hats to Cahey. The men appear to be middle-class Irish with money to lend to ideas. Mr. O'Toole is there: he pumps Cahey's hand and asks how everything is going. Cahey finds a seat but then everyone stands around him and begins singing the song penned by the editor of *The Nation*, Timothy D. Sullivan, a song most Irish consider as the unofficial national anthem.

> "'God save Ireland,' said the heroes
> 'God save Ireland,' said they all
> Whether on the scaffold high
> Or the battlefield we die
> Oh, what matter when for Erin dear we fall

"Never till the latest day shall the memory pass away
　Of the gallant lives thus given for our land
　But on the cause must go, amidst joy and weal and woe
　Till we make our Isle a nation free and grand

"'God save Ireland,' said the heroes
　'God save Ireland,' said they all
　Whether on the scaffold high
　Or the battlefield we die
　Oh, what matter when for Erin dear we fall.

At the end of the song, the men find seats, but the atmosphere has changed from one of business as usual to one of we have to get this done. Men are serious about uniting Ireland. As the rhetoric and emotions ebb and flow, Cahey remembers a similar meeting in Galway, one that introduced him to the ideas of Irish independence and Irish unity. That meeting seems so long ago, yet the sentiments and the intent of the Irish men gathered in this New York meeting hall are the same.

Various men speak and are applauded and encouraged by the audience. Then Cahey stands and moves to the front of the room. The room is loud and boisterous, aroused by the previous speakers. The presiding man who has organized the meeting raises his hands to quiet the room. "I believe Mr. Harrington has something to say." He nods to Cahey and backs up.

Cahey takes his essay out of his coat pocket and unfolds the pages. He reads his essay to the assembled men.

53

As Cahey enters his own house with Danielle, who has joined him for the walk at the end of their workday, he is greeted by Frederick saying, "You are late."

"Yes, I am," says Cahey, "but what a day, what a day. New stalls are ready so I had to go and get some of the horses and start moving them back into the Exchange. With all the motorized automobiles and the cable cars, the horses were a bit spooked and it took time. Then I—"

"Okay, you had a busy day," interrupts Frederick.

Cahey pauses as he places his cap on the hook at the door and turns to look at Frederick. "And how was your day?"

"Yes, well, I have something to tell all of you."

"I thought as much," says Cahey and sits at his place at the table playfully pulling the braids of one of the twins. "Uncle Frederick has something to tell us." The girls giggle and Sophie gives Cahey her "don't start" look. Cahey turns his attention to Frederick. "Yes, what is it?"

Frederick hurries over to Danielle and takes her hat and receipts and pulls out a chair for her. She sits.

"Well, I have been invited to attend the Alfred Stieglitz's 291 Gallery opening for photographs tomorrow night."

"That's great," says Danielle. "But doesn't Stieglitz usually show art?"

"Yes, he does, but there is a new movement that's been in Germany and Austria for years, but Stieglitz is now bringing it to America. Artists such as Rodin, Cézanne, Toulouse Lautrec, Picasso, Braque, and Brancusi were introduced to the American audience through Stieglitz's gallery. Now Stieglitz wants to legitimize photography as a fine art form."

"What is the new movement?" asks Cahey.

"Pictorialism." Frederick's excitement shows in how he pauses to let the word sink into his friends' ears.

Cahey watches as his friend beams with his shared information. "And?" asks Cahey, allowing Frederick to continue with his excitement.

"Pictorialism is a way to show photography is truly a fine art. He's calling these photographers 'Photo Secessions' with Edward Steichen, Gertrude Käsebier, and Clarence White exhibiting their work. These photographers use a high degree of craftsmanship in making photographic prints. They use exotic emulsions, fine quality papers, and painstaking techniques that produce effects in their prints similar to the work of the Impressionists."

Frederick is still in his lecture mode when Cahey interrupts. "So great, you have a chance to see these."

"And you. I have four tickets and want you, Danielle, and Sophie to go with me tomorrow night."

Frederick is looking at all of them as they stop and look back at him.

"What to do with the twins?" asks Danielle before Sophie gets a chance to ask.

Sharon is helping Danielle serve the table. "I can stay over tomorrow evening with the twins."

Sophie moves over to the stove near Sharon. "What do women wear to exhibits? I have only the dresses from Boston I wear every day. Nothing nice."

Sharon laughs and puts her arm around Sophie's shoulders. "I think maybe we should go shopping tomorrow. I have a Sears Catalogue downstairs in the office; we can take a look at what you might like before we head out. And we can take the twins on the outing after the lunch food is delivered." She turns to Danielle, "Sophie and I are going shopping tomorrow after the lunch food is delivered. Do you want to go with us?"

Danielle smiles, glances at Frederick and nods her head. "Yes, I can get the servers to clean up the tent, so it should be fine to leave a little early."

Sharon then looks at Cahey. "Are you interested in joining us?"

Cahey sees the smiles on the women's faces. "No, but I can see you know I have the funds to pay and will happily do so. My way of saying 'thank you'."

"Then it is all set," says Frederick, who sits and begins eating with relish. "Dinner is great, Sophie."

Cahey looks at his friend with a question but then sees how cheerful the women are talking about fashion and where to go to shop the next day. His day with the horses is left far behind. He pulls another braid on the twin nearest him. She squeals and dinner resumes.

Sophie gets up and goes over to the fireplace mantel. "A letter came for you today."

Cahey opens the envelope and reads. It is from Colm.

Dear Cahey,

I hope this letter finds you well. I write with bad news. Seámus has died. I am so sorry to tell you but you were always like a son to him. He has said so many times. He was buried yesterday. Pádraig is all but grown and is eager to take over more responsibility at the distillery, but that is another bit of bad news. The distillery is moving towards using the new trucks to transport the ale to the pubs. Mr. Persse feels it will reduce costs of taking care of the animals twenty-four hours a day and replacing them when they are injured or aged. So, more bad news, he wants to end your contract of using the horses to make deliveries. I need you to advise Pádraig and Michael as to what to do. I have talked with Michael and he said since Mr. Persse talked with me that I should be the one to write you. Please forgive such bad news and lots of it. I do not know how to help with this one. Take care,

Your friend,

Colm

Cahey is quiet. The friends around the table sense that the letter is the bearer of bad news. Cahey looks up and everyone is staring at him.

"Seámus, the man I told you about who was like a papa to me, has died. Colm has written to share the news with me."

Frederick stands and walks over behind Cahey and places both his hands on Cahey's shoulders. "I am so sorry."

"I'm fine, really. I know people don't live forever, but I am so far away and cannot help. I feel so helpless."

As he buries his face in his hands, one of the twins speaks up, "Uncle Cahey, are you okay?"

Cahey looks up. "Yes, I am fine, but there is other bad news. Mr. Persse, the owner of the distillery, is replacing the carts and horses with trucks. I have to do something with the horses and that means there may not be a job for Seámus's son, Pádraig."

Frederick moves and sits back down at the table. "I heard that there is a mechanic's school opening to learn how to work on these automobiles. It will be a big industry one day."

Sharon speaks next, "I saw in the *Herald* that there will be stations for gas and stations for repairs. That will be an opportunity for those who need jobs."

"Yes, but that is here in New York where everything moves faster than light. What about in Ireland?" says Cahey.

"If they have the trucks, they will need the same thing there," says Sophie.

Cahey agrees. Maybe Pádraig can get training in the new mechanics so he can take care of the trucks at the distillery and still keep his job. He has to think about all of these things, but he has to think quickly and respond to Colm and let Michael and Pádraig know what he is thinking. The first thing he plans on doing is to assure all of them that he will do something. The second thing is to contact Mr. Persse and ask his advice on what to do with the horses. The third thing is to find some way to get Pádraig the training he needs.

Cahey stands in the middle of the dining room in the midst of a whirlwind of activity as the ladies prepare for the exhibit's opening reception. All day at the house people have been coming and going. Cahey finds Sophie preparing food much earlier than usual. He leaves quickly to allow them space to get things done.

When he returns, he finds that they have gone shopping and are in the process of getting their new clothes ready for the event. Cahey and Frederick make haste to complete their toiletries knowing that the ladies would take over the bathroom. They remove themselves from the kitchen and the chambers and camp out in Cahey's office downstairs. Much activity can be heard from upstairs. The twins run about. The women call to each other from different rooms. Finally, one of the twins comes to the top of the stairs and calls out to the men to come up for dinner. Cahey and Frederick find the meal is on the dining room table with no women in sight.

Just as Frederick goes into his chamber to dress, Cahey hears Sharon call out as she comes up the stairs. She has books borrowed from the library for the twins to read. The twins come immediately knowing that she also has sugar treats from the sweet shop.

Cahey clears his throat. "I guess I better get ready." He goes into the parlor and shuts the door. He can hear Sharon talking with the twins and deciding which book to read first. When he emerges, he has on one of the latest suit fashions that Marie had talked him into buying. Sharon gives a whistle. Cahey grins. "Men can dress up too, you know."

Frederick appears in his best suit. "I don't get a whistle?"

Instead, Sharon asks, "Girls, can you believe this is Uncle Cahey and Uncle Frederick?" The twins continue to stare at the two men they have seen only in work clothes suitable for the stables and the photographic dark room. As the men wait for the ladies, Cahey updates Frederick on what he has accomplished that day concerning Ireland.

"I telegraphed Colm, Michael, Pádraig, and Mr. Persse. I assured the men that I am prepared to do what I can to help. I asked Mr. Persse for his advice. I have already received a reply. He suggested that I contact Mr. Lynch and ask if he would like to buy the horses. I thought that was a great idea, so I telegraphed Mr. Lynch right away. I am waiting to hear from him. As to Pádraig, I suggested that he locate a mechanics school nearby. Maybe there is one opening in Galway; and I would see to the fees. I am waiting to hear from him.

The men are silenced when Sophie in her emerald gown and Danielle in her blue plaid open the door to the bed chamber and come into the dining room. They have coiffed their hair and have woven in matching ribbons. The men stand up immediately.

Frederick steps over to Danielle. "You look absolutely amazing." Danielle takes his extended arm and together they go down the stairs.

Cahey is quietly looking on as Sophie gathers the twins and kisses them good night. She thanks Sharon for all the help she did in shopping and now staying with the girls. When she turns, Cahey remains silent, extends his arm, and together they walk down the stairs to join the others.

The evening weather is lovely so they decide to walk.

"Thank you for the dress."

"No need to thank me. You have earned it with all you do at the house. You prepare meals for all of us, keep the house in shape, shop for the food, take care of the girls, and see that our laundry is clean and pressed. You do a lot to run this motley group of people living at Sniffen Court. Frederick and I both thank you."

They walk for a block or two in silence.

Sophie clears her throat. "I want to tell you that I got a telegram today from the fisherman's group in Boston."

Cahey remains silent and allows Sophie to tell him the information, but Sophie is slow to share her news. They continue to walk and finally, Cahey encourages her to speak. "How do you feel about the information in the letter?" He turns and glances at Sophie. Tears are running down her cheeks. "Sophie, what is the matter?"

"They still could not confirm whether or not Séan is dead. There is no evidence of his boat or his body. They cannot confirm him gone until seven years from the date of his disappearance."

"Well, that is at least something."

"Something? The twins and I must go on for the next seven years not knowing if he is alive or dead and if dead, how he might have died, and if alive where he might be that he did not reach out to find us?"

Cahey stops. He gently grabs Sophie's arm and she swings back toward him. "Sophie, don't worry. You and the twins will be taken care of. Don't worry."

"I cannot let your generosity continue in this way. I want to return to Ireland and raise my girls there in the village with my mother and other family members."

"Ah, you want to go home."

"Yes. I want to go home."

Sophie turns and begins walking to catch up with Frederick and Danielle. Cahey lingers but at the crosswalk catches up with the others and gets in stride. Home? He doesn't quite know what home is anymore. With no family and no home-land, he feels that home is being developed right there at Sniffen Court with Sophie, the twins, Frederick, and their other friends dropping in and out. How does he find home?

They arrive at the 291 Gallery. Many others have arrived before the group. The four of them pause and Danielle leans over to Frederick. "Are we late? You said seven o'clock and it is just now seven, yet all these people are here."

"We are fine. You will see."

The four enter the gallery and the guests move easily out of the way to accommodate them. There is a shout from the back of the room. "Frederick is here." People turn and look at Fred-erick as do Cahey, Danielle, and Sophie. The guests burst into applause with comments of "well done" and "great art."

Cahey looks about. He sees Marie with an escort. She curt-seys ever so slightly towards him.

Then Mr. Stieglitz pushes through the crowd and reaches out to greet Frederick. He then turns to the other guests, "I would like to present Mr. Frederick Davidson, the artist of the exhibit."

All eyes are on Frederick. Cahey grins and claps Frederick on the back. "Well, sir, you kept this a secret."

In front of them are photographs that Frederick has rendered and finessed into wonderful impressionist paintings. The photos are of the people living in Sniffen Court: a group shot around the dining table, Sophie in the kitchen, the twins reading in the big chair in the office downstairs with Sharon working at the desk, Cahey staring out a window, Danielle and Sophie serving dinner. The photos are dreamlike with soft edges and subtle contrasts.

As in a trance, Danielle and Sophie walk toward the photos. They study each image and without so much as a word, move to the next one and the next one and the next one. Cahey stands slightly behind them and watches as Frederick shakes hands and talks briefly with other guests who want to meet the artist. He sees Frederick watching as Danielle and Sophie move along to view the photos.

Frederick turns to Cahey and the women. "Well," he says hesitantly, "what do you think?"

Sophie is the first to answer. "They are absolutely brilliant."

Danielle smiles, "They are too brilliant for words."

Cahey throws an arm around Frederick's shoulders. "So, this is what you have been working on for so many hours in the darkroom. And we thought you were just overbooked with your job. Why didn't you tell us?"

"I wasn't sure I could pull it off. You like everything I do, so I brought it to Mr. Stieglitz to get an opinion is all."

"He obviously liked what he saw. But why didn't you tell us the exhibit is all about your work?"

"I wanted it to be a surprise."

"Well, you certainly surprised me. This is indeed brilliant."

The four friends bask in the praise heaped on Frederick. There are wine toasts and small plates served. Finally, Cahey suggests that someone there take a group photo of the four of them so that Frederick can be in the photo. Mr. Stieglitz has a photographer who agrees and who gives Frederick the image. Later, when Frederick develops it, Cahey studies the group carefully. He sees Danielle with her hand tucked around Frederick's arm, and then there is his arm around Frederick's shoulders. Sophie is standing next to him with her hands folded in front of her. The image captures all of their faces beaming except Sophie's. She is smiling but cannot hide her sadness.

55

F all moves into winter. The holiday season catches the household at Sniffen Court in full swing. Cahey is sitting at the dining room table with a cup of tea. He is in a thoughtful mood. The house is quiet and he thinks about how the year has played out. Though Cahey's racing business continues, so has the work at the Exchange with new horses arriving every day. His Irish Services ends. Mr. Lynch bought his horses and moved them down to Spancil Hill and gave Cahey a fair price for all of them. The draft selling side of the business had been sold to Colm and Michael when Seámus died. They kept Pádraig on to run the operation. Cahey extends the offer of the training to Pádraig, who responds that he needs time to think about it.

The Exchange, after the fire, has been totally rebuilt and includes a self-service buffet. Danielle is asked to manage the buffet, but she says she really enjoys the freedom of being a business owner. There are plenty of parties all up and down Fifth Avenue and in the homes of the wealthy New Yorkers where she has been able to broaden her business. Both her mother and papa have joined her as bakers and Sharon has become a partner and quit the hotel. She manages the bakery's accounts as well as Cahey's. With his and Frederick's help, the women buy one of the abandoned Victorian houses where they host events in the downstairs parlors. The two women live upstairs and operate the business from there and in the huge kitchen at the back of the house. They call their business: Lavigne and McGee Bake Shoppe, which is a mouthful, but they want their names and heritage to be represented. They specialize in French pastries and Irish bread.

As he drinks his tea, Cahey glances around the room; he sees Frederick's new art on the walls. The art is gaining in popularity and therefore increasing in value. Frederick is doing well. Though he still takes photos of everyday events, he has begun to expand into taking more photographs of the horses that Cahey grooms and works with, especially at the race-course. These photos are turned into art prints. The horse owners are the first to buy, but many race fans want prints of their favorite horses. The business is brisk especially now at the holidays. Requests come in every day for yet another horse print.

Sophie has decorated the house for the holidays. Cahey has a tree in the dining room corner for the first time. Evergreens are over the doorways and around the windows. The twins have woven strips of paper into various ornament shapes and painted them bright colors. Sharon arrives at least twice a week to take care of his books, to instruct the twins on various weavings, and to bring them paint to decorate the ornaments.

Having Sophie and the twins in the house has been an easy adjustment. Cahey is comfortable having her around. He has grown protective of the twins. Sophie moves about the house, cleaning, cooking meals for the people in the house, washing and ironing, and taking care of the twins. She plans Christmas dinner, and as the day gets closer, the activity in the household

increases. There are secret hideaways of gifts and covered packages that are whisked out of sight.

Christmas morning arrives. Cahey awakens to the smell of
Sophie's hot griddle cakes and sausages with a side dish of figs.
Frederick and Cahey tumble with the twins until Sophie calms
everyone down and they sit for breakfast. Danielle arrives in
the middle of the morning with packages, small cakes which
her parents call petits gâteaux, and treats for the twins. Sharon
comes midday with chestnut dressing and gravy to go with
Sophie's turkey. She too has packages, which she places under
the tree, including a wrapped tube.

Dinner is served with toasts made all around.

"Thank you for all that you have done this year to make our
lives better than ever," toasts Frederick.

"And may next year be even better for all of us, here together," says Cahey.

Everyone drinks but Sophie. Cahey looks at her with a
raised eyebrow. "Is there something wrong?"

She looks away. "No, nothing is wrong. Let's have dessert."
And she is up removing plates and dishes to the kitchen.
Everyone helps tidy the table. Sophie brings over from the side-
board a chocolate cake, an apple pie, and a plate of sugar
cookies the twins had helped to make. Danielle adds her box of
small cakes. Frederick pours out little glasses of brandy for the
adults. The scene is one of sharing, gift opening, and friendly
chatter. All the presents are distributed and opened except for
the tube that Sharon brought in.

"This is for you, Cahey," she says and offers the wrapped
tube to him.

He glances first at the tube and then at her face. She is grin-
ning and excited. "Open it!" He tears into the paper, opens the
end of the tube, and out slides a rolled-up cloth. As he unfolds
the cloth, he sees what it is and unfolds the Irish flag in one
swift motion.

"Well done, we need a bit of something Irish in this place, it will go over the fireplace!"

Frederick punches Cahey gently on the arm, "I'm already outnumbered, here. What are you saying, 'something Irish'?"

As preparations are being made to hang the flag, Sophie slips out of the room. She comes back with two wrapped packages. "We are not quite finished," she says. She hands one of the packages to Frederick and the other to Cahey. Both men open the packages at the same time. Inside each is a quilt. Frederick's quilt is made of Scottish plaids. "I was not sure of the clan's colors, will these do?"

Frederick beams his biggest smile of the day. "Will they do? This is amazing! When did you have time to make this?"

A shy smile comes over Sophie's face, but she is quiet. "What do you think about yours? Cahey?" she asks "It is the traditional King Quilt in memory of the village where we once lived and the people we knew there."

"The village has a quilt pattern?" asks Danielle.

"No, but the village has a king," explains Sophie. "Ryan Ó Ruadháin was the king and also Séan's grandfather. So, I made the King Quilt so you can remember that visit so many years ago when I first met you as a young man fishing with King Ryan and Séan." Sophie hesitates but stops.

"I will treasure it." Cahey holds the quilt to his chest. "There is more?" He walks over to stand in front of Sophie.

"Yes. *Go gcuire Dia an t-adh ort.*"

"*Nuair a bhíonn tú ag fágáil?*"

"*Amárach.*"

"*Rah Dé ort.*" Cahey turns and sits at the table.

"Wait!" interrupts Sharon. "I understand some of this. Sophie, why are you leaving tomorrow?"

Sophie tells them about the telegram and not knowing if Séan is alive or dead and how he will not be declared dead until he is missing for seven years. She wants to return to her village in Ireland and raise her children there. The money Danielle has paid her to help with the catering business has been saved and she has purchased tickets to leave.

The friends sit in silence. Frederick is still holding his quilt. Cahey folds his and puts it on the chair near the Christmas tree.

Sharon speaks first. "I will be sad to see you go, but I understand how you made the decision. *Rah De ort*, God be with you." She goes over and gives Sophie a big hug.

Everyone loosens up then with hugs and begin to talk about the arrangements, trunks, and getting to the dock. The twins are dancing around with excitement on their voyage across the sea.

Cahey stands and goes to the front window and looks down the lane. His new family is changing and people are going away. He has no choice but to change with them, but it fills his heart with sadness.

56

Cahey offers to help Sophie pack but choosing what to take does not consume a lot of time. Other than a few new clothes and items for the twins, there is little that Sophie brought with her from her time with Séan in Boston. Frederick offers her one of his paintings and wants her to choose. She stands a long time in front of each painting now hung around the dining room. Finally, she stops in front of the group photo taken at the exhibit. "This one, this is the one I want. Then I will have a memory of all of us."

"Great. I'll wrap it carefully and put it in a crate." Frederick takes down the art and disappears downstairs.

Cahey sits at the table with a cup of tea. He is suddenly tired and not sure of his path anymore. He has allowed circumstances to dictate his future. He has concentrated on building his future in America and now that future is changing. He walks over to the fireplace and looks long at the Irish flag hanging there.

Sharon sees him studying the flag. "I don't know what you are thinking, but I feel you are not here in your thoughts."

Cahey smiles. "You are right; this flag reminds me as to why I came to America but does not answer the question of why I have stayed."

"Being Irish is not easy there or here."

"I know that so well." Cahey walks over to the window and looks out at the New York he has gotten to know. Sharon sits silently watching him.

"There is an Irish proverb: 'It is in the shelter of each other that people live'." She pauses. "You and Frederick have provided such a place here for people to live. You should know that."

Cahey nods but keeps looking out the window.

"What was your home like in Ireland?"

His face changes with his memories. "I grew up in a cottage by the sea. It was cold and crowded with all of us. I left after mum and papa died and my brother guided my two sisters to Dublin. I went to Galway and worked for a distillery. My knowledge of horses got me the job." Cahey remembers Seámus, Michael and Sheila, Colm, and then Micil. He is quiet for a time.

"And where did you live in Galway?" Sharon pursues Cahey's past, the one he has remained silent about.

"I lived in the distillery lodging for workers, a small room where I studied and practiced writing and...." He stops and turns to walk over to the fireplace. On the mantel he has carefully placed Micil's journal. He picks it up, opens the leaf and reads out loud, "'I'll be listening for you.' It's what Micil wrote before she died."

Sharon remains still but looks away from him. "That explains a lot," she says. "I have seen the journal but did not know it was from someone in Ireland." She pauses, then asks, "What do you miss?"

Cahey holds the journal gently in his hands. "I miss riding horses and writing letters." He pauses and looks up from the journal to see Sharon. "I miss the shoreline and the language. I miss Ireland as much as ever."

"You can go back to Ireland, you know."

Cahey thinks again. He remembers the hunger, the desperation, the lack of education, and the serious illnesses like the one that killed Micil. No, going back is not his future. "I know, but my life is now here. This is where I must look for my future. This is home." And he replaces the journal on the mantel.

The morning passes too quickly. Two wooden boxes and a trunk are loaded onto the cart. Cahey pays a man to take the cart to the dock for them. He hails a carriage for Sophie and the twins; Frederick and Cahey will see Sophie and the girls off. Sharon and Danielle said their goodbyes after Christmas dinner.

At the dock, the passage tickets are collected and the wooden boxes and trunk are loaded onto the ship. Sophie is in a stateroom with the girls since they are traveling alone on this trip. Farewells are said. Cahey turns to Sophie one last time. "If there is anything you or the twins need, you will contact me, yes?" Sophie nods. "And you will see Colm when you arrive. He will meet you at the dock and get you and the twins to the village. He has made arrangements to borrow a cart."

"Yes, Cahey, I will do all you ask." She smiles and reaches up to touch his cheek. "You have been a wonderful friend. Thank you."

Cahey turns, his face bright red, and he heads down the gangway. Halfway down he turns, "*Go dtí go gcasfaimid le chéile arís.*"

Sophie smiles and waves, hiding her tears, "Yes, until we meet again."

Cahey does not leave the dock area until the ship has pulled in the anchor and has moved away from the shore. He and Frederick walk the long way back to Sniffen Court. The house is quiet. Both men poke around downstairs, not wanting to go up into the empty rooms, but as the evening gets darker, it is time to go upstairs. Cahey opens the bed chamber where the twins and Sophie had lived. Sophie had cleaned the chamber and moved all his belongings into the room. His new quilt, the King Quilt, is on the bed. He goes into the kitchen; Sophie has left a stew on the stove ready for their supper. Freshly baked bread is wrapped in a damp towel next to the stew. She seems to have thought of everything except how not to miss her and the twins.

Both men slump through the next week. They do what they have to do for work, and when they are home, they sit with cups of tea and stare at the emptiness of the house. Sharon comes in and out downstairs doing the books, but Danielle has only been by once. She announced that she would be back when there was better humor in the household; that was days ago. The days turn into weeks and then into months. The men work long hours and when they are home, they continue to sit with tea and look at the emptiness of the house. Frederick is away most evenings, and Cahey has fallen into his earlier habits of reading or sitting in his office trying to write.

One day in early April, Cahey is drinking tea and reading in the dining room. Frederick comes in and sits down at the table with him. "Cahey, it's time we get busy doing things at night again. Spring is here and we need to get out and do things."

"Like what?" asks Cahey, not at all interested in doing things.

"We used to go to all the openings, the theatre, the museums, and the racecourse, which you still go to but only on business. We need to have some fun."

"Fun? You are gone a lot in the evenings. Aren't you out with Danielle having fun?"

"But I miss going out with you. And yes, I have been going out with Danielle, but I want you to go out too. You are miserable, just sitting here drinking tea and reading."

Cahey puts down the newspaper he has been reading. "What do you suggest?"

"Now you're talking. There is a hotel at 43rd and Broadway that is offering a musical revue and dinner. Let's book a table and go tonight."

"Tonight? But I have to check in at the Exchange this afternoon."

"That's okay; I will swing down that way and book a table."

The men part and continue their day. Cahey heads toward Longacre Square and to the Exchange and Frederick stops into the Cadillac Hotel to book their table. The seating is at nine with the revue to follow. Both men return to Sniffen Court in time to change into suits appropriate for an outing. The evening is clear; they decide to walk.

Frederick begins to talk. "This has been a busy year."

Cahey nods, "Yes it has."

"So many changes."

Cahey is silent as they continue to walk.

"I have something else I want to tell you."

Cahey continues to walk. "Yes, what?"

"I have been thinking about Danielle. I would like to ask her to marry me."

Cahey stops abruptly in the middle of crossing a street. "That is wonderful, Frederick, absolutely wonderful. When?"

"I thought I would ask her tonight. I have invited Danielle and Sharon to join us at the hotel."

Cahey is taken aback. "Another one of your surprises and you didn't say anything."

"I wanted to be sure how we would continue."

"So, what are your plans?"

"If Danielle says yes, we will plan the wedding and then plan the next part: where to live."

"I see. We own the house at Sniffen Court together. I am not sure I would want to be there alone."

"Yes, I assumed that, and because of your financial contribution into Danielle's business and their purchase of the house for business, you own that as well."

"What are you suggesting?"

"As partners, I would like to continue to live at Sniffen Court with Danielle and you. My artwork has really paid well this year. So, I have another surprise for you."

"For me?"

"Yes. I will tell you what it is after dinner when the ladies are with us." With that, Frederick picks up his pace and it is all Cahey can do to keep up with him.

The ladies are in the lobby waiting for them when they arrive. They are shown to their seats and order dinner. Both women are dressed for the evening and feel like they are truly celebrating but don't know what. When the dinner plates have been cleared, before the revue, Frederick stands up from the table. Sharon and Danielle are chattering away. Frederick kneels beside Danielle. She stops talking and looks his way. She looks puzzled as to why he is kneeling. The band gives an introductory drum roll. Frederick takes out a jewelry box and puts it in front of Danielle.

"Danielle, I am in love with you and would like to have you be in my life forever. Will you marry me?"

Sharon covers her mouth with her hands as she watches Danielle's reaction. Danielle reaches for the box and opens it; inside is a diamond ring. She lifts it out of the box and hands it to Frederick. "Yes, I will marry you. Put it on." The band strikes up a stirring song and their kiss is long and intense.

Cahey is pleased for his friend. Though he and Danielle had a bumpy start when they met, he has admired how she and

Frederick have gotten along and developed such happiness between them. The two couples talk until the revue starts. Danielle sits with her arm linked inside of Frederick's where the ring glistens in the lights. She keeps looking at it.

After the revue, there is dessert and coffee. Cahey orders brandy for him and Frederick and they sit and enjoy listening to the women talk about wedding plans. Since both are planners, food and organization are not a problem. Frederick takes Danielle out onto the dance floor as the band strikes up "East Side West Side." Everyone sings along.

"Down in front of Casey's old brown wooden stoop

On a summer's evening we formed a merry group

Boys and girls together we would sing and waltz

While Tony played the organ on the sidewalks of New York

"East Side, West Side, all around the town

The tots sang 'Ring-around-Rosie', 'London Bridge is falling down'

Boys and girls together, me and Mamie O'Rourke

Tripped the light fantastic on the sidewalks of New York"

As the song ends and they return to the table, Frederick says to Danielle, "I thought I might ask you something else."

"What else?"

"I thought we might live at Sniffen Court and keep Cahey company. He is a major owner in both places, and we seem to do well together. What do you think?"

"I think that is a great idea. What do you say, Cahey?"

"Wait, what about me?" Sharon asks. "I share a room with Danielle and I will be all alone."

"The house is full of people," reminds Danielle, "Mama and papa are downstairs and people are always about. Plus, you will have your own space for the first time."

Sharon smiles and agrees. Having her own space might be nice for a change.

"And what do you say, Cahey?" repeats Frederick.

"Absolutely!"

"Then it is settled," says Frederick. He fumbles through all his suit pockets and pulls out a formal sheet of paper. "Now, on to your surprise," he says to Cahey, handing the paper to him.

Cahey unfolds the sheets. It is a deed to a farm on the Hudson River, twelve miles north of the city, thirty acres.

"What is this?"

"It is your weekend and summer getaway where you can ride horses and work with your own training techniques. It is our gift to you but does have a few stipulations."

"Stipulations?"

"Yes, first, it is jointly owned by all of us just like the Sniffen Court house, the catering business house, and now the farm. Second, you get to name it whatever you would like."

Cahey is unable to say anything. Finally, he reaches out and grabs Frederick around the shoulders, "Thank you, *a charra,* thank you." The hug the two men share shows a deep caring and a long friendship.

"Shall we go take a look this weekend?" asks Frederick.

After the dinner and revue, the four friends leave the hotel but the crowds outside are huge. People are standing everywhere. "What's going on?" Cahey asks a police officer outside the hotel door.

"People are here to watch the fireworks from the top of the Times Building," he says. "Didn't you know that Mayor McClellan signed a resolution on this day, April 8, 1904, to change the name of this area from Longacre Square to Times Square?"

"And why are they doing this?"

"Adolph Ochs wants it is why. That's his building right there on the triangle."

"The newspaper building?"

"That's right; *The New York Times* is now located on Times Square."

"But why the crowds?"

"Mr. Ochs has organized a celebration of the square with fireworks at midnight to celebrate. Isn't that the craziest thing? Better stay and see this because it won't last another year. Too dangerous, too many people, too expensive. They won't celebrate like this again, not here, mark my words."

The friends find a place to watch and Frederick leans over to Cahey. "And who will manage the farm for us?"

Cahey smiles. "I got a telegraph from Pádraig yesterday. He's on the next ship to New York. He would like to work with the horses here rather than train to be a mechanic. I think he would be perfect for the job."

The four of them stand and watch the ever-increasing firework display. The colors streak overhead. Pops and shrieks of the firework missiles fill Cahey's ears. The star-like patterns cover the sky then fade and blend into the darkness.

Sharon leans over to Cahey. "Frederick and Danielle look so happy."

Cahey nods. He does see how happy they are. All the years that Frederick and Cahey have shared in New York shift through Cahey's thoughts. They have come a long way from that collision on the ship to growing friends into a family. And now with a wedding and a new farm, change is happening again, but they have survived the changes and the thin times. His hope is that they will continue to survive. Cahey sees Danielle's arm is linked onto Frederick's, who is clasping her hand draped on his arm. Their heads are close together as they look up at the light show in the sky. Cahey remembers Micil's arms around his waist as they rode Colleen over the meadow from the beach and how they created cloud pictures in the sky, looking up together with their whole future ahead of them. A particularly loud firework breaks his memory.

Sharon leans over closer to Cahey. "Do you ever think about getting married?"

The last of the fireworks display bursts out over the top of the buildings and everyone cheers, all but Cahey.

57

T he weekend is planned. Early Saturday morning, the four friends climb into a wagon Cahey has arranged to take them up to the new farm. Rather than take the train, he insists that horses need to see the land first. Frederick laughs. "It is all about the horses, isn't it, Cahey? That is why we live in a stable."

Winding up to the farm on the Hudson River, they arrive to find the sun shining and a light blue sky overhead. As Cahey drives the wagon through the double-wide gates, he sees a white wooden fence lining the lane leading to a two-story cottage. An apple orchard on the left is covered with blooms in pink clusters as the buds begin to open in the middle of April. On the right is a meadow edged with trees in the distance.

Cahey stops the wagon in front of the cottage. The women climb down and take a picnic basket onto the porch. Without going inside, Cahey starts unfastening the horses from the wagon.

"What are you doing, Cahey? We will need to return to the city," says Frederick.

"But not before we see the thirty acres. And what better way to see it than to ride?" Cahey looks over at Frederick. "You do ride, don't you?"

"Ah, my friend, after all these years, you know I ride."

The men work together to unharness the horses. They swing onto the bare backs and begin their ride around the farm. There is a stable. There are outhouses for storage and a large red barn. There are paddocks that can be used for a garden and for a temporary place to put a horse.

They ride the horses away from the barn and through a back pasture. Frederick beckons Cahey at the top of a hill. "Cahey," he calls and motions for him to come.

Cahey rides over. At the top of the hill, he looks out to see a meadow with beech trees and lavender. The scent fills the air. He sits on the horse and listens. "I can hear the river."

"Me too. Let's go see it."

Cahey takes off after his friend.

As they reach the Hudson River, the two men pause and look at the flowing water. They sit in silence, just listening to the river and feeling the breeze. "Have you come up with a name for the farm?" asks Frederick.

As Cahey looks over the meadow and listens to the river, his memories flood him with images of Ireland. He thinks about the love of his life—he can see Micil sitting under the beech trees. He sees the fair where he did one of the best things he has ever done: buy his first horse. Without even thinking about what he is saying, the words spill out of his mouth, "Spancil Hill. The farm will be called Spancil Hill."

THE END

ACKNOWLEDGMENTS
FROM LEARA RHODES

Music is so much a part of this novel due to my love of live music and the people I have met in Ireland. Kate Neilan rented her Airbnb and introduced me to her parents, Tom and Maureen Neilan, who live on a farm outside of Gort, Ireland. Maureen gave me wonderful biscuits and tea. Tom shared stories of growing up on farmlands in rural Ireland, taught me how to buy horses at a fair, and invited me to a session at a local pub with Charlie Piggott, a founding member of De Dannan, a traditional Irish band, where I fell in love with both them and their Irish music.

Sue Booth-Forbes at Anam Cara Retreat in the Beara Peninsula near Eyeries, Ireland will forever be the friend every writer wants to have. She opened her house and introduced another part of Ireland to me by telling me stories I will never forget, stories about fur coats and farm cheese. The first night I arrived at Anam Cara, the creative women staying there at the time were waiting in the hallway for me to arrive in the rain at ten in the night; we were off to the pub where an older woman taught me how to dance the military two-step. And then there is Tig Choili, a pub in Galway where I bought a t-shirt and wear it often to remind me of how much I enjoy listening to sessions at a pub.

My ancestors came from Ireland and though I did not know them, I feel as though I did through the survival skills they passed down through the generations. I saw those skills in my mother and now in my daughter and her daughters. My daughter, Jessica, has been my greatest advocate. She has listened and responded with the feelings I needed to hear at the time. She has my heart forever.

I am forever grateful to my publisher, who without a doubt believes in people and gave me a chance to tell this story. She has been a cheerleader with great insight and honesty.

Any historical discrepancies are mine. I tried to be true to the era, the facts, and the events of the day. The characters are all my imagination including what they did. It is a story about survival and how our ancestors may have done it better than we are today.

My sister-friends have been with me through many years. I thank them for listening and being there for me: Louise Benjamin and Lee Wenthe. I also want to thank my younger friends who have listened and encouraged: Lilly McEachern, Stacia Price, and Maruja Bogaard. A special thank you goes to Shannah Cahoe Montgomery for a wonderful photo shoot in the garden and Sydney Wakeford for building a website that represents who I am.

CREDITS GO TO THE FOLLOWING:

Author photo | Shannah Cahoe Montgomery

"Spancil Hill" | Written by Michael Considine sometime between 1870 and 1873

"The Dawning of the Day" | Written by Edward Walsh, translation by Na Casaidigh

"Fisherman's Son and the Gruagach of Tricks" | Written by Jeremiah Curtin, 1890, published by Sampson Low, Marston, Searle & Rivington, London

"A Nation Once Again" | Written by Thomas Osborne Davis and published in The Nation on July 13, 1844

"The Boyhood of Finn Mac Cumhal and The Song of Finn in Praise of May," 9th Century Poem.

"The Boyhood of Finn Mac Cumhal" [Chapter 9]. Rollston, T.W. The High Deeds of Finn and other Bardic Romances of

Ancient Ireland. 1910. Public Domain through Project Gutenberg.

"Connemara Cradle Song" | The song uses the same air as "Down in the Valley." According to Pat Conway's book The Very Best Irish Songs & Ballads, (Dublin: Walton Manufacturing, 1999), page 44, "Connemara Cradle Song" was written by John Francis Waller (1809-1894). The song was popularized by Mayo-born Delia Murphy (1902-1971), who apparently claimed copyright for it in 1951.

"Piping Tim of Galway" | The person or people who wrote "The Galway Piper" are forgotten to history, though it's known to have been published as early as 1740.

"Kilgary Mountain [Whiskey in the Jar]" | The song is delivered as a light-hearted celebration of debauchery and is usually a communal singalong. At some point in the colonial period, the song was carried to the United States, where it was popular for its irreverent attitude toward British officials. Some American versions deal with American characters in American settings such as the Ozarks or Appalachians.

"God Save Ireland" | Written by Timothy Daniel Sullivan, 1867

"The Sidewalks of New York (East Side/West Side)" | Written by Charles B. Lawlor with lyrics by James W. Blake, 1894

ABOUT THE AUTHOR
LEARA RHODES

Leara Rhodes has been a writer since college in Philadelphia, where she received her master's and doctorate from Temple University. She has been a journalist, editor, freelance writer, and university professor teaching writing. During her academic career, she published three books and numerous journal articles. She was awarded a Fulbright to Haiti and named the first educator inducted into the Georgia Magazine Hall of Fame. Her summer teaching programs included two at the University College Dublin and two at Trinity College, University of Oxford.

Leara lives in Athens, Georgia, and prefers to garden, cook, travel, or spend time with her family and friends when she is not writing.

To learn more about Leara, visit her website: Leararhodes.com.

WATCH FOR LEARA'S NEXT NOVEL

The Darkest Midnight in December

Coming Fall of 2024